THE LORD I LEFT

SCARLETT PECKHAM

The Lord I Left

Ebook ISBN: 978-1-64197-124-9
Print KDP ISBN: 979-8-60236-307-4
IS Print ISBN: 978-1-64197-138-6

NYLA Publishing
121 W 27th St., Suite 1201, New York, NY 10001
http://www.nyliterary.com

The Lord I Left

SECRETS OF CHARLOTTE STREET
BOOK THREE

SCARLETT PECKHAM

PRAISE FOR SCARLETT PECKHAM

"An astonishingly good debut...The whole book is a breath of fresh air, both a complex, layered story and a soaring romance with two very real people at its heart." — *The New York Times Book Review* on THE DUKE I TEMPTED

"Peckham's meticulous character work pays off in spectacular, grandly romantic fashion and The Duke I Tempted ends with particularly cathartic and hard-won happily ever after." — *Book-Page* on THE DUKE I TEMPTED

"If you want something to speed your heart and stop your breath as you read beneath the covers, with only the meager flashlight beam warding off the enveloping night — then you have a rare treat in store." — *The Seattle Review of Books* on THE DUKE I TEMPTED

"With her ability to tread the line between the most diverting of historical circumstances and a progressive level of sex positivity that makes me want to sing her praises from the rooftops,

Peckham proves herself one of the most exciting romance authors on the rise." — *Entertainment Weekly* on THE EARL I RUINED

"A beautifully written, character-driven story that expertly unravels a big misunderstanding, and surprises with its twists and turns and wicked secrets right up until the end." — *NPR* on THE EARL I RUINED

ABOUT THIS BOOK

He's a minister to whores... She's a fallen woman...

Lord Lieutenant Henry Evesham is an evangelical reformer charged with investigating the flesh trade in London. His visits to bawdy houses leave him with a burning desire to help sinners who've lost their innocence to vice—even if the temptations of their world test his vow not to lose his moral compass...again.

As apprentice to London's most notorious whipping governess, Alice Hull is on the cusp of abandoning her quiet, rural roots for the city's swirl of provocative ideas and pleasures—until a family tragedy upends her dreams and leaves her desperate to get home. When the handsome, pious Lord Lieutenant offers her a ride despite the coming blizzard, she knows he is her best chance to reach her ailing mother—even if she doesn't trust him.

He has the power to destroy her... She has the power to undo him...

As they struggle to travel the snow-swept countryside, they find their suspicion of each other thawing into a longing that leaves them both shaken. Alice stirs Henry's deepest fantasies, and he awakens parts of her she thought she'd foresworn years ago. But Henry is considering new regulations that threaten the people Alice holds dear, and association with a woman like Alice would threaten Henry's reputation if he allowed himself to get too close.

Is falling for the wrong person a test of faith ...or a chance at unimagined grace?

AUTHOR'S NOTE

A note on content, for sensitive readers who like to know.

(If you prefer to be surprised, skip this part.)

This book contains the following: explicit sex; kink and hierophilia (look it up!); feelings of guilt and shame concerning sex; prostitution (both practitioners of and debates about the legality of); parental mortality; toxic families of origin; religious faith, including questioning of and alienation from; allusions to body image issues; and quite a lot of truly despicable cursing.

DEDICATION

For Sarah E. Younger, whose faith in me—and in this series—is one of my great blessings.

CHAPTER 1

Mary-le-Bone, London
January 1758

The London morning smelled of smoke and had the look of a sketch crudely rendered in blunt charcoal. Icy sludge dripped from sodden eaves into the rivulets of muck that passed for streets, sloshing Henry Evesham's newly polished boots.

It was an ominous morning to begin a journey. Which was appropriate, given Henry's destination.

"I'll just be a moment," he told Elena Brearley's groom, handing off the reins of his too-fine, borrowed curricle. He walked briskly from the mews to Charlotte Street, stopping at the solemn door of the house marked twenty-three.

It still struck him how little Mistress Brearley's townhouse resembled its forbidding reputation. When he'd first come here, he'd imagined a spired fortress acrid with the stink of brimstone and noisy with wails of pain. Not this quiet, stately residence, more like an exclusive members club than the lurid whipping house of his imagination.

Henry flicked his knuckle against the door, tense at who might open it. He exhaled when, small mercy, the tall, black footman in the powdered wig appeared, rather than the petite, white woman with the intense brown eyes.

Dove's eyes, he'd thought when he'd first seen her. *Dove's eyes,* he'd thought again when she'd glared at him as he left this place last week.

But no, alas, that was not accurate. If he was being honest with himself—and he'd vowed to be rigorously honest with himself—Alice, for it was untruthful to pretend he did not recall her name—had glared not because he'd *left* but because he'd fled, bolting up the stairs and out the door as if his life depended on it.

(No. Not his life. His soul.)

"Good morning, Stoker," he said brightly to the footman. By now, they knew each other, the denizens of Charlotte Street and Lord Lieutenant Henry Evesham.

Still, the servant went through the customary stiff-lipped ceremony that bartered entrance to the door.

"Your key?" Stoker asked, holding out his hand.

Henry rummaged in his overcoat for the elaborately worked iron, its end marking his identity with a sigil of a cross affixed in thorns. The fearsome whipping governess Elena Brearley, he had discovered, was not above a joke.

"Keep it," Henry said. "I shan't be back after today."

If this announcement meant anything to Stoker, the man did not betray it, only stepped aside, allowing Henry entry. "You're not expected," Stoker said in his usual hushed tone. "The establishment is closed today."

Henry smiled cheerfully, for this was precisely the reason he'd chosen today to come. "I hoped that since you're closed Mistress Brearley might be free for a brief word. In private."

He followed Stoker at a distance down the corridor into the bowels of the house, inhaling its scent of vinegar and polished wood. It was nothing like the way most brothels smelled, an odor of stale gin and pomander masking the livelier, human scents of lust. He'd visited enough *bagnios* in the past two years—fine ones with half-dressed painted ladies offering entertainment and strong spirts, low ones offering little more than dirty cots for rutting—to know that this place was as unusual as its mistress claimed.

He was aware of her particularities by now—the codes of discipline and discretion Mistress Brearley believed made this place safer than others of its kind. It was her mission to persuade him that wider adoption of her ways would reduce the dangers of the flesh trade for whores and culls alike.

He was not sure he was convinced. But he recognized in her a seriousness of purpose that beat in his own breast.

They were both evangelists.

Stoker led him up a flight of stairs to a large parlor. Velvet curtains blocked the daylight and a fire roaring in a man-sized hearth gave the double-vaulted room its only light. It was, as always, midnight in this room, though outside the morning bells had just struck eight.

Elena Brearley sat still and regal, writing at her desk. She paused and lifted her eyes in greeting. "Henry."

"Lord Lieutenant," he corrected, with a wink. It was a little joke between them, his insistence on a title that he knew Elena Brearley would never utter. Her establishment observed a different hierarchy than the one outside its walls. The only title honored here was Mistress Brearley.

A touch of wry amusement curled around the edges of her

mouth. "I did not expect to see you here again." She looked at him directly, her gaze expansive and forgiving, like she knew the precise makings of his soul—every virtue, sin, and limitation.

He did the only thing he could before such a gaze, which was to pretend he did not notice it, that it did not make him want to flinch.

"Ah, yes, my apologies for my haste in taking leave last week," he said. "I belatedly remembered I was overdue for an appointment at the Lords. I hope your girl was not alarmed at my abruptness. Thank you for seeing me, nevertheless."

She smiled at his lie, saving him the trouble of mentally reproving himself for it. "Of course. You know it delights me to find myself of service to an emissary of His Majesty's government."

She always spoke to him in this mordant tone, as though they were on opposite sides of an irony so vast that it could only be amusing, and they both knew it. It made him want to tell her all his secrets, though that would be perverse—the man of God confessing to a whore.

"I am grateful for all of your assistance," he said. "It has been immensely helpful in preparing my report to the Lords."

"I wait in suspense to learn your recommendations."

"I'm delivering the report in a few weeks. I'll see to it you receive a printing."

His remit as Lord Lieutenant was to investigate the toll of vice upon the innocents of London and propose ways to fight the scourge. He'd done careful research for two years, haunting houses of ill repute and interviewing everyone from palace courtesans to alley trollops to those who bought their wares. All that was left was to weigh the evidence and decide whether stricter punishment or progressive reform would best serve London's streets. Whatever he decided would make enemies of half the city

—either the brothel-keeps and harlots who wished to ply their trade in safety or the moralists who hoped to drive them out of sight.

Mistress Brearley continued to look closely at him, as if she might make out from his posture whether his report would prove him to be an ally or an adversary. "I do hope you will consider all that we discussed as you form your conclusions," she said, searching his eyes.

He dodged her gaze. Despite his prayers for moral guidance, he did not yet know what he would do.

He was conscious of the city's factions watching him for clues. But he had swum in ambiguity so long that his own beliefs—once so unshakable he had made his name espousing them in fiery print—had become murky and disordered. He was a man divided.

"Your proposed reforms will certainly be among my considerations," he said blandly.

"That is heartening. But do also remember what we spoke about last week."

He stiffened. He had inquired as to her prices—a standard question he'd forgotten to ask on earlier visits, given her insistence on speaking of condoms and physicians and license fees and guilds—and she'd replied that the price would depend on the nature of his desires.

"I have no desires," he'd said briskly. (*Liar,* he'd dutifully accounted to himself as he'd done so.)

"I was speaking rhetorically," she'd answered, using a tone that was not so different from the one he'd used on the men whose lives he'd upended during his time at *Saints & Satyrs*. A tone that said *we both know what you are.*

"But if that is true, Henry," she'd gone on thoughtfully, "I do wonder if it's just. A man tasked with reforming the flesh trade, one would think, has a responsibility to understand the yearnings at the heart of it. Does he not?"

"One can judge a crime without committing it."

"And one can possess a desire without indulging it," she'd replied, staring at him entirely too long. "As a man of God, I'd assume you value empathy."

He'd been silent, unwilling to engage her on this point, for he was here to ask questions, not proffer whatever lesions dotted the purity of his relationship with sin for her inspection.

He'd been relieved when she'd dropped the matter and summoned her girl to give him a tour of the premises.

But he'd been wrong to be relieved. For if Mistress Brearley had sensed the secrets buried in his guts, Alice had brought them roiling to the surface by doing no more than entering the room. Ever since he'd first set eyes on her, with her petite frame and faraway expression and enormous, doleful eyes—

Yes, he knew what yearning was.

Elena cleared her throat, reminding him that she was waiting for an answer.

"Of course I recall our conversation. And I appreciate your advice."

"Then I won't repeat myself. But I urge you to think of the good that you can do. The suffering you might prevent."

On this, they agreed. It was a call from God, his mission, and he was grateful for the chance to do work of lasting moral consequence. That he'd found the work to be a trial—that it tested his ethics and compassion, necessitated he walk the tempting pathways of a sinner—made him certain the sacrifice was worthy.

He sighed, and ceased the effort of trying to look official. "I rarely think of anything else, of late. That, I promise you."

She nodded. She always seemed to believe his good intentions despite the threats he'd made against her in his previous line of work. He admired this about her—her capacity for forgiveness. He was not sure he would be so charitable, were their positions reversed.

"How can I help you today, Henry?" Elena asked.

He tried to look extremely casual, though this was difficult, in her hard-backed wooden chair. "In my haste to leave on my last visit I wonder if I misplaced a book. I must travel to the country to write my report and I hoped to retrieve it before I left, if you've come across it."

"A book?"

"Yes—leather, bound, handwritten. It contained my notes."

It was his journal, actually, but he could not bring himself to admit to Mistress Brearley that he had left such an intimate personal artifact here, where anyone might read it. He suspected it had fallen from his satchel when he'd gone running out the door the week before.

Mistress Brearley shook her head. "I would have sent it back to you had I discovered it. Our respect for discretion extends to exotic creatures like Methodists, same as it does to flagellants and whores." She smiled.

He was relieved she hadn't found it. God alone should be privy to the writings in that book.

He must have dropped it somewhere else after he'd rushed off in his ooze of guilt. Losing it in some anonymous alley or bankside muck would be infinitely preferable to losing it here. It would diminish his authority for such people to know the nature of his private struggles. And if they knew, they might expose him.

He bowed and took a slip of paper from his pocket. "Please write to me at this address should it turn up. Thank you for your time. I must be on my way."

He moved toward the door, but before his fingers reached the knob, it flew open with such force that the wood cracked against the plaster wall behind it.

He jumped back just in time to avoid being struck on the chin. The serving girl, Alice, rushed blindly past him toward her mistress's desk, breathing like she'd taken a bullet to the lungs.

Mistress Brearley stood abruptly. "Alice, what is it?"

Before, the girl had always seemed impassive, betraying no emotion beside an occasional touch of perverse playfulness beneath the solemnity of her appearance. Her beauty was in the intelligence of her eyes, which danced in a way that made you long to know the private thoughts that made them flicker so.

But now, her eyes were wild, and she clutched a piece of paper to her sparrow's chest so tight that her knuckles glinted blue. Her hands, he noticed, were so small he could fold both of them inside one of his large paws. (But he should not be thinking of fleshly contact with a woman. Not ever, but especially not now, when the girl in question was so upset she could hardly breathe.)

"It's my mother," Alice choked out. "She's suffered an attack. Her heart. My sister writes—" she frantically shook her head, as if unable to speak the dire words aloud, and held the letter out to Mistress Brearley.

"We expect she has but days," Mistress Brearley read aloud. "Oh, my dear girl."

"My sympathies," he murmured, without thinking.

Alice whipped her head around, and he realized, belatedly, she had not noticed he was here.

"Oh—I was not aware you had a—" She edged closer to her mistress without finishing the thought, her expression indicating she would have been more pleased to see a beggar pustuled in contagious pox than Henry.

He no doubt deserved that look, and longed to shrink away,

but the minister in him could not help but see the anguish in her shoulders and wish to comfort her.

"Miss Alice, I'm so sorry you've had bad news." He pushed a chair toward her, for she seemed unsteady on her feet. "You should sit down," he said in a low, soothing voice. "You've had a shock. Perhaps you'd like to pray?"

Alice looked up at him in bemusement, then quickly turned back to Elena without answering, as if she could not waste time in making sense of him. "I have to get back—my sisters ..."

Elena came and bolstered Alice against her arm, rubbing her back. She stood half a foot taller than the girl, whose head would not meet Henry's breastbone.

"I'll need to find a mail coach right away," Alice said, speaking rapidly. "It's at least three days home and if I miss it today, I may not get there in time to—"

A sound escaped her that was not speech so much as heartbreak.

"Breathe, my girl," Elena murmured. "I'll have the boy run and fetch the timetables to Fleetwend while you pack."

Fleetwend. The name was familiar to Henry. He'd been there once, on a revival.

"Fleetwend's in Somerset, no?" he asked. "On the River Wythe?"

Elena looked at him over Alice's head. "Yes, that's correct Alice, is it not?"

Alice nodded a tearful assent into her sleeve.

He felt a chill run up his spine. *God is great.*

Her town was only a few hours drive beyond his father's house. This was no coincidence. He had lost his journal for a reason: so that he might be in this very room, on this very day, when he happened to be on his way to Somerset just as a young woman found herself in desperate need of passage there.

Joy in God's providence warmed him like a flame had been kindled in his belly. He needed this. A reminder of the foundation of his faith.

He inclined his head down to Alice's height, so that he could speak softly to her. "I'm headed that way, Miss—" he did not know her surname.

"Hull," Mistress Brearley provided.

"Miss Hull. If you do not mind traveling by open carriage in cold weather, it would be no trouble to take you to your family."

Her face twisted, in some reaction he could not precisely read, but which was not gratitude.

"I could not impose upon your kindness." Her eyes darted to Mistress Brearley's, as though looking for confirmation.

"'Tis no imposition whatsoever," he said in his most reassuring voice. When she did not look soothed by his tone, he stepped nearer and tried a joke. "I'm a minister by training, Miss Hull. We never turn down the chance to play the Good Samaritan."

His quip did not a thing to ease her look of worry. She stepped backwards, away from him. He remembered, too late, that his prodigious stature was not often regarded as soothing by petite young women. He was crowding her. He moved away and rounded his shoulders, making himself smaller to give her space.

"I'm afraid I can't promise much comfort, but I can get you to your family by tomorrow evening. You have my word."

Alice once again gave a beseeching look to Mistress Brearley, but her employer looked reflectively at Henry. "Alice, the mail coach will take twice that much time in winter weather," she said quietly. "You'd do well to consider Henry's offer."

Some silent understanding passed from mistress to maid, and Alice dropped her shoulders, immediately acquiescing to her employer's wishes.

"Thank you," she said, turning to him, her face resigned. "If you will grant me a moment, I will gather my things."

"Of course," he said.

She quickly left the room. Even in distress, her movements were as precise as the words of a poem. Not a single footstep wasted.

"You are very gracious to look after her," Mistress Brearley murmured, her eyes following Alice. "She's the eldest child and the family will need her."

"'Tis my pleasure to do a kindness for a woman in need."

And a recompense, to make up for the sinful thoughts he'd had of her. And perhaps, more selfishly, a way to reassure himself he was still the godly man he wished to be. The one he had so nearly lost to the lapses that had gripped him this last year.

He would get her home.

He would not fail himself, nor Reverend Keeper, nor the Lord.

Not again.

CHAPTER 2

Singing stops the tears, Alice's father had taught her as a girl, whenever she'd skinned her knee or suffered a child's momentary sadness. *Sing a little song, and before you know it, you'll be smiling.* And so, as she climbed the steps to her room at the top of the house, she forced out the first tune that came to mind.

My Pin-Box is the Portion
My Mother left with me;
Which gains me much Promotion,
And great Tranquility:
It doth maintain me bravely,
Although all Things are dear:
I'll not let out my Pin-Box
F'less than forty Pounds a Year

Mama would murder her for singing vulgar tunes at such a time—take it as proof that despite her daughter's supposed London polishing, Alice was still strange, like Papa's people. Even in the best of times, Mama'd hated the broadsheet ditties Alice's father had always hummed as he'd tinkered in his workshop. Her mother preferred ballads. The kind about death and doomed love affairs and the forgiveness of the Lord.

But none of those subjects were likely to keep Alice from crying, so she opened the door to her chamber and sang the next verse louder as she found her traveling satchel and began to gather her possessions.

My Pin-Box is a Treasure
Which many Men delights;
For therewith I can pleasure
Both Earls, Lords, and Knights,
If they do use my Pin-Box,
They will not think it dear,
Although that it doth cost them
A hundred Pounds a Year.

Her voice caught as she yanked her formal receiving dress from its hook. It had been made for answering the door at Charlotte Street. She would likely need it for her mother's funeral.

Her mother's funeral.

Her hands shook too badly to fold the garment properly. She pressed her face into the fabric.

How could this be? A month ago her mother had been her usual forceful self, sending preserves and knitted mittens and a pointed letter declaring it time for Alice to come home and have herself made Mrs. William Thatcher before some other, cleverer, girl claimed the title first.

Alice had resented it, this unsubtle hint that she should end her time in London and return to the drab life that awaited her in Fleetwend, where everyone thought her perverse and loose and willful. She'd made excuses not to come for Christmas, sending a box of candied cherries in her stead.

Candied cherries. Of all the awful things.

She'd thought if she stayed away long enough her mother might come to prefer the money her daughter sent home from London to the prospect of William Thatcher for a son-in-law.

And if not, she'd thought that she had time to seek forgiveness.

Years and years to make her case by a slow process of simply not returning.

But she'd been wrong. If the doctor was correct in his assessment, her mother had, at most, a week.

She pulled her trunk from beneath the bed and rummaged through her letters and books until she found a silver chain buried at the bottom. She fished it out and rubbed the harp-shaped pendant on her dress. Her father had given this necklace to her mother when they'd married. When Alice left for London, her mother had pressed it into her palm. *He loved you so, child. And so do I. Don't forget it.* A sentiment so shocking in its uncharacteristic sweetness that she'd not been able to answer. She'd buried the necklace in her trunk and hadn't looked at it since she'd arrived here.

Now it was dull and tarnished.

She kissed the little harp, feeling like the most ungrateful girl who'd ever lived. "Forgive me, Mama," she whispered, looping the chain around her head and under the high collar of her dress. "Wait for me." Her voice was hoarse with the sadness that seemed determined to seep out as tears, so she squeezed her eyes shut and started up another verse.

I Have a gallant Pin-Box,
The like you ne'er did see,
It is where never was the Pox,
Something above my Knee:
O 'tis a gallant Pin-Box,
You never saw the Peer;
Then would not want my Pin-Box
For forty Pounds a Year.

Elena peered into the room, holding a cloak. "Oh, Alice. Only you would sing bawdy songs with grief." Her mistress's face, usually as serene as the surface of the moon, was taut with concern.

Alice shrugged, grateful that Elena never cared when her behavior was strange. "Better to sing than to weep."

Elena looked at her tenderly, like she was going to embrace her. Alice shook her head and darted over to rummage in her satchel, because Elena's kindness would make the tears fall down, and once they came they wouldn't stop.

Elena knew her well enough not to press emotion on her. She tipped up Alice's chin instead. "In any case," she said with a sly smile, "don't let Henry Evesham hear you singing about your pin-box."

The thought of shocking the judgmental lord lieutenant lifted Alice's mood. She returned Elena's mischievous expression and leaned into her ear to sing her favorite verse.

The Parson and the Vicar,
Though they are holy Men,
Yet no Man e'er is quicker
To use my Pin-Box, when
They think no Man doth know it;
For that is all their Fear
Although that it doth cost them
A hundred Pounds a Year.

ELENA THREW BACK HER HEAD AND LAUGHED. "HUSH! IF EVESHAM hears you, the poor man will go running for the street again."

"The poor man," Alice scoffed. "Please. It's scarcely worse than the filth he wrote in his paper."

Evesham had found fame as the editor of the evangelical news rag *Saints & Satyrs,* which he used as a pulpit to decry London's sins and vices. He'd nearly exposed this club two years before, riding the pressure on their necks to a plum position for himself with the House of Lords, who'd made him a lieutenant tasked with investigating the flesh trade.

"Do you really think it's wise for me to travel with him? After all he's done to us?"

Alice had been horrified when her mistress had invited Evesham to the establishment to learn more about their practices. He'd promised them discretion, but the more he knew about this place, the more evidence he had to imperil all their lives.

Elena just smiled in that mysterious way she had, like she'd already read the ending to the story of your life. "He's the pious sort, Alice, but I suspect he's a decent man. You'll be safe with him."

"I don't doubt for my safety. Just my sanity, stuck beside a sneering Puritan."

"I believe he's a Methodist," Elena said mildly.

"Whatever he is, he looks at me like rancid meat, and I am too distraught to pretend to be pleasant to him." Her voice quavered. She was tempted to sing another verse about her pin-box to steady herself.

Elena only shrugged. "Well, you ought to try. He's traveling to the countryside to write his report, and I sense he's still undecided on his findings. Perhaps you can help sway him to the merits of reform. You'll have the advantage of the final word. It could be an opportunity."

Alice did not need to be reminded that Evesham had the power to make things far more difficult for them if he urged harsher laws. She was flattered her mistress thought her capable of influencing his views. But she did not for a moment believe it to be true.

"I doubt the lofty lord lieutenant would welcome my opinions on the law. He acts like merely breathing the same air as me is sinful."

"You might be surprised," Elena said. "You never know what lurks beneath the surface of a man." She paused, and bit her lip. "Though, perhaps you'll agree his surface is ... remarkable. Ironic, that a man so disdainful of the flesh should be so singularly blessed in its bounty."

Alice groaned, relieved she wasn't the only one who'd noticed Evesham's looks—his burly arms, his lantern jaw, the almost obscene fullness of his thighs beneath his breeches.

She shot Elena the smallest hint of a smile. "It isn't right, a man like *him* looking like *that*."

Elena's eyes twinkled. "At least you will be able to enjoy the scenery he provides, if not the company." She held out the cloak. "Here, take this for the journey. It's terribly cold."

Alice took the heavy garment, a lustrous, purple velvet lined with ermine. It was the kind of robe a queen might wear—no doubt one of the many outrageously fine gifts from Lord Avondale that Elena stored unused and unacknowledged in her dressing room. Elena found Avondale's relentless attempts to win her affection tiresome, but Alice thought the intensity of his devotion to his whipping governess was rather touching.

What do you want, Alice? Mama was always demanding in her letters. *You're never satisfied.* Here, she'd found it. She wanted a life like Elena's. Freedom to rule over a kingdom of her own, surrounded by people who would delight in her eccentricity, rather than wishing it away.

Elena patted her hand. "Come. Evesham is waiting. Write to me as soon as you can and take the time you need with your family. We'll delay your training until you are able to return."

Alice nodded. She did not say what she feared: that her training as a governess would never happen, for the life she had been planning would not be possible if her mother died.

She wouldn't think of that right now. For now, she must simply get home.

She followed Elena down the stairs, pausing at a shelf of books the artisans here passed among themselves. She treasured this modest collection of well-paged tomes on history and philosophy. The presence of ideas had been a second form of payment here, and the one she'd miss the most. She grabbed two volumes she'd not yet read, not much caring what they were, and tucked them in her bag.

Downstairs, Evesham was waiting by the stairs. His bright

green eyes rose at the sound of her footsteps. "Ah. There you are. Allow me to take your bag."

He lifted it as though it were no heavier than a house cat. Perversely, she felt a little thrum at the sight of his long legs ambling toward the door. Perhaps because she had the stature of a dormouse, something in her always lit up in the presence of large men.

She immediately snuffed it out. She would not do Henry Evesham the great honor of lusting after him.

"The groom brought Henry's curricle around," Elena said. "And Mary will bring some bricks to warm you."

Alice stepped out the door to see a vehicle more fit for a fashionable gentleman of leisure than a renegading man of God—a slight, gold-lacquered thing on thin wheels pulled by two elegant horses.

Evesham held out his hand to help her step from the mounting block to the seat. Noting her expression, he let out a sheepish laugh. "Not what you were expecting."

Alice shook her head, surprised he was perceptive enough to see what she'd been thinking.

"Not my usual conveyance," he allowed, smiling. "It's borrowed—but it's built for speed. We'll be in Fleetwend by tomorrow night with any luck."

He stepped up into the curricle, causing the entire seat to shift with his size, and Alice to topple against his shoulders, which were as wide as two of her.

"My apologies," he murmured, whipping his arm to his side like she might pollute his clothing.

She inched away, offended that he should recoil when it had been him who jostled her. She tucked herself into Elena Brearley's regal ermine, wishing it could protect her pride from his judgement.

Mary, the old cook, came and piled steaming bricks around Alice's feet, and a warm flask in her lap. "Cider for the chill." She lowered her voice. "With a touch of gin in it to warm you, if the likes of hisself will let ye touch the stuff."

Mary shared Alice's opinions on the wisdom of consorting with the likes of Henry Evesham. All the servants did.

Henry smiled at Mary. "One could not judge Miss Hull for drinking whatever she likes in such circumstances," he said in a kindly tone.

Alice glanced over at him. His cheeks were flushed. She wondered if he made this false display of charm because he was embarrassed he had flinched from her. Or perhaps it was because he sensed how everyone here resented him for the way he had threatened their livelihoods and walked about their home as if it —*they*—might infect him with low morals.

She took Mary's hand and squeezed it. "Thank you."

"I'll be thinking of you, child," Mary said.

Elena held up a hand. "We all will. Travel safely."

"Onward, then," Henry said, taking the reins. "You must be eager to get home."

"Yes," she whispered.

But as Charlotte Street receded behind them and the curricle wobbled its way over the cobbles heading north, she knew it was a lie. It had been years since she'd thought of home with anything like longing. The tension between herself and her mother had grown so sharp after her father's death it had been like the pitch of tuning fork, a note that always trembled in the air. *Don't be odd, you little changeling. Stop wandering off, don't mourn so, never look at men that way. You'll become unruly like Papa's people and give your sisters strange ideas.*

She was not ready to leave Charlotte Street.

Because she knew—had always known—what leaving here would mean.

It would be a kind of death. And she wasn't ready.

She'd only just begun to feel alive.

She shut her eyes and began to hum a filthy song about a high-prized pin-box, if only so she would not weep.

CHAPTER 3

Henry's father had often bitterly complained that Henry was so dogged in his principles he ran roughshod over practical reality. Observing Alice Hull hunched to the furthest edge of the curricle, shrouded in her cloak and humming joylessly beneath her breath, he wondered if perhaps he'd been over-moved by the spirit in insisting on driving this young woman in a small vehicle on a two-day journey in bad weather.

It was clear she loathed him.

He held himself rigid, hoping if he kept his elbows wedged against his sides, kept his knees pressed up to his breastbone like a mantis, he might demonstrate he desired nothing more than her comfort, and win some small measure of her trust.

But she had not so much as looked at him. They'd been on the road ten minutes, and he was already sore.

He distracted himself with trying to make out the tune she hummed. He didn't recognize the melody, but there was a pleasant timbre to her voice. He wondered if she hummed to fill the silence—and if so, if he should speak to her.

But what should he say? The rude way he behaved last week would make the usual pleasantries seem awkward, but to acknowledge the rudeness seemed more awkward still. Normally he took pains to move through the world respectfully, even when he disapproved of the parts of it he walked through. But that day last week, he'd been in such a state that he'd run all the way from Mary-le-Bone to the Thames and then across the bridge to Southwark, repeating Reverend Keeper's counsel in his head: *vigorous exercise quiets an unruly mind.*

It hadn't worked.

A gentle rain began to fall, veering sideways in the chilly wind. He glanced at Alice, worried she'd be cold. She looked like she was trying not to cry.

Poor girl. What would ease his mind, were he in her position?

Prayer.

But he was not her minister, and she hadn't asked, and he did not wish to be presumptuous. Better to begin with lighter conversation.

"What's that song you're humming?" he asked her.

"You wouldn't know it," she said. She did not resume the tune, and the silence between them seemed heavier than the clop of the horses' shoes against the cobbles.

"I didn't mean to stop you. You have a lovely voice."

She said nothing. Her silence was excruciating.

"I'd planned to stop for the night in West Eckdale," he told her. "There's a pleasant inn there, if that's agreeable to you."

She nodded.

"And we'll take luncheon at a public house at noon. Though tell me if you'd like to stop before then for your comfort."

As soon as the words left his mouth, he regretted the intimacy of what he'd just suggested, for they were little more than strangers. He wracked his mind for something more to say, but he'd only ever conversed with fallen women to interview them about their work, or to pray with them when they came to him in supplication, wishing for God's forgiveness. He could not fathom what he and Alice Hull might have in common.

He wished he had not spoken to her at all.

The curricle hit a puddle that he hadn't seen, tossing them both up an inch into the air. He landed back on the padded bench with a thud, his arm falling heavily on Alice's. Her teeth clicked with the impact.

"Are you all right?" he asked, scrambling away so as not to crush her.

But it was too late, because he'd already felt the softness of her cloak, the slightness of her body beneath it. Already noticed that she smelled sweet, like milky tea with honey.

He did not allow himself sweet things.

(Not anymore.)

"I'm fine," Alice said, scooting so close to the side of the curricle that she was nearly hanging out the door.

"Had I known I would have a passenger, I would have hired a more spacious chaise for the journey."

"I'm grateful for any transport. You need not concern yourself with my comfort." She was polite, but stiffly so, as if the effort of being civil caused her strain. He wondered if this was due to her grief, or her suspicion of him.

"In that case, I'll focus on my own discomfort," he said, shooting a rueful grimace at his knees. "I feel like a grasshopper in knee breeches, crammed into this little cart."

She turned to him and smiled, a sly smile, like a cat might wear. "Aye. Quite a delicate contraption for journeying on country roads in winter, this."

She was just polite enough not to mention that the situation was made worse by the fact he was a giant. Kind of her.

Her voice held the Somerset twang he had grown up with, and her words the bluntness he knew well from his father's people. He didn't mind her directness. He was pleased she was saying anything at all.

"Yes, it's quite a delicate gig for going anywhere," he agreed. "I borrowed it from Lord Apthorp to economize on the expense of travel. I'm saving to marry, once I've fulfilled my duties to the Lords."

He flushed. Why had he told her that?

"Congratulations," she said tonelessly.

He flushed deeper, realizing she'd misunderstood him. "Oh. No, I have not yet had the honor of asking for a lady's hand. I meant only that I intend to ... to find a helpmeet and start a family of my own. Soon."

Reverend Keeper had counseled him to marry, urgently, to avoid another scorching lapse. *'Tis better to marry, Henry, than to burn.*

He glanced at Alice again, to see if she had reacted to his strange admission, but she just stared out at the passing streets, like he'd said nothing. She no doubt had more pressing things on her mind than his bachelor status. He was being an oaf, babbling about himself. He offered her the only comfort he could think of.

"Alice, would you like to say a prayer? For your mother?"

She looked down at her lap, her face inscrutable. "If what my sister wrote is true, my mother is past the point of prayer."

"Prayer is not merely to ask comfort for the ill, but also solace for the bereaved."

"I don't pray," she said flatly.

How impossibly sad. "That need not stop you now," he assured her. "It is never too late to seek a relationship with God. Or to re-sow the field, if it has fallen fallow, as it were."

"With respect, Mr. Evesham," she said curtly, "I am long past saving."

His heart ached at so young a person believing she had consigned herself to Hell. The vehemence of her voice bespoke a history. People did not turn their backs on God without a reason, and sometimes that reason was in fact the way towards faith.

Was this part of the Lord's plan? Had Alice been put in his path for a greater purpose than mere transportation? Was he meant to remind her of God's love?

He hesitated, thinking of a delicate way to tell her no one was past saving. But suddenly she turned and looked him directly in the eye for the first time since they'd left Charlotte Street.

"But then, you know that already, don't you, Lord Lieutenant? Your views on my character seemed clear enough last week."

Her eyes held his, demanding he acknowledge her words.

Demanding he remember what he'd sworn to himself he would not think about again.

His cheeks went hot.

He had offended her by not acknowledging what had happened. A misjudgment, for of course it was better to make amends than sit in silent guilt, and to convince himself otherwise was intellectual dishonesty. He'd chosen *his* comfort over hers. He must make it right.

"Miss Hull, I worried it would be ungentlemanly of me to even speak of such a thing, so forgive my silence, but I am sorry for my unmannerly behavior last week. It weighs on me. You were only doing me a courtesy and I regret the disrespect I showed to you by leaving so suddenly."

The resentment in her expression become something sharper, like amusement. "Quite a mouth you have on you, Lord Lieutenant. Right poetry."

He was taken aback. "Well, I am a minister. We do sermonize."

"And I keep order at a whipping house. You need not apologize to the likes of me. I've seen far worse behavior than a scandalized man running away in fear. But let's not pretend you think I'm the type for prayers."

Oh, bother and bog. He'd made it worse.

"I was not afraid," he felt compelled to say, though his tone sounded fussy even to his own ears. "Not precisely."

In truth, he had been terrified—not of her, but of himself. But he certainly could not explain the distinction, for her comfort on this journey would not improve if she knew what he'd been thinking, then and after, night after night.

"Ah. Ashamed, then?" she countered.

And then it was his turn to stare fixedly, determinedly ahead in silence.

For maybe she already knew what he'd truly been thinking as he'd fled.

And that would be far, far worse.

CHAPTER 4

Her accusation quieted the lord lieutenant.

Good.

Prayer was Alice's least favorite topic, and she did not wish to discuss her low opinion of the Church with the likes of Henry Evesham. She preferred to spend her final moments in London taking in the crowds and shops and smells and sounds of life. She already mourned the barkers' cries and the clattering of carts, the lopsided eaves and medieval walls and twisting alleys in which one could get lost half a mile from one's doors.

She should be grieving for her mother, but what she grieved was London.

"Do you attend a church, Miss Hull?" Henry asked.

She tore her eyes away from the streets, begrudging his intrusion into her sadness. The man's determination to engage her on religion was so relentless she would be impressed by his determination, were she disposed to credit him with any favorable quality aside from looks.

"No."

"I saw you looking at that chapel—" he gestured at a church

she'd scarcely noticed they were passing— "and I thought to mention that if you are looking for a congregation, I worship with many former members of your trade."

Members of her trade? She knew what he implied, but she disliked that he would not say the words directly, like they would filthy up his mouth.

"You worship with other housekeepers?"

He furrowed his brow. "I meant…" He coughed. "Er, that is, prostitutes."

"I'm not a whore, as it happens," she drawled, not because she cared that he might think she was, but because it would be pleasant to embarrass him for making the wrong assumption. "My wicked nature extends to giving tours and polishing keys."

Of course, she was training to do more. But the precise nature of her ambitions seemed irrelevant, now that she was doomed to be an organ maker's wife in Fleetwend. A fate from which church, unfortunately, could not deliver her.

"My apologies," he said quickly. "I only mentioned it because many of the girls I've met during my interviews feel they are estranged from God by the nature of their livelihood, and they needn't be. You could attend a meeting, if you desire an accepting place to worship."

"Lord Lieutenant, what women like myself are most commonly estranged from is a decent income. Whoredom is not caused by a lack of faith in God. It's caused by the desire to eat. You'd do well to understand this, if you wish to improve our lot with your report."

He straightened, clearly taking umbrage. "I do understand that the motive to sin is complicated. It *always* is. I did not mean to imply otherwise. I run a charity for prostitutes, and their welfare is important to me. I merely wanted to offer you—"

She held up a hand. "Sir, if your intention is to preach to me on this journey, I shall have to take my chances with the mail coach. I am grateful for your offer to drive me home, but my soul is not your concern."

Her voice rose more than she liked. She knew she should be doing what Elena said, trying to make a friend of him, to influence his views. But the clergy had lost her good opinion long ago, and she lacked the patience in her current state of agitation to feign tolerance for foolish bluster.

Henry looked like he'd been slapped. "I see. Forgive the intrusion."

He looked back out of the road, rearranging his face into a bland expression. She disliked how good he was at that—covering up his pique. She'd never had the skill of hiding her own feelings. She comforted herself that his face was not nearly so intriguing when he made it so unfeeling, and she was less inclined to steal glances at him and wonder who this 'helpmeet' was he wished to marry.

She could gaze at London instead. The streets were wider now that they neared the edge of town, lined with trees and farms instead of people. Her grief expanded with the open road. London was the opposite of Fleetwend, where every encounter in the village square was heavy with familiarity that went back generations. Somehow, she'd left the place her people had lived for a century and found herself at home.

And just as suddenly as she'd found it, she was leaving it.

She knew she would not have this place again. The furtive, selfish steps she'd been taking to make her life here permanent would not work if her sisters were orphaned. They could not afford her mother's house without her widow's annuity, and even if they could, Eliza was too young to look after it alone. The girls were Alice's to care for, and she could not care for them while training to be a governess.

It had been wild to consider it. She'd always known her real future was in Fleetwend. But she had not known, before she left, that there was another world—one that dazzled her, filled her mind with so many thoughts she sometimes felt like she was flying through the air.

She wished she had not learned.

To know and give it up was so much worse than never having known of it at all.

She began to hum the tune about the pin-box. Henry Evesham drove in silence.

Except for the rumbling of his stomach.

She pretended not to hear the sound, but she noticed him go pink at the evidence of his mortal body needing sustenance. He said nothing, but after an hour of this he cleared his throat.

"I could use refreshment," he said. "Would you like to stop for luncheon?" He glanced at her from the corner of his eye, as though he was nervous to look at her full on.

"The very idea of food makes me feel sick," she said, without thinking.

He looked at her with alarm, like he had mistakenly offered her poison instead of nourishment. Oh dear. She had not meant to snap at him. Politeness was apparently beyond her in this state. *Sense* was beyond her.

"But *you* must eat," she said quickly. "Let's stop."

He helped her down from the carriage and insisted on leading her to find a comfortable seat by the hearth indoors. It was hot beside the fire after hours in the cold, and the sudden comfort lulled her.

She closed her eyes and snuggled down into the plushness of the ermine cloak. The weight of it upon her shoulders was almost like a man's embrace. She hugged herself, and let the feeling carry her out of this stuffy inn and into a half-dreaming state, where she was not fleeing London, but tucked in bed in Mary-le-Bone, with a fire roaring in the hearth and a lover's arms draped around her neck.

Her lover touched her gently on her back, murmuring something sweet to her, her name, some tender words of caring. She sighed and murmured back to go away and let her sleep, and he touched her more insistently, rousing her awake. She smiled and moved to kiss him, for if she did, perhaps he'd let her doze.

But when she opened her eyes—

CHAPTER 5

Henry hated to disturb Alice from her pleasant little nest beside the fire. At rest, the watchful intensity that radiated from her was absent. She looked delicate and beautiful, especially when she let out a long, contented sigh.

But they could not afford to waste the daylight.

"Alice," he said. She didn't stir.

"Alice?" Naught but a grunt.

At a loss, he reached out and gently, ever so gently, placed his hand on her shoulder. "Alice."

She murmured something sleepy and he put more pressure on her back.

She sighed some girlish protest, lifting her head up toward his so sweetly that he leaned in closer, on instinct. His gaze fell to her lips.

And then her eyes fluttered opened and went wide, and she yelped and clutched her cloak over her mouth.

Henry bolted backward, nearly knocking over a table behind him.

"I'm sorry!" he said, aghast at himself for looming over her that way. “You fell asleep. I was trying to wake you.”

“It’s all right,” she muttered, looking at her shoes. “I was dreaming of … I thought you were someone else.”

He tried not to speculate about who she’d imagined was shaking her awake, with that earthy smile on her lips and those …

(Dove’s eyes.)

He handed her a parcel wrapped in paper, trying not to seem like he’d nearly fallen in a trance in a busy public room of a well-trafficked inn. “Bread and cakes and bit of cold ham, in case you’re hungry later.”

“Thank you,” she said, looking surprised. The fact that she evidently thought he’d meant to starve her did much to restore his sanity.

“Come,” he said. “The horses are waiting.”

Outside, the rain had worsened. He frowned up at the sky. “Will you be all right in this?”

She scoffed. “Yes, of course. It’s just a bit of rain, not piss.” She raised a brow, like she expected him to admonish her for her coarse speech, but a fat raindrop landed in her eye. She cursed, and another drop landed on her cheekbone, just beneath her sooty lashes.

“S’pose that’s the Lord, smiting me for cursing in the presence of a vicar.”

“I’m not a vicar,” he said absently. His thumb twitched with the desire to reach out and wipe the drop away. Which, of course, he didn’t.

Alice charged away, pulling her cloak over her head. She hoisted herself into the curricle without his assistance. They drove away in silence, though, after a time, she seemed to be in a better mood.

“I rather like it,” she declared, leaning her head out from beneath the awning and catching a raindrop on her tongue.

"The rain?" he asked, trying not to stare.

She licked her lips and settled back. "Mmm. It smells so clean, especially out here, in the countryside. Tastes like winter."

He was relieved she was making conversation as though nothing odd had happened, even if the conversation itself was strange. "You prefer the countryside to London?" he asked, unsure how to reply to her assertion that winter had a flavor.

She stopped smiling. "No."

She rummaged in the bag of food he'd given her and took out a hunk of cake. She sniffed. "Mmm. Cinnamon," she said happily. She tore off a small corner and took a bite. "'Tis very good."

He'd thought it would be—it had looked moist and rich, studded with nuts and candied ginger. She broke off another corner and offered it to him.

"No thank you," he said. "I don't eat sweets."

"I love sweets. I'd live on sweets alone if given the opportunity."

"I haven't a taste for them," he said. (A lie.)

Alice munched reflectively. "It tastes like the cake my sister Liza makes at Christmastide, when she can get the sugar."

He was curious about her family. "Mistress Brearley mentioned you have sisters. I am sure they will be relieved to see you. Family is a blessing at a difficult time like this."

She only nodded, chewing.

"I have a sister myself," he went on. "I haven't seen her in years. It will be a grand thing to spend a fortnight with her in the country."

She swallowed. "Why such a long time?"

He sighed. "My father disapproves of me. Thinks I'll harm her chances for a husband."

"You?" she sputtered with such force that crumbs flew out of her mouth. "The Lord Lieutenant!"

He tried to keep any bitterness out of his voice, for it would not do to dishonor his father, whatever their disagreements. "He did not approve of my leaving the Church to scribble on Fleet Street and rave in the streets, as he put it."

His father had been furious that Henry had turned down a position as a vicar in their shire—a position his father had strategized and traded favors in order to secure for him—in favor of leaving his curacy to join with a loose circuit of Methodists, and support himself by writing. He'd demanded Henry reconsider.

But faith was not a consideration. It simply was. His allegiance to the principles of Methodism had made him whole. His heart craved a closer communion with God than the Church of England offered.

"Well," Alice said, chewing, "he must be eating crow now that you've risen so nicely."

Henry doubted it. He'd dearly hoped that securing the position as Lord Lieutenant—a higher honor than a vicar, much more like the high church bishop his father had always hoped he might eventually become—would make the man finally see that his refusal to take orders was not a rebellion. But two years had passed with no more than occasional letters from his mother. He'd spent his holidays with cousins, or with friends. He'd been shocked to receive an invitation home to attend his nephew's christening.

"He certainly prefers it to my previous occupation," he allowed, hoping that much was true.

Alice chortled. "Don't we all."

He sighed. He would be the first to admit that his time at *Saints & Satyrs* had not been his finest moment. He'd begun his role with grand ambitions to meld his faith with his mission to bring morality to London's streets—to expose sin, hypocrisy, abuse. But the more his circulation rose, the more his publishers wished for wild stories to drive it ever higher, and the more his ethics became subject to negotiation. He'd become apuff with his own vanity. He'd lost his way.

He'd welcomed the work for the Lords as a chance to return to work of moral value.

But with it had come the new temptations.

Bodily ones.

None of which he cared to share with Alice Hull.

Alice chewed meditatively, having progressed from cake to ham. "Well, then, if he's not fond of you, why are you visiting?"

"He's hosting a small party to mark the birth of his first grandchild. My brother's son. I believe that is the reason for the invitation. Since it coincided with the conclusion of my investigation, I decided to take time in the country to write my report. Spend time with my family."

He hated this gulf between them, especially now that it was coming time to have a family of his own. He'd done everything he could think of to ensure that this trip went well. He'd borrowed the elegant curricle from Lord Apthorp so that he would not anger his father, who was sensitive to appearances being from low origins, by arriving in a badly sprung rented chaise or, worse yet, on the mail coach. He'd sent ahead his mother's favorite tea from London, his brother's favorite tobacco, his sister's favorite chocolates.

He said a silent prayer that this visit would go well. *Dear Lord, please bless us with a warm connection and better understanding, so that love and harmony may flourish in our hearts at last. Grant me the strength to honor my father. Grant me his forgiveness.*

"Pardon?" Alice asked around a mouthful of cold meat. She'd taken off her gloves to eat and he noticed her hands were turning blue. It was considerably colder on the wooded road, especially in the rain.

"I didn't say anything."

"Your lips were moving."

"I was praying."

She wrinkled her nose and returned her attention to her luncheon.

"Would you like me to say one for your mother?" He suspected he knew the answer, but he felt compelled to try again.

"No, thank you," she said around a bite of ham.

"Very well." He'd say one for himself. *Please Lord, let me get your child Alice to Fleetwend in time to say goodbye—*

"She'd be quite proud of me, conning passage home from the likes of you," Alice said, interrupting his thoughts. "She's always after me to cozen to the quality."

"You hardly conned me. And I'm hardly the quality."

"Oh, you're quality as far as Margaret Hull's concerned, Lord Lieutenant." Each breath sent out puffs of steam into the air, which gave the playful tone she'd taken a somewhat puckish, elfin quality that made him want to stare at her.

"What's your mother like?" he asked.

She shivered violently, and he wondered if it was the chill or if he'd erred in asking her to speak of the woman she was worried about.

"Oh … a proud character. Right about every subject she's ever had the pleasure of announcing her opinion on. Tough as a piece of sterling. Hair just as silver, though she'd beat my knuckles with a spoon for mentioning it."

She laughed softly. Sadly. "She disapproves of me. Thinks I disport myself too freely with the boys and poison my sisters' minds with my coarse tongue and strange ideas."

He felt foolish for thinking he had nothing in common with Alice Hull. For he knew exactly the combination of affection and pain in her voice.

"It's difficult," he said.

"What is?" she asked, shivering again.

"How much one loves one's parents, even when one is at odds with them."

Alice said nothing, making him feel a bit foolish for speaking so freely.

The roads had become muddy, and the horses moved more slowly, kicking up muck in their wake. Alice breathed in through her nose, and he felt her tremble beside him.

"Alice, are you well?" he asked softly.

"I'm fine," she said, through chattering teeth. But she did not look fine. He could see her shaking as she stiffly jammed her fingers back into her gloves.

"You're cold. You're shivering. I'm worried you'll take ill."

"The trouble is not my health," she snapped, glaring at him. "It is the fact that my mother is dying, and I am four counties away."

He chewed at the inside of his cheek.

She sighed deeply. "I'm sorry. I'll be just fine."

But he slowed the horses so that he could meet her gaze directly.

"Really," she protested. "Please drive on."

"I'm so sorry, Alice," he said. "I'm so sorry you must endure this."

She grit her teeth and looked away from him. "It's no fault of yours, unless you have the power to stop country women's hearts."

He sucked in his breath. "I regret I lack the power to fix the weather or your mother's health. I meant it's your suffering I'm sorry for."

"Then please stop adding to it and understand I *don't wish to bloody talk.*"

CHAPTER 6

Henry did not reprimand her sharp tongue nor offer to pray for her withered spirit.

Either might have been preferable, for instead he just looked stricken and fell silent.

She would rather tumble out the side of the curricle than cry in front of him, so she struck up her humming. She shut her eyes and put her breath into it, blocking out awareness of anything save the sound of her own voice.

It lulled her into sleep, a state she'd always found easy to lapse into, particularly when she wanted to be alone. This time, she did not dream.

When she woke it was to the carriage stopping. She started. Henry was down on the ground, fumbling with the harnesses. It was dark, and cold, and they were outside another inn.

Alice yawned, and Henry looked up at her. "Ah. Awake at last." He offered her a hand to help her down. She took it, and noticed how strong and steady his grip was, like she was leaning on an iron rail.

"We'll stop here for the night. I secured a private room for you." He hesitated. "Told them you're my sister, if they ask."

"Thank you," she said. She felt guilty enough for shouting at him earlier that she did not bother to inquire as to why he minded whoring but not lying. "I'll just get my bag."

"I carried it upstairs. They asked if you wished for supper, but I thought you might prefer a tray to dining in the public rooms. I asked them to bring you something warm. I hope you don't mind the presumption."

"No, thank you."

She was surprised that he'd taken such pains after the harsh words she'd spoken to him. She should apologize. But the idea of it exhausted her, so she pretended she was accustomed to such kindness. That she was so spoiled from fine treatment she didn't even notice it. That she was the type of queenly girl she'd once flattered herself she might someday become.

Inside the inn was warm and bright. Henry pointed to a door at the end of the hall and handed her a key.

"They've lit a fire for you and there should be clean linens." He gestured at the room beside hers. "I'm here. Should you encounter trouble please don't hesitate to wake me. I sleep lightly, and will hear a knock."

It struck her that he must think her delicate, because of all her napping. The truth was that she was as sturdy as they came—just excellent at sleeping. Sleep was the only privacy one had when one shared a narrow bed with two squirming sisters, and since childhood it had been her best escape. Save, of course, for music.

"Thank you," she told him, meaning for the room, for driving her, and for enduring her poor temper.

"Of course." He paused, his face drawn with concern. "Good night, Alice."

She nodded. "Good night."

She shut the door so she would not have to withstand his look of pity. Her room was small and sparely furnished, but clean and neat. A step above the inns she used to stay at with her father as a girl, where bugs would skitter across her skin and bite her ankles. She removed her rain-damp cloak and changed into her nightdress. A maid came and brought her a steaming bowl of soup and a loaf of hot brown bread with butter. She ate a bit of it, dipping the bread into the broth, but she had little appetite.

She tried not to think of her mother.

She tried not to think of how frightened her sisters must be.

She tried not to think of the terrifying suddenness with which life could rip you open, snatch away all that was good.

She wished she were at home, tucked among her sisters in their bed, falling asleep to the sound of their breath and snores as she had done back before her father died. Back when they had all been together and secure and happy, and it had been no shame to be the strange one of the lot because life itself was not a risk.

She'd prayed at night, back then.

Back before she'd realized prayers were wasted breath.

She would not think of that.

She needed to soothe her mind, lest the bad thoughts take her.

It was too late for singing, so she fished inside her satchel for one for the books she'd borrowed and retrieved the one on top. The pages were coarse, the cover plain brown leather, with no author's name or title.

She opened a page at random, and found that it was not a history, as she'd assumed. It was not a book at all, in the formal sense, though it was bound like one. It was some sort of account or journal, handwritten in the precise script of a clerk.

I have walked a great distance tonight to calm my mind, yet still, it churns with sinful thoughts. It brings me such despair to think that no matter how I endeavor to rid myself of frailty it emerges—as though my capacity for weakness is my most enduring strength. I shall pray for greater resolve, though I sometimes wonder if He tires of my prayers.

How odd. She could not imagine who among the artisans at Charlotte Street might have written such words. She flipped to the back cover, looking for a name, but there was only a date in the same precise hand, followed by a list of duties.

1. Practice intellectual honesty!
2. Account regularly to Reverend Keeper!

It went on just as cryptically, with strange, depressing edicts. The next page was even worse.

Daily Regime for Renewed Perfection of the Mind and Spirit

0400: Wake and morning prayers
0430: Brisk walk, one mile
0500: Physical exercises for strength of body
0545: Breakfast
0600: Prayers and Bible study
0700: Commence work
1200: Luncheon
1230: Resume work
1900: Supper
1930: Brisk five mile walk
2100: Prayers and Bible study
2200: Sleep

SHE SQUINTED AT THE BOOK IN PURE HORROR. IMAGINE KEEPING such a schedule if one did not *have* to. She was no stranger to rising at dawn or to long days of labor—but if she could avoid them, she most certainly would.

All the time devoted to prayer reminded her of Henry, and his hourly offers to turn the curricle into her private chapel.

He was so strange.

There was a kind of charm to him— a touch of nerves, a dab of humor, a flash of kindness—beneath his arrogant exterior. She had not seen this side of him when she'd answered the door on his occasional visits to Charlotte Street, when he'd always seemed pained to be there. She'd certainly seen none of it when she'd given him his tour the week before. He'd spent the whole time with shifty eyes, looking at her as though she was a spider who might lay eggs in his ear at any moment.

It had offended her, for she'd done nothing salty—merely shown him the rooms and listed the services performed there, even humoring his insulting questions as best she could.

"People *request* such things?" he'd asked, looking queasily at a riding crop.

"Men ask for *what?*" he'd marveled, gaping at a dildo.

But in the middle of the tour he'd stopped talking altogether. And then, suddenly, he'd shoved past her and gone bolting up the stairs, looking so utterly disgusted you'd have thought she'd offered to rut him for a sixpence, and had foul breath besides.

At first, she'd been certain she'd done something wrong and landed them all in gaol. But then, when nothing came of it, she'd realized he'd not been so much scandalized as revolted.

And it made her bloody angry. For who was he, to come to *their* place, and judge *them*?

But now he was buying her cakes and coddling her health and begging for the privilege of praying for her mother?

Perhaps *she* was not the odd one in their traveling party.

She put the book aside and closed her eyes. They felt heavy from a day's effort not to cry. From the bitter cold. From life itself.

Her mother had liked to scold her as a girl that there were always pleasures to be had, if one could find the strength of will to look for them.

She focused on the quiet crackling of the fire, the faint pressure of the quilt above her body, the pit-pit-patter of the rain. How nice it was, she forced herself to notice. How pleasant, despite everything, to be warm and snug in bed when it was cold and wet outside.

Her mother had been right.

She let her comfort carry her away.

And when she awoke it was to darkness and the aching quiet of the countryside and the bleakness of the future. The awful, awful truth that this silence would be her life now.

Empty. Hopeless.

She gasped against the weight of fear that pressed the air out of her chest.

She couldn't breathe.

CHAPTER 7

After a light supper, Henry put on his coat and went outside for his evening constitutional. The rain had stopped at last. He walked along the carriage road, using a lamp to light the way. These days, he never slept unless he'd walked at least five miles, careful to observe Reverend Keeper's prescriptions for building ramparts against sin.

"You've lived too long amidst low morals, Henry," the reverend had pronounced, not unkindly, that awful night six months ago when Henry showed up at his door, shaking and stricken from what he'd very nearly done. "'Tis a noble thing you're doing, helping rid our city of its sinful ways. But you must buttress your faith against Satan's temptations, lest they overpower you."

Reverend Keeper had advised a rigorous course of biblical perfection to ward off the worldliness that had crept into Henry's thoughts and habits during his years of secular work. A daily regime of exercise, prayer, Bible study, meditation and rigorous abstention from worldly pleasures, all carefully recorded in his journal.

The routine—the same one he'd observed when he'd first

joined an evangelical fellowship at University—gave him more strength. But it had done little to relieve his growing doubts about his mission to the House of Lords. With every passing day, the report, and the quandary it posed, seemed a heavier millstone about his neck.

Should he, as Reverend Keeper so fervently believed, use his power to suffocate the flames that fed prostitution, and its attendant vices? Or should he be more conscientious to the argument Alice had made so forcefully in the curricle. *Whoredom is not caused by a lack of faith in God. It's caused by the desire to eat.*

He had done enough research to know that, in the practicalities, Alice was not wrong.

But did such practicalities matter, when it came to making laws? Should law protect the body or the soul? Reflect the highest ethics of the nation and of God, or protect its weakest parties, even if that necessitated turning a permissive eye toward sin?

Surely it was closer to the spirit of Christ to be compassionate? But how could he in good conscience remove obstacles to vice? Leaving aside his own morals, his credibility as a reverend would be laughable if he openly advocated for fornication.

And he wanted to be a reverend.

Didn't he?

(Yes? Should the answer not be clearer? Should it not even merit question? *Oh Lord, help me.*)

Did he not feel most weightless when he put himself in God's hands, and most dutiful when he shared His word? Did he not enjoy counseling, worshiping, preaching?

(He did! He did!)

But then, if he was meant to be a man of God, what was it that had flared in him when he'd followed Alice Hull through the hallways of Elena Brearley's club? Why had he nearly choked for air?

Well, he hadn't, not at first. The first room she'd shown him had been a kind of dungeon, with stone floors and a wooden rack against a wall fitted with iron bars and shackles.

"A place for torture?" he'd asked, unsettled.

"A place for pleasure," Alice had contradicted, laughing softly when he'd shuddered.

"Many of our members join the club because they've heard rumors of this room. I've seen men fall to their knees upon entering, in gratitude, because of how closely it matches what they've dreamt of."

He'd wanted to say that desiring the act did not excuse the sinful nature of it. But she'd turned and unlocked another room across the corridor, a chamber lined in burgundy velvet. It contained a number of poles and hooks, across which were strung an elaborate network of ropes, like the web of a spider.

"Some of our members enjoy suspension. Some enjoy tying others, or being bound."

He'd hardly been able to look.

Another door, this one a schoolroom. "For when a governess has caught one of our dear members being naughty."

He wrote senseless notations, trying to keep his expression neutral, so as not to betray his shock.

Another door revealed a bathing room with an elaborate mirrored dressing table. "Some guests enjoy performing acts of service. Playing at being a lady's maid or a valet. Others like to command—to be pampered and groomed like a king."

That was when he'd begun to doubt himself. When his squeamishness had begun to feel like something else. For the bathing tub had sparked a memory of the night that had sent him racing to Reverend Keeper's.

He'd quickly retreated to the hall, not wishing to linger in a place that ushered in unwanted memories of dissipation that would awaken what should not be in his heart.

He'd been relieved when Alice led him to the last room in the corridor. Until she'd opened the door, and the hall had filled with the scent of something spicy and familiar.

Incense.

He'd felt a presentiment of dread, but he'd followed her inside and found himself frozen at the unholy sight of what was in that room. Stained glass panels on the walls. Kneelers. And at the front of the room, an altar.

Of all the things. It was a sacrilege to put an altar in this place. A fake church in a house of sin. *What kind of person would—*

(He would. He would.)

He could hardly breathe, shocked that the execrable, sinful, sacrilegious stirrings he loathed himself for sometimes feeling might be shared by other men. Enough of them that there was an *entire room devoted to it in a whorehouse.*

"What happens here?" he'd forced himself to choke out.

"Acts of worship," Alice had said quietly. "And acts of penance."

His mind swam with ideas of such rank sinfulness his skin prickled, and he turned his back away from the image.

But the thoughts had come anyway.

Hands on him. Perfumed ablutions. A woman kneeling at—

Hellfire.

Hypocrisy.

Damnation.

That's when he'd gone lurching for the door.

He was hot, just recalling it. He shrugged off his overcoat, never mind the flurries of ice that had begun to drift down from the sky.

He walked in the icy night and prayed. He walked, and prayed, and walked, and prayed until finally he was cold again, and his mind was clear, and he was so exhausted it was all he could do to climb up the staircase of the inn and remove his boots and collapse onto his bed.

He was nearly asleep when he heard a cry through the wall.

He stilled, straining to hear.

"No," the voice whimpered.

He lifted his ear to the wall above his bed.

It was Alice. She was gasping. Sobbing in such a way she strained for air.

Poor child. He ached to hear her.

"Alice," he said, making his voice deep and loud so she could hear him through the wall.

No response, save for the sound of crying.

He pounded the wall with the heel of his hand. "Alice, don't despair. I'm here, and God is here."

The sobs continued brokenly.

He thumped the wall again. "Alice, that's my hand. Knock back if you can hear me."

After a brief pause, there was a wan, hollow-sounding tap.

"Good girl. Good girl." He thumped again. "Hold your hand there, and I'll do the same, and we'll pray."

He pressed his palm against the plaster, willing calm and God's grace and succor to her, willing his spirit to pass through to her, so she might take comfort. Even if she did not share his faith, he wanted her to know she was not alone. If she could not perceive that God's arms held her, she could at least know Henry's were only through the wall.

"Alice, pray with me," he murmured. "The Lord is my shepherd. I shall not want."

He heard no speech, only whimpers. Nonetheless he recited the psalm. And when he was done, he recited it again.

Even though I walk through the valley of the shadow of death,

I will fear no evil,

For you are with me.

He continued to recite the words long past the time her sobs abated, almost as if he said them to himself.

CHAPTER 8

Alice awoke as she'd fallen asleep: on her stomach, with her fingers resting against the wall next to her head.

The room was frigid with no fire, and she could see her breath. She snatched her hands beneath the covers and blew on them for warmth.

It was dark outside, but she could hear the sounds of horses and people in the stable yard. Henry would no doubt be eager to leave, but the very idea of stepping into the bitter air was painful. She heard her mother's voice, that old refrain from childhood. *Out of bed, my slug-a-lag. The day's half wasted.*

She smiled. Oh, Mama. The sadness that had pierced her the night before felt less unbearable with the promise of a new, fresh day.

Or perhaps it was the lingering comfort of Henry Evesham's prayer.

She did not know why it had calmed her so. Maybe the repetitive nature of the psalm. Maybe the simple kindness of Henry, a near-stranger she'd been rude to, trying to assuage her grief in the middle of the night. Maybe the memory of praying with her mother as a child.

Whatever it was, it had soothed her.

It shook her, how much it had soothed her.

She wanted to thank Henry for that small peace.

She supposed she could begin by getting out of bed.

She closed her eyes and threw off the counterpane, yelping at the icy air. She danced across the floorboards as she pulled her dress and boots over her stockings, cursing, and hastened downstairs. She found Henry in the dining parlor, eating gruel.

It was strange to look at him in the morning, boyish and young after a night's sleep. He glanced up and saw her coming and his face changed. He looked at her like she was the one dying.

She detested pity.

She strode forward with a jolly, stomping gait, rubbing her hands. "Ah, bless the fire in this room!" she said loudly. "Woke up frozen from toes to tits."

She expected her vulgarity to shock the sympathetic expression off his face, but he ignored her cursing and just looked at her with worry. "Alice. How are you?"

His voice was so concerned that she felt embarrassed by what he knew about her.

"Hungry as a bear," she said, turning to look for a serving girl so that he would not see her blushing.

"Were you able to get any rest?" he asked.

The intimacy in his tone made her more mortified, but there was no serving girl about, so she slapped a smile on her face and nodded. "Oh yes. Quite comfortable, this inn. Better than the ratholes I grew up with. Though chilly on the waking."

He pushed a basket of warm bread and rolls toward her, looking worried. She busied herself slathering butter and preserves over a puffy, fragrant roll and taking an eager bite.

The mingled tastes of yeast and cream and tart, sweet berries hit her tongue, and she sighed with pleasure she didn't have to feign. She wondered that Henry ate only porridge, despite the bounty of delicious confections for the taking.

"Oh, you must try this jam! Heaven."

He shook his head politely. "I prefer a simple diet."

She shrugged and poured milk—fresh, not the watered kind—into her mug of coffee. She took a sip and let the warmth restore her.

Henry had not stopped watching her. She wondered if he was inspecting her table manners.

Well, better that than remarking on her hysterics the night before.

And if he watched her, she could watch him, which she would not mind as he had a pleasant face to look upon as one took the morning meal. He'd shaved and combed back his hair—which he wore unfashionably long, without a wig. It suited him.

He noticed her observing him and flushed a bit. She smiled rather boldly, just to see how he'd react.

He coughed.

She laughed softly into her roll as she lifted it up to her mouth.

Henry took a timepiece from his waistcoat and grimaced. "We should get on the road before there is a queue in the stable yard."

He was right. She swallowed and stood, brushing crumbs off her dress. "I'll settle with the innkeeper."

"No need. I've paid our bill."

She reached into her pocket for her coin purse. "How much do I owe?"

She hoped it wasn't very much. She was already concerned about the expense of the funeral. She sent her wages to her mother, keeping little for herself. She had not planned for a disaster and had nothing to fall back on, no reserve.

Henry waved her coins away. "It's no trouble."

She bristled. "I will not accept your charity. You must let me pay my share."

It was clear that Henry did not live in poverty—his clothing was well made, if modest, and he had the hearty build of a man who was not starved. Still, she doubted he had much wealth to spare, being a public servant and a member of the low church, with its emphasis on charity. Besides, she was not his responsibility. She was already taking more of his benevolence than she liked by accepting his ride home. Not to mention his politeness, in the face of her poor manners. His prayers, murmured through the wall. His kindness, which made it difficult to remember he was a threat.

Rather than answering her, he stood up. "We should set off."

Very well. She would leave coins tucked in the pocket of his satchel when he next stopped to change the horses.

They stopped in the cloakroom to retrieve their winter garments. It was bracingly cold away from the fire. A shock to the chin and the nose.

She yelped at the assault of the cold air and buried her face in her ermine.

Henry frowned. "I should have warned you. It's bitter cold today."

"You've been outside?"

"I always begin the morning with a stroll. It's good for the constitution."

"But it's scarcely six o'clock. When did you rise?"

"Four. I always rise at four."

It must be some kind of predilection of the rich and educated —making a study of self-denial. She'd seen such tastes on Charlotte Street—a hunger to pretend to be lower than one's station. She hoped that were she ever possessed of abundance she would have the good sense to *enjoy* it. To dine on cream and sleep 'til noon and buy a pianoforte and play the dreamy songs that always filtered through her thoughts. She'd buy a cozy house of her own in London and a hundred books.

She'd live in a nest of music and ideas, answering to no one.

Henry helped her into the curricle. "Are you warm enough?" he asked, climbing up beside her.

"Toasty as a roasting lamb," she sputtered through chattering teeth.

He frowned, seeming unsure how this was possible. "You're … over-warm?"

"No, Henry. It would be impossible to be over-warm in this weather. I was attempting to amuse you with irony."

She burrowed deeper in her ermine, so that only her eyes were exposed to the cold air. Her body ran cold at the best of times. She longed for warmth.

Henry, she noticed, barely seemed to shiver. A man of his build no doubt generated as much warmth as a brazier. She stole a look at his coat—an expensive wool by the looks of it—and ardently wished she could crawl inside it. Nothing like the warmth a man gave off, when one was freezing.

She slid a little closer to him, wondering if she might steal a bit of his heat for herself. She paused, waiting for him to object, but he did not seem to notice. She edged a little closer, until she could make out the feeling of his arm against her cloak. She paused, hoping if she went very, very slowly she might snuggle even closer, when a gust of wind came at them and buffeted her face with icy air.

"Bleeding cursed cockles," she hissed, shrouding her face in Henry's shoulder.

"Alice, please don't curse," Henry said so sharply she looked up.

His expression was aghast, though she could not make out if it was at her language, or at his own outburst, or at the fact that she was nearly in his lap.

She had not meant to shock him, nor to pounce on him. But now that she had, well. She rather liked it.

"I'm sorry," she said. "But it's like the frozen steppes of Hell out here today."

He gasped.

Literally gasped, like someone had punched him in the ribs.

"Alice," he pronounced clearly, gravely, the way one might say it if one were training a dog. He moved away, detaching his body from her grip.

She slunk to her side of the carriage, pouting. She supposed she should take care not to further traumatize him with her corruption before he'd delivered her to Fleetwend, since he was doing her a kindness, and since it would not serve her to earn his ill will. She could be well-mannered for a few hours, even if she was an awful changeling child who had a dying mother and no feeling in her limbs.

Perhaps.

"Another hour and we'll be at the next coaching inn," Henry said gruffly. "You can warm up by the fire."

"I'm fine," she sighed. "I wasn't complaining to you, just to the world in general. Ignore my rotted whinging. We haven't time to spare. I need to get home to my sisters."

He clicked his tongue, urging the horses into a slightly faster clip, though they were already at a trot.

"When is the last time you saw them?" he asked her. "Your sisters, I mean."

Her heart gave a little gulp. Too long.

"It's been over a year. I rarely return home."

The time in London had flown by—feeling at once like an era, rich and memorable, and at the same time like a minute, over before she'd realized it had passed.

"That must be difficult," Henry said.

Since he already found her thoroughly wicked, she would not tell him that the most difficult thing was that it had not been difficult at all.

It had been glorious.

The pinnacle of her life.

"When did you last visit home?" she asked, preferring to deflect the question than to further indict her character.

He hesitated. "Five years."

She sucked in her breath. This was genuinely shocking.

"I've seen my mother at my cousin's house. But my father has not wished me home."

She could not help but shake her head. "Half a decade!"

"Yes, and not a day has passed that I did not wish it could be different. 'Tis a sad thing, to be away from one's family."

She sighed, not entirely agreeing but knowing that to object would further convince him of her wickedness. "Yes."

"Why don't you return more often?" he asked. "Does Mistress Brearley not grant you leave?"

She tensed at the implication her employer was anything but generous. "She grants me a week's leave twice a year. As she does all her servants and artisans. But my family relies on my wages, so I prefer to work rather than to take it."

"Artisans?" he asked, looking confused.

"The governesses and masters and others who see to members' needs."

He nodded quickly. "Ah, of course. Prostitutes."

Perhaps she *could* remember he was a threat.

"Call them what you like—they don't mind. But what they

do requires more skill than rutting. It takes talent to read a person's desires, even more to fulfill them, especially when it comes to ropes and whips and other things that can cause harm if not practiced with great care. Catrine, the rope mistress, was an acrobat who performed at the Theatre Royal. Eloise trained fine horses before she trained fine men to serve her—"

"And what of you?" he interrupted. "How is it that you came to work for Mistress Brearley?"

As he asked the question, a drop of something cold and wet landed on her nose.

Snow?

No, surely not. It rarely snowed this far south, even in the winter. She glanced up at the sky. It was flat and gray, cloudless and low.

"Mistress Brearley is a relation of my father's family. I wrote to her seeking a position when my father died. It was my mother's hope that I would go to London for some polishing. Learn to keep a gracious home for my future husband." Stop being so damned odd and dreamy and wanton-skirted, or at least exhaust the impulse away from home, where she would not destroy the family's prospects.

The expression this provoked from him could only be described as "ill." "Your mother wished for you to prepare for matrimony by working for a whipping governess?"

Alice chuckled at his tone. "I assure you she was not aware of the nature of the establishment when I took the position."

A tendon in his jaw spasmed. "Mistress Brearley lied about the position? I would have thought her above such tricks. *Despicable,* entrapping innocent girls."

"No she certainly did not. Elena told me the truth when I wrote to her inquiring for a job, and I kept it from my mother.

Mama would have forbidden me to go and I had no other connections in London."

"Alice, *why*? Why would you wish to work in such a place, knowing what it was?" He sounded like this idea physically pained him.

She could not believe she had imagined she was growing to like him. She must have forgotten his talent for making her very, very angry.

"First of all, Henry Evesham, for the first year I did little other than order meals and mind the maids, no different than I would keeping any house. I scarcely think it's a crime. But even if I *did* sell more than that, it would be because I *chose* to—because the sale would earn me at least three times what I can get in service—and I would be *grateful* for the chance. We cannot all become rich men of ease and leisure through the noble art of casting others' private lives into the papers for public mockery and titillation."

If a man's jaw could become detached from his face, Henry Evesham's was trying. He was no doubt shocked by her opinions, but she flattered herself he was also shocked by her fluency in expressing them, when she wanted to. She had picked up many things at Elena Brearley's house and one of them was a taste for vigorous debate of others' dubious notions of morality.

Those stories Henry Evesham had made his name writing—those about her mistress's establishment and those about the gin-swillers, the gamblers, the adulterers—were devoured because they gave the public the thrill of the illicit. Which meant, if they were pointing fingers, the man of God was selling something sinful too.

"I will grant you that the tone of *Saints & Satyrs* was designed to elicit a strong response," Henry finally said. "But the purpose was not to titillate."

"Then what was it? To make a name for yourself and your fine rhyming verses?"

"No. To open the public's eyes. To provoke a clarity about the nature of the ills that plague our city so that something can be done. And to expose the complicity of those in power who turn a blind eye to it—or indulge in it themselves."

"You circled around Charlotte Street for months, though we hurt no one. There's no shortage of actual violent, dangerous, murdering criminals marauding around London and abusing whores, if exposing crime was your true purpose."

He said nothing, but his jaw was working like he was grinding his teeth.

Well that was fine, for she had *plenty* to say. "I know all the details, Henry. I know how you made a bargain with Lord Apthorp to print the confessions of his sordid past to spare our other members. Is that so noble? Extorting a man's privacy in exchange for mercy?"

He closed his eyes. "I had an obligation to my publishers to grow our circulation. Their demands got out of hand."

He opened his eyes and looked at her, and she sensed from the urgency in them he was, for some reason, desperate to be believed. "When I could afford to, I left."

"Ah," she said triumphantly. "You took what work you could to make your living? So do those of us who work on Charlotte Street. And other places that are far less fine and pleasant."

If this priggish man could not understand that the sex trade was just that—a *trade*—and one of the few open to unschooled women, he had no business casting judgment upon it.

Several more drops of snow fell on her nose, and she pushed them off, furious at this man and at the weather and at the disagreeable quality of life in general.

Henry cleared his throat.

Oh, wonderful, she had won herself another sermon.

"I stand by my mission," he said primly. "My paper did much good. But there were several instances in which I acted beneath my own conscience and allowed my vanity to get the better of me. I do regret that, and I have asked for God's forgiveness. I'm sorry if I hurt anyone you care about."

She had not expected him to concede.

She liked it.

"You should be sorry," she said, pleasantly smug.

"But," he added forcefully, "I will not pretend I approve of the fornication and whipping and … I fear to speculate whatever else … that goes on in your Mistress's establishment. Nor will I pretend to believe you can work there without a moral reckoning."

"Again with the rutting and whipping," she laughed, just to be difficult.

He looked from left to right, as if hoping one of the frozen trees was hearing this and could assure him he had not lost his mind. "You cannot *deny* that is the purpose of the place. You gave me the tour yourself."

She turned to him with the devil's own smile on her face. "Oh I *remember the tour*, Henry. You needn't remind me."

His face went so red she could scarcely make out his eyebrows from his forehead.

Good.

"What Mistress Brearley offers her members, Henry," she said sweetly, "is the freedom to indulge their deepest desires, with no harm, no shame and as little risk as possible."

"Yes," he countered, looking at her dead in the eyes. "Any *sin* imaginable."

She felt the hairs along the back of her neck prickle. Her

mother always said she was like a cur when she was angry, and she felt like one. She wanted to bite him.

"We observe our own morality," she shot back. "Which is to do no harm and take our pleasure without guilt or shame or *risk of exposure in the papers.*"

He blinked. "You do not truly think one can *invent* one's own morality?"

Oh, he was exasperating.

"Is that not what laws are? Morals invented by men with grand houses and fine robes?"

"Laws are a code of justice, based on Christian principles and upheld by the King," he said pedantically.

"Laws are made up by men. Plenty that is moral is not legal, and plenty that is legal is not right."

She smiled, pleased at her own philosophizing. He looked up at the sky. Probably commiserating with the Lord about her blasphemy and rotten soul. But when he looked back at her, his face was contorted into a smile, if a pained one.

"You're rather a quick wit for a woman who insists she is nothing but a lowly housekeeper."

She did not like to admit it, but she was pleased by this assessment from a lofty type like him. This debate reminded her of the meandering conversations she enjoyed with Elena as they read the papers and discussed the business of the house. It had been a worthy education.

"I merely have a decent head for logic and a fine mouth," she said.

He laughed softly, but the smile quickly left his face. "Alice, I do understand what you are saying. You believe people should have the freedom to practice what they wish safely and in peace, separating notions of decency from notions of harm. Many people I've interviewed agree with you."

"What I'm saying, Henry, is that 'tis in your gift to make the streets safer for those who do not have the luxury of working for Elena Brearley." She paused, thinking of the stories she'd heard passed around. Girls and mollies beaten. Culls who didn't pay. Brats, pox, pimps. Not to mention the Henry Eveshams of the world, who judged you as a pestilence for doing no more than trying to make bread.

Henry sighed. "I take my responsibility seriously, Alice. But there is also the question of morality, and I take that seriously as well. I'm curious: how do you personally account for God's morality, working in such a place?"

He posed this question with such earnest sincerity she could not help but bark out an irritated laugh. "*God's* morality? Well, Henry, I suppose I don't account for it at all."

He looked at her in disbelief.

"Henry, I have two sisters, a dying mother, and no money to speak of. We'll lose our cottage without my mother's widow's portion. Liza could work in service, perhaps, but Sally isn't yet nine years old. What do you think happens to girls like us, if no man rushes in to marry them? Where's God's morality in that?"

"If you need help, Alice—"

"I'm not asking for your bloody charity," she spat. "I'm just asking you to remember there are lives at stake. Mine. Elena's. All those girls you interview when you make your sober rounds and scribble down your notes, looking like you might be ill."

He glanced sadly at her eyes. "I am concerned about them, Alice. Gravely concerned. I take my work seriously. I promise you."

She relaxed slightly, for he did look earnest.

"But have you no concern for your mortal soul?" he asked softly.

She wanted to lift her arms and scream in frustration.

Charlotte Street was more sacred to her than any church, and for reasons Henry Evesham would never understand. And unlike the church, Charlotte Street had never betrayed her.

"My soul is not your concern," she muttered. "I told you that yesterday, and I meant it."

He nodded. For a minute, he was blessedly silent.

"It's just that I," he murmured, his voice faraway, as if lost in private thought, "I couldn't bear it."

"Bear what?" she snapped, not at all delighted he had resumed this conversation.

"Living in estrangement from the Lord. Surrounded by so much sin."

He looked at her raggedly, as though the very idea upset him. He seemed *sincere.*

As if he feared for her.

As if he could not imagine what it was to live imperfectly.

As though he had never felt desire.

But she had worked on Charlotte Street long enough to know that *everyone* desired something.

Including, she was certain, Lord Lieutenant Henry Evesham. She had seen the look in his eyes as she'd shown him the chapel room in Elena Brearley's cellar, and if she was not mistaken, they had flashed with something she recognized before he'd run off in his fit of horror: yearning.

Read them, Elena always counseled artisans in training. *Look into their soul and see what they long for. Answer their hunger.*

She decided to put her training to work. "You said you're looking to marry."

He nodded. "Yes. Soon, I hope."

"I see," she drawled. "Then I expect, as a bachelor, you're a virgin? Pure as the dawn?" She smirked, waiting for him to admit his hypocrisy.

His mouth fell open. He flushed a deeper red.

"I don't see what relevance—" he finally sputtered.

Oh.

She had not expected that. Most of the clergy that came to Charlotte Street kept their belief in the purity of the flesh strictly theoretical. But she could tell by his stammering he wasn't lying. He *was* a virgin.

What would that feel like? To be a man his age, to walk daily among *bagnios* and bawdy houses, and shudder in revulsion at the idea of making love?

"Me," she said softly, looking in his eyes, "I couldn't bear it."

"Bear what?" he asked.

"Oh, Henry," she murmured. "Don't you ever want touch? Pleasure?"

Something dark flashed in his eyes. He tore them away from her face, looking pained, though whether it was anger at her prying or the pull of unmet need, she couldn't say.

"No," he said crisply. "I'm perfectly content. There is ample pleasure to be found in living virtuously. And if you *please,* Miss Hull, I beg you not to discuss this any further. I *beg* you."

His voice shook. She glanced at him and realized he was shaky and upset. She instantly regretted she'd let herself get carried away. Her emotions were everywhere—bouncing between despair and anger and provocation. She felt like a witch, like a demon, like a spirit untethered form the world. She could not feel her fingers, much less her sense of decency.

"I'm sorry," she said finally. "You're right. I'm not myself. I did not mean to upset you."

A drop of snow fell into her eye, like Henry Evesham's God was rebuking her for lying.

"No," she corrected herself. "I *did* mean to upset you. Because I am upset and I wanted you to understand why."

His shoulders fell. He nodded. "It's only natural to feel aggrieved. I appreciate your honesty. I won't forget it when I'm writing my report."

They drove on in uneasy silence, an unpleasant tension between them. It only grew as the snow began to fall in earnest. By noon, snow had accumulated on the roads, causing the wheels to skitter.

It was rather beautiful, the way it shrouded the trees in pretty veils of white and danced lazily about the air. But she could not pretend she did not know what bad weather meant. She glanced at the horses, worried for the ice packing in their hooves.

She was certain, from his silence, from the tension in the way he held the reins, that Henry worried too. But they both stared ahead, as if by not acknowledging what was becoming more obvious by the quarter hour, they might prevent it from becoming true.

She began to hum about her pin-box, to keep herself from spinning out the possibilities into dreadful visions. She hummed low, improvising on the tune to keep her mind occupied.

Beside her, she heard a rumble. Henry was humming too.

She glanced at him, and he gave her a weary, close-lipped smile. His voice—a tenor, by the sound of it—met hers, and formed a harmony. When she went up an octave, and improvised a measure, he found the counterpoint as easily as if they'd sung the song a hundred times.

She began to laugh, both in joy at the companionable pleasure of the harmony, and at the outrageous notion that the pious Lord Lieutenant was unwittingly crooning the melody to a song about the cunny of an unrepentant whore.

He smiled. "Is my voice so amusing?"

"No, Henry," she answered honestly. "Your voice is lovely."

Below them, the carriage creaked, the wheels straining.

Henry's face tightened, then collapsed into something like despondency.

Finally he sighed, and looked over at her with a posture of defeat.

"Alice, I'm not going to be able to get you to Fleetwend in this weather."

CHAPTER 9

Henry had developed a theory about Alice's humming: She hummed the way he prayed.

To ease her worries. To be alone inside her thoughts—or perhaps to be released from them. To turn them outward, so that inside, she had peace.

And so he hummed too, because prayer eluded him just now. He felt defeated.

All day, he'd studied Alice like she was a verse of scripture he was trying to illuminate. Her broken sobs the night before. Her seeming inability to acknowledge her vulnerability and grief in the light of morning. Her joy in simple, earthly pleasures—raindrops, hot buttered rolls. Her fierce convictions about her work, and his, and her impish delight in rattling him. The way she was sometimes so intense it felt like her gaze might scorch him—and sometimes so dreamy that had he not been acutely aware of her body's nearness, he would have thought she'd floated away when he wasn't looking.

He could not remember the last time he had met a person who

made him contort his mind to comprehend her—to pin her down as this or that. There was a singularity to her that seemed to defy classification. An originality that was precious—worth protecting.

And he was failing at it.

He knew it was not his fault that the weather had turned too severe to finish the journey, but he felt responsible. And disappointed, for he had hoped it was within his gift to lift the burden of worry from Alice, rather than to contribute to its protraction.

(And was there not, if he was honest, a selfish motive too? Had he not wanted her to look at him and know that, whatever their philosophical differences, he had come to her aid? Had he not wanted her admiration, or at least her gratitude?)

(He had. Nay, he still did.)

But he had only added to her worries.

Why had he debated with her? If the Lord wished for Henry to remind Alice of His love for her, surely discussing sin and punishment was not the way. He should have told her of the way the Lord could hold you. The comfort of the endless, awe-inspiring sacrifice of Christ.

He'd done exactly as his father always said: put principle ahead of people.

And now he sat beside this girl he'd failed, braced in the shameful echo of the words he'd known were true for an hour, but had not been able to bring himself to voice until this moment: *I'm not able to get you to Fleetwend in this weather.*

He snuck a glance at her, fully expecting to see contempt written on her face for his inability to do what he had promised. Fully feeling he had earned it.

But she merely looked up at the sky and nodded.

A realist, apparently, Alice Hull. He was not sure why this surprised him.

"There was a sign for an inn a half mile away. Leave me there and I'll catch the next mail coach that comes through once the snow stops. You've been more than generous in taking me this far."

"No, of course not. We're near enough to my father's house to make it there. I'll take you with me and as soon as the roads are passable, we'll drive on to your mother's. If the weather clears overnight, we could get there by mid-morning."

She looked at him like he had sprouted horns. "You want to take *me* to your family home?"

He nodded, not acknowledging the implication of her question, though he knew very well what she must be thinking.

"It's no imposition," he said quickly. "They have plenty of space."

She laughed softly. Lack of space would not be the reason for their objection to bringing home a woman such as Alice, and her eyes made clear she knew this as well as he did.

"And how were you planning to explain where you'd collected the likes of me, Reverend?"

Well, he couldn't.

He had offered to take her to Fleetwend assuming that he could deliver her to her door without anyone who knew him learning he'd driven a woman of questionable character alone across the countryside. If it became gossip, there would be the question of propriety—perhaps damage to his reputation. But more immediately, he could not set off this delicate reunion with his father on the wrong footing. Which meant he could not tell his family who she was.

He would have to lie.

He'd known this, abstractly, but it felt much worse now that he had to suggest a deceit aloud.

"I will introduce you to my parents as a widow. Mrs. Hull. A member of my fellowship on her way to visit her ailing mother."

The unsavory nature of the request felt sour leaving his mouth —not least because it would no doubt confirm her view of his questionable ethics.

"I mean no offense," he added quickly. "Truly. It's just that … my father is sensitive to the appearance of things, and he would not approve of me driving an unchaperoned maiden." He did not add that if his father knew the nature of the work of this particular unchaperoned maiden, he would without question throw them both out of his house, and likely never speak to Henry again.

Nor would he be discreet about his reasons why.

Rumors could get back to Reverend Keeper. It was imperative Henry prevent gossip. His future depended on the Reverend's belief that he was reformed.

Alice drummed her fingers on her knee. "I will not cause trouble for you Henry. You may say whatever you like. But I'm confused. Is it not a sin to lie to one's own family?"

He sighed. "It is. But the greater sin would be to leave you stranded when your mother is ailing, and it is in my gift to take you home."

"Ah, I see. You uphold your own morality." She scrunched up her mouth, a pronounced twinkle in her eye.

He had to grant her grudging respect. He, too, liked to gloat upon winning arguments.

"I see your point. But I would argue that my father's objections are not rooted in morality. My father would disapprove of my driving you home because it lacks the appearance of respectability. From a moral standpoint, I know that I would not behave in such a way that your respectability or mine would be called into question, whatever the appearance. The appearance is not what is important to me if the intention and result are good."

She looked at him earnestly. "I'm teasing, Henry. I understand your relationship is strained. I'll do whatever I can to help you. Whatever you need me to say or do, just ask."

Her sudden sincerity touched him. He prayed there would not be call to ask—that the weather would clear with the sunrise, and he would have no further cause to perpetuate untruths.

"Thank you, Alice."

She shrugged. "Such are the advantages of an immoral woman."

Despite his low mood, he laughed. She smiled broadly, like she was pleased to have amused him. That is, until he drove past the forested outer grounds of his father's land, and the rolling hillocks came into view. On the highest of them sat his father's house, grand and large enough for ten families, all its windows lit with candles. Such a waste.

"Foreskin of Christ!" Alice uttered, gazing at it like it was something tasty she could eat.

He nearly choked. "Alice, *please.* You mustn't speak that way."

She continued gaping, unperturbed. "You live *here*?"

He shook his head. "Not me."

Her eyes had gone as large and round as sixpence in her dainty head. She'd obviously not been expecting him to hail from an estate like landed gentry. And in truth, he didn't. His father had purchased the estate when Henry'd been eleven and already at school. The glass-monger's airs in buying the old priory were met with great scorn by the other landholders in the area, who laughed at the enormous, modern house he built on the land. That Charles Evesham was richer than all of them made no difference then, and Henry doubted it made any now.

But his father had not believed the contempt of his betters would last. He'd thought he could buy respectability. And perhaps, in a way, he had—for Henry's brother had married well, and his mother planned to bring his sister out next year in London.

"Good thing I'm wearing my furs," Alice pronounced, grinning merrily at him.

Despite himself, he smiled.

Alice pointed at the spires of the snug, stone building to the west of the main house.

"What's that?"

"The old priory. It's the original structure on the estate."

"What does your family use it for?"

"Nothing in particular. Storage. It's mostly empty—the chapel has some pew-boxes and a decrepit old organ my sister likes to pretend she can play."

Her eyes remained fixed on it. "It's beautiful."

It was, and yet the sight of it filled him with unpleasant memories of his father chasing him and his friends out of it when they'd gathered there to worship, accusing Henry of holding a conventicle that would get them all arrested.

He looked away.

As they neared the house, the grand front door burst open and his sister, Josephine, came running out of it in only her gown. She waved her arms and beamed as she dashed down the steps past a waiting footman.

"You're here!" she cried, as he slowed the curricle to a stop. "Oh, Henry, I thought you would never arrive. I've been watching at the window for hours, worried the snow would keep you."

He hopped to the ground and pulled her into a long, tight hug. Despite their difference in age he and Josephine had been close as children. They still exchanged letters, but since the last time he'd seen her she'd transformed from a girl into a polished young woman. It made him sad that he had missed it.

"Where's your coat, goose?" he asked. "You'll catch your death."

From over his sister's shoulder he noticed Alice wince at the word death, and he immediately reproached himself for speaking so insensitively of mortality when its specter haunted those she loved.

Josephine released him and turned to look at Alice. "Why, you didn't tell us you were bringing a lady home," she whispered. "Don't tell me you've gone and eloped. Father will have a fit."

The idea of being married to Alice Hull brought a flush to his cheeks that he could feel despite the bracing air and the flecks of snow that tumbled off his eyebrows.

"No," he whispered back. "This is Mrs. Hull," he said in a louder, warmer voice. "She's a member of my church. Her mother lives nearby and is ailing. I hoped to take her home on my way here. But the weather has not cooperated."

Alice bowed her head and accepted Henry's hand to be helped down.

"Pleased to make your acquaintance, Mrs. Hull," Josephine said, flashing a big, bright smile at Alice, who smiled back. He noticed Alice held herself erect and demure, without a trace of the impish cast to her features she had displayed in cursing at the size of his father's house.

Foreskin of Christ was not a swear he'd heard uttered in even the worst kind of brothel, and Alice Hull was only coarse when she wanted to be.

Which meant she'd said that just to provoke him.

Why?

I'm teasing, she'd said. Did that mean that she liked him? Considered him a friend? Or did she do it because she still mistrusted him?

Why did the answer seem so important?

(Because you—)

Josephine grabbed his arm. "Come inside! The cook made you rum pudding and I've been salivating over it all day."

He refrained from noting that he did not allow himself rum or pudding.

Instead, his stomach knotted with his nerves, he followed his sister up the stairs into his father's house.

CHAPTER 10

Alice could feel the tension radiating from Henry as they walked inside the house. He was nervous and trying not to show it. It was a state she knew well from observing new members at Charlotte Street, but not one she had expected from a grown man, walking into his family's home. It made her a little sad, how uncertain he seemed to be here. She hoped, for his sake, that his visit would be a warm one.

She tried to keep a subdued expression on her face as servants took their coats, for she did not wish to embarrass Henry by marveling too openly at the extraordinary splendor of the house.

But it was difficult, because the place was like a monument to luxury. The carpets were brilliant and plush beneath her feet. The elaborately carved woodwork gleamed under hundreds of wax candles set in enormous, sparkling chandeliers and delicate, etched sconces. Every surface was bedecked in crystal vases and intricately painted bowls and fanciful glass ornaments. She wanted to run off and explore, to count the rooms and examine the gilt-framed portraits and run her fingers along the tapestry-paneled walls and sniff the hothouse flowers and weigh the delicate china ornaments in her palm.

"My dear, my dear," a tall, red-haired woman cried, rushing into the room to greet them. She grabbed Henry and clutched him to her bosom with obvious relish. "Oh, my boy, how very happy I am to have you home at last!"

"I'm happy to be here, Mama," Henry said. The smile of pure gratitude on his face nearly broke Alice's heart.

He'd clearly gotten his build and hair from his mother's side, for Mrs. Evesham was nearly as tall and broad as her son. She squeezed him for so long that, after a moment, he seemed to shrink a bit with embarrassment at the outpouring of maternal affection. It was a gesture she recognized from having made it many times herself.

Don't do that, she wanted to tell him. *Be grateful for her love for you. For her health.*

Henry's eyes scanned the vast and empty hall. "Where are the others?" he asked.

Mrs. Evesham straightened, and the joy seemed to leave the room like a candle being snuffed. "Your father and Jonathan are in the study having brandy."

"Of course," Josephine added, with a look that indicated this was their usual practice, and one she found trying.

Henry's stomach growled loudly, causing his mother to laugh. "Ah, still my hungry Henry," she said affectionately.

Henry winced, clearly not fond of this pet name.

Mrs. Evesham did not seem to notice. "Fear not, supper will be in an hour. In the meantime, I'm sure you'll want to freshen up. Henry, your room is just as you left it. And Josephine, would you show Mrs. Hull to the bedchamber next to yours? I'll think she'll be more comfortable there, instead of alone in the guest wing."

"Thank you," Alice said. "I'm so grateful to you for your hospitality." She did not add that she doubted there was a single room in such a house in which she would not be comfortable, right down to the scullery closet.

Josephine smiled warmly at Alice, gesturing for her to follow her up the grand staircase.

"You'll want to dress for supper," she said kindly, taking in Alice's drab gown. "Father's quite formal about his table."

Bollocks. All she had beside her service dresses was her dark receiving gown, more apt for a funeral than a rich man's formal banquet. She didn't mind looking odd for her own sake, but she wanted to be as good as her word in not causing trouble for Henry.

She wished she'd had time to ask him questions. How would a proper Methodist widow dress? How would she behave? Who would she have been married to? Would he have been handsome? Would Mrs. Hull have been his queen?

"Oh, I'm in mourning, you see, and—"

Josephine nodded. "Of course. If you haven't packed for company, perhaps you'd like to borrow something of mine? I'm a little taller than you"—this was an understatement, for Josephine shared her brother's height—"but my maid could pin up the hem in a few minutes."

"Thank you, if it's not too much trouble."

Josephine laughed. "Not at all. Baxter will be pleased to have another victim of her vicious hairdressing. Don't say you haven't been warned."

Alice laughed too, though she was surprised that Henry's sister's manner was so cheerful and warm. It did not match the formality of the house, nor her polished accent.

Josephine led her inside a room with an enormous bed, three times as wide as the small one in Alice's garret at Charlotte Street.

It had four carved wooden posts and was surrounded by curtains held open with frilled ribbon.

"I'm just next door if you need anything," Josephine said. "Baxter will bring a gown to you and I'll come and fetch you for supper."

"Yes, please. Thank you, Miss Evesham."

Josephine smiled and shut the door.

Alice went to the floor-to-ceiling looking glass and examined her reflection.

She looked like a hedge-bird—more appropriate for begging at the stable door of this palace of a home than for sleeping in it. Her gown was rumpled and her hair was matted up in torrents from the hooded cloak. Her mother would have a fit, her looking such a shambles in a place as fine as this. *Alice, girl, pin up your hair and act the lady.*

Hearing Mama's voice so clearly in her mind knocked the wind right out of her. She remembered the words Henry had murmured through the wall the night before:

Even though I walk through the valley of the shadow of death,

I will fear no evil,

For you are with me.

She had not prayed in years. But the soothing nature of those words called out to her, and she knelt before by the fire and clutched the little harp that dangled from the necklace at her throat.

I'm coming, Mama. Please wait for me.

The words did not feel like enough. She tried again.

Dear God:

Was that how one prayed properly? Was it like writing a letter?

I know I have not been a faithful correspondent, and it's selfish of me to resume our acquaintance only to ask you for a favor. But please, if you receive this message, let her live. Grant me the time to say goodbye.

God gave no sign of having heard her, but the door swung open and a woman marched in carrying a beautiful blue gown embroidered elaborately with lavender blossoms.

"You Mrs. Hull?" she asked.

Alice nodded.

The maid curtsied. "Baxter, madam. Miss told me to pin you into this. Let's get you undressed."

Alice had not been dressed by someone else since she was a child, and she did not know what to do. But Baxter's fingers were so brisk that before she knew it she was out of her drab gown and dressed in a fabric as soft as clouds that smelled of rich people.

"Now, your hair," Baxter said. "This flat look doesn't suit your wee head."

Alice was not sure whether to laugh or cry at this observation. Her hair was not her crowning glory, especially after a day in the rain and snow. "Not much to be done about that. My hair is lank by nature."

"Not when I'm dressing it, it's not," Baxter said, with a wink. The woman sat Alice down at a pretty gold table and began doing violent, painful things to her scalp, something between massage and torture. Baxter used her comb to tease the strands into whorls that she held in place with hairpins, moving them rapidly from the pocket of her apron to her mouth to Alice's increasingly tender head.

"There we are," she said, stepping back, so Alice could see herself in the mirror.

"Oh my," Alice breathed at her reflection. The dress was not immodest but cut much lower than the high-necked gowns that made up her Charlotte Street wardrobe. The dark blue set off her eyes, making them more violet than brown. But her hair was the real miracle. Baxter had removed Alice's middle part in favor of an intricate high chignon that swooped elegantly above her hairline, making her look, if not tall, positively regal.

Baxter winked, smoothed Alice's gown to fall more gracefully about her shoulders, and left as briskly as she had arrived.

Alice could not help casting a sly smile at her reflection. She looked like quite the Lady Miss. Perhaps *this* was her sign from Henry Evesham's God, for her mother would cackle with pure glee at the looks of her right now.

Josephine came to get her and led her downstairs to a formal parlor where the family was gathered. "Prepare yourself for the festivities," she said in a dry whisper.

Despite the sumptuous surroundings and flickering candles, the mood in the room was palpably grim. A thin, impeccably dressed gentleman wearing a powdered wig seemed to be presiding, and beside him was a man who could have been his twin, were he not several decades younger and his own wig quite a bit taller. They were locked in a low conversation with Henry, who had to bend at the waist to match their shorter stature, and did not appear to be enjoying himself.

When he saw her, he broke away, looking at her with an expression almost like bemusement. She stiffened, worried that she had already done something amiss that might expose their lie.

"Why Mrs. Hull," he said, his face breaking from perplexity into a cockeyed, boyish smile that made him look extremely handsome, and nothing like a minister. "Blue suits you."

He'd never looked at her like that before. Like he was just a man, and she was just a woman.

"You look well yourself." But then, he always did.

He smiled—a quick, private smile—more to himself than her.

Josephine looked from him to her and Alice paused—she'd forgotten the girl was right beside her. Evidently so had Henry, for he quickly stepped back, assuming a more formal posture.

"Let me introduce you to my family," he said, leading her to the pair of men. "Mrs. Hull, this is my elder brother, Mr. Jonathan Evesham, and my father, Mr. Charles Evesham."

She curtsied and said "good evening" and was relieved when both men gave her polite, dismissive bows and returned to their conversation.

She turned her attention to a collection of pale china vases placed on the nearest table, painted with purple flowers that resembled the ones embroidered on her dress. "So pretty," she said offhand to Josephine, so that Henry would feel free to rejoin his father's conversation rather than worry about putting her at ease.

"Why thank you," Josephine said with an enormous smile. "I painted them myself."

"I've seen similar in a little shop in Mayfair, but yours are so much finer. What talent."

Josephine looked immensely gratified. "Papa fabricates them for me in his factory. I have a mind to sell them, but he believes I will never find a husband if I appear to have an interest in trade."

"Men have such odd notions," Alice sighed. She froze, for perhaps that was not the right thing for a proper widow to say.

Josephine just rolled her eyes. "Truly."

"Why, the Lord Lieutenant has arrived!" a woman's voice called from across the room.

Alice turned, and saw that the voice belonged to a drawing of a wealthy woman in a newspaper. Or rather, a woman who looked exactly like a drawing of a fashionable lady, with glossy dark hair piled in such an elaborate fashion above her head that it made the handiwork Baxter had performed on Alice's tresses seem rudimentary. She wore a beautiful silk dress in a chestnut shade that matched her hair, and amber jewels set in yellow gold, so that when she moved it was like the colors of autumn swirled about the room.

"Olivia, have you ever met Mr. Henry Evesham?" this vision said to someone behind her shoulder. "He wasn't at our wedding."

A second woman walked in quickly to catch up with the first, and she was equally striking, though her hair was blond, and her gown was a deep, saturated pink adorned with fine, whispering feathers.

Alice knew that women like this existed, theoretically, but she rarely came across such creatures in the wild. The wealthy women who held keys at Charlotte Street did not come to the establishment in such regalia. She tried not to stare, despite desperately wanting to.

Henry looked perplexed to be the center of these two ladies' attention, though the rest of the family looked on as if nothing was out of the ordinary. Alice watched as he was introduced to the blond woman, Miss Olivia Bradley-Hough of Bath, who Alice gathered was the cousin of the other woman, who was married to Henry's brother and who the family called Isabel.

Josephine introduced Alice to the ladies, who gave her gracious smiles. The elder Mr. Evesham signalled to the servants, who opened a door to a long, grand dining room. Inside, the table was dressed with more dishes than Alice had ever seen at once. The spread was thoroughly delightful, arranged on gleaming silver platters in towering heaps that seeming to quiver in excited anticipation of being eaten.

Alice felt the long day of cold and worry melt away in the face of such a feast.

This was going to be fun.

She was shown to a place between Henry and the senior Mr. Evesham, who headed up the table. Josephine sat across from her, and Miss Bradley-Hough sat at Henry's other side, beside Jonathan Evesham, who would be handsome were it not for a pinched expression that made him seem permanently cross.

As soon as everyone was seated, a retinue of servants emerged, graceful as ballet dancers, holding more trays of food, which they proffered to the guests. A footman went around to fill their cups with wine. When he reached Henry, Henry politely waved him away with a soft "no thank you."

"Why, no wine Mr. Evesham!" Miss Bradley-Hough said, laughing. "How sensible you are. The gentlemen of Bath are forever in their cups at supper. It drives my mother to fits, trying to keep her cellar filled."

"She should host more Methodists," Henry quipped. "We're mostly a temperate lot, easy on the purse strings. If she'd like to set an example, I'm sure we can arrange for a revival."

Miss Bradley-Hough laughed, but Alice noticed Henry's father scowling at the exchange.

Another servant came by with a mousse of fish and Henry waved that onward too, taking none. He piled his plate with potatoes in cream sauce and a dish of greens. When a platter of pork filets in butter came by him, he waved that away too. He did the same with a big, beautiful leg of lamb that smelled like heaven itself.

With each dish he declined, his father became more visibly annoyed.

"Take some lamb, Henry," he ordered his son in a voice pitched low enough, Alice suspected, to avoid being overheard by Miss Bradley-Hough.

"No thank you," Henry said pleasantly, instead accepting a dish of jellied fruit.

"A man cannot subsist on potatoes and jelly," his father hissed.

Henry looked taken aback. "I prefer not to eat meat, as you know," he said calmly.

"You'll make yourself ill," his father barked. His voice lacked the educated smoothness of his children's and his wife's. His accent reminded her of the blacksmith's in Fleetwend, Mr. Flaiff, who'd gown up poor in Bristol.

Henry laughed—a forced kind of laugh that held no amusement. "I have not eaten the flesh of God's creatures in years, and I have yet to waste away."

"Indeed," his brother said slyly, leaning over Josephine so as to better hear the conversation. "He's built like an oxcart as it is. If he ate properly, I imagine he wouldn't fit through the door."

Henry's mouth curled up in an utterly acidic smile. "Quite," he said evenly.

"Well I've never met a gentleman who lives on vegetables!" Miss Bradley-Hough remarked, no doubt trying to smooth away this disagreement—an act of graciousness that Alice thought admirable. "Are you also a vegetarian, Mrs. Hull?"

Alice glanced down at the generous portion of red-blooded, silky lamb she'd heaped on her plate, and hoped a meatless diet was not some characteristic of Henry's sect that would expose their lie about her being a member of his worship circle.

"Evidently not," Alice said to Miss Bradley-Hough, jauntily spearing a piece with her fork and putting it in her mouth with delectation.

Beside her, Henry laughed appreciatively.

In truth, she could not imagine turning down such luxurious food. She was shocked when the plates were cleared, a whole new array of dishes was brought to the table, and the process repeated.

As the dishes came around the two lady cousins chattered of this and that—evidently they had both grown up in Bath, and Alice gathered they were quite popular there. Isabel Evesham seemed to be doing her best to forward a friendship between Henry and Miss Bradley-Hough. Oddly, Isabel's husband seemed to be doing his own best to block his wife's efforts—to the obvious agitation of his father. Meanwhile, Josephine and Mrs.

Evesham told Alice of their preparations for the Christening, as though none of this was happening.

Observing the Evesham family at supper was like watching a game unfold, without quite knowing what the object of it was.

"Tell us of your work in London, Henry," Isabel said. "It sounds so very important."

Henry's fork paused in the air. The entire family stopped talking.

"Yes, how is your little flock these days?" Jonathan asked. He'd been drinking heavily throughout the meal, and his words had grown thicker and less clever with each sip. "Still giving farmers' wives conniptions in the streets?"

"Not as often as I like," Henry said smoothly. "My work for the House of Lords leaves little time for preaching."

Jonathan turned to Miss Bradley-Hough. "Olivia, my brother has always had quite a way with women. He makes them faint, y'see. Claims they're moved by the spirit of the Lord, but—" he paused to take a swig of claret—"I've always said it was boredom at the sheer duration of his sermons."

He chuckled at his own joke, smiling at his wife's cousin as if he was certain she would also find this very droll. Miss Bradley-Hough looked nervously down at her plate. Henry's face continued to be fixed in an expression of sardonic boredom.

Alice had lost her appetite.

Imagine, not seeing one's family in years, only to be subjected to drunken mockery within an hour of arriving. And mockery that came at no provocation. Alice's mother could be critical, but at least she did not behave that way for *sport.*

"The Lord Lieutenant's sermons are in great demand in London nevertheless," Alice interjected, looking Jonathan Evesham directly in the eyes and employing the arctic tone she'd perfected under Elena Brearley's tutelage. "People gather from across the town to hear him on Friday afternoons. 'Tis why he was made a deputy of the House of Lords."

"He was made a deputy," Jonathan rejoined, "because he traffics in obscene tales under the guise of Christian virtue."

At the word 'obscene' Miss Bradley-Hough jumped a bit in her seat, causing her elbow to catch a passing platter of duck in brown gravy. Alice watched in fixed horror as the tray overturned in a colossal arc through the air and rained a cascade of sticky, orange-scented sauce down the front of her beautiful pink gown.

The scream she let out was, Alice thought, a rather fitting conclusion to the meal.

Isabel leapt up and rushed around the table to come to her cousin's aid as a cavalry of servants scurried about, attempting to staunch the worst of the damage. The whole chaotic party rushed out of the room, leaving two empty seats, and the rest of the Evesham family looking stunned.

"Jonathan, what has come over you?" his mother hissed from the end of the table. "Speaking of such things in front of a lady of Miss Bradley-Hough's breeding." She glanced at Alice. "And our guest, Mrs. Hull."

Jonathan waved his hand expansively and rolled his eyes. "'Tis only the truth. Imagine, he could have been a bishop. Instead he traffics in hysteria and hellfire, yet condemns his own family for peddling porcelain."

"I don't condemn anyone," Henry said heatedly. "I only suggested you not sell to traders headed to Barbados, as—"

"Oh please," Jonathan Evesham spat. "You can spare us your moralizing. Save it for your sermons."

Alice could see Henry forcibly restraining himself. His shoulder blades stood out beneath his artfully tailored coat, like they might burst through the fabric.

The senior Mr. Evesham held up his hand. "Enough, Jonathan."

"No wine, no beef, no wife, no life," Jonathan went on merrily, smacking his lips in satisfaction at his little poem. "But then, I suppose he has his choice of wayward women with whom to spend his lonely nights."

"What an utterly preposterous statement," Alice burst out.

Henry met her eye and subtly shook his head at her, as if to say *don't get involved*—but his fingers clenched his glass of milk so tightly that she wondered how it didn't shatter. She was so angry on his behalf that she wanted to leap up and push his brother into the remaining puddle of duck sauce. Instead she channeled this impulse into lowering her voice into the flat, belittling tone she'd perfected answering Elena Brearley's door.

"It is true, sir, that Mr. Evesham is highly influential in London for his ability to provide solace to the suffering," she said. "But he also strikes a great deal of fear into the hearts of drunken louts as result of the rather significant power at his disposal. Some might argue such a combination is terrifying enough to command respect. But then, one has to be clever enough to see it."

CHAPTER 11

It turned out that a fearless, sharp-tongued woman trained by an expert in dressing down males who considered themselves superior was an effective accessory to bring to a family supper. Oh, the surge of pure, radiant affection he felt for Alice as she glared at his brother, like Jonathan was no better than a flea.

His entire family stared at Alice, as if not sure whether to be angry or afraid of her.

His mother, clearly noting that there was little hope of returning to civility, stood up before the verbal altercation could become more heated, or another dinner guest could wind up covered in roast fowl.

"Ladies, shall we leave the gentlemen to brandy and retire to the drawing room?"

"I will join the ladies," Henry said, rising. He shifted his eyes to his brother. "After all, as Jonathan points out, I don't drink."

"Stay," his father ordered. "We have things to discuss."

His mother signaled to Josephine and Alice to follow her out of the room. Alice shot him a questioning glance. He smiled at her reassuringly, touched, if a bit ashamed, that she was worried about leaving him in a room with his own family. Imagine, he had worried *she* might lower him in his family's esteem. He should have been worried his family's crass behavior would lower himself in hers.

It no doubt already had.

As soon as the others were gone, his father turned to his brother, rage written on his face. "Jonathan, if you have any sense at all you would not malign your brother in front of Olivia after everything I've done to fix the hash you've made of things."

Henry dearly wondered what Jonathan had done.

(He hoped, God forgive him, it was something unutterably terrible.)

"Olivia should know Henry consorts with whores if she's going to marry him," Jonathan shot back, before Henry could ask.

Marry him?

Oh.

Now he understood why he was here.

Not for a christening.

To pay the eternal debt.

To be given one last chance to prove himself of value to the family empire.

He should have assumed there was a cynical purpose to the invitation. His father had been eager to forge an alliance with the Bradley-Houghs for a decade, for they owned his largest competitor in the southwest of England. This revelation should not slice through him. But he could feel the stoic expression he'd managed to maintain withering on his face. He felt flattened.

"So that's why you summoned me," he said to his father, trying not to sound as disheartened as he felt.

His father rolled his eyes heavenward, as though to even

imagine otherwise was foolish. "Of course that's why I summoned you."

"It won't work," Jonathan told their father, reaching for his wine. "Olivia won't have a gelding."

His brother smirked, enjoying his own wit.

It took every ounce of every promise Henry had ever sworn to himself or God or Reverend Keeper not to stand up and suffocate his brother with his ridiculous three-tiered wig.

Instead, he calmly folded his serviette and rose from the table. "Sir," he said in a low voice to his father, "I'll come to discuss the matter with you in the morning." He looked meaningfully at Jonathan. "Privately."

"Sit down, Henry," his father commanded. "We'll sort this out here and now."

"No, sir," he said, somehow managing to keep his tone polite but firm. He was far too angry to have this conversation with anything like filial respect, and he did not wish to say something he might regret. And he certainly was not going to say another word in front of Jonathan.

He bowed. "Good night, sir."

"He's never been worth a pence that you invested in him," Jonathan slurred before Henry'd even reached the door.

Henry stepped into the hall and shut the door behind him, so he would not have to hear his father's response. He held himself still, trying to breathe.

It had been so naive to come here thinking anything would be different. In his relief at being welcome home again, he'd let down his defenses.

It *hurt* to be reminded. He wanted to go to his room and lock the door so no one could take a look at him and see that he'd deluded himself into thinking he was *wanted* here.

Alice emerged from the privy closet at the end of the hall and saw him standing at the far end of the corridor. She paused, inclined her head, and smiled at him like she was his dearest friend.

Because she pitied him.

He forced a smile on his face. He couldn't stand for her to think him pitiful.

But as he fell into step beside her, her expression went arch rather than sympathetic. She leaned up on her tiptoes toward his ear.

"I see why you're so afraid of Satan now," she whispered. "It's because you have his own sotted demon for a brother."

He put his knuckle to his lips to keep from laughing out loud, but it still came out in a snort. Thank the Lord for Alice Hull. For her sharp tongue and fortifying presence.

Alice cracked an impish smile, pleased at his mirth. "I pledge you this, Reverend," she went on. "Shan't find anything as wicked as the likes of *him* on Charlotte Street."

Josephine stuck her head out of his mother's parlor door and beckoned to them. "Henry, come! Mama wishes for music."

He offered Alice his arm to escort her in. "I apologize you had to witness that display," he said, recovering his composure.

She hooked her arm in his. "Don't fret for me. Had myself a bit of venison so tasty I'll remember it to my heirs. I only regret your brother ruined my pudding."

"It was kind of you to come to my defense. Thank you."

She lightly, every so lightly, squeezed his forearm. "Well, I owed you. For last night."

She pressed her lips in a tight line, like saying this had cost her. "It was a comfort to me," she added, looking down at the floor.

She didn't want his pity either.

Oh, they were a pair. He wanted to say more, to prolong this moment of such intimate friendship with his unlikely ally (for that was what this was, was it not? Certainly not more than—)

His sister called his name again, and he swallowed the thought and opened the door.

At least his mother's drawing room was pleasant on this winter night. The walls were hung with portraits of her side of the family—hearty, red-headed people that looked like him—and the furnishings were comfortable, less grand and formal than the ones his father liked. It had always been his favorite room in the house.

His mother came forward, offered Alice a chair, and placed a hand on his shoulder. "Henry, darling, will you sing for us? I've missed our musical evenings."

This was her way of apologizing to him for the scene at supper, he knew. And so he smiled back at her and nodded, though singing was the last thing he wished to do. He did not want his mother to fret. The position she was in was not an easy one.

"Of course," he said. "But only if Josephine will play for me."

Josephine leapt up and went directly to the pianoforte, where she began rifling through a book of secular music.

"Actually, I wrote a new hymn," he told her. "It's to the tune of—"

"Oh, not a hymn!" his sister groaned playfully. "I think we have all earned a bit of levity after that *lovely* meal." She waggled her brows at him, placed her hands upon the keys and played the opening bars of a cheerful country song they had loved to sing as children.

Alice smile in recognition at the music. "*Good Morning, Pretty Maid*. I used to sing it as a girl with my sisters."

"Then you must sing the part of the maiden!" Josephine said, delighted. "I am much better at playing than singing, as Henry can attest."

Henry had been going to object to the frivolity of the song, which a man such as himself should no doubt be seen to disapprove of. But Alice seemed pleased, and he knew she liked music, from all her humming. Why not have a little lightness, after such a trying day?

"Oh, very well."

He stood at the center of the room, waiting for the cue. Josephine gestured for Alice to stand beside him. Before he could think better of them singing the song *to* each other, his sister began the bars of the first verse.

Well, what was the trouble in having a little merriment, after what they'd all endured? He turned to Alice and pretended to doff his hat as he sang the opening lines.

Good morning, pretty maid,
Where are you going?

He bowed raffishly at Alice to amuse his mother, who clapped her hands at his antics.

To range these fields so fair,
There's no man knowing,
I think too bold you are,
To range these fields so fair,
In danger everywhere,
Thou charming maiden.

His mother laughed and clapped, while Alice regarded him with mingled amusement and disbelief at his playacting the role of the pompous farmer as he sang. But when the next verse came, she gave him a coy curtsy, opened her mouth and let out one of the most pleasant alto voices he had ever heard.

A charming maid I am,
Sir, she replied.
Without any guile or care,
To no man tied;

She held out her hand, bare of a wedding ring, as if its bareness were a boast.

My recreations are to range
These fields so fair;
To take the pleasant air,

Josephine paused the music dramatically, and Alice paused too, narrowing her eyes to deliver the final line with vigorous, cheerful scorn.

Thou boasting stranger.

HIS MOTHER THREW BACK HER HEAD AND ROARED IN AMUSEMENT. Not to be outmatched, Henry puffed himself up for the farmer's response.

A farmer's son I am,
Your nighest neighbor,
Great store of wealth I have,
By honest labour;
So if you will agree,
Soon married we will be,

HIS SISTER ONCE AGAIN PAUSED THE MUSIC AND HE REMEMBERED, slightly too late, how his verse ended. Nevertheless, he clutched his hand over his heart, looked Alice in the eyes, and delivered the final stanza.

For I'm in love with thee,
Thou charming maiden.

ALICE ROLLED HER EYES COMICALLY AND STOMPED HER FOOT.

A farmer's wife must work,
Both late and early,

Like any toiling serf,
Therefore believe me.
I don't intend to be
A servant bound to thee.
To do thy drudgery,
Thou boasting stranger.

She sang with such defiant flourish it was like he really had proposed to her. Josephine played the last few notes raucously and his mother rose to her feet, applauding.

Mama laughed so merrily that tears stood in her eyes.

"Oh, Mrs. Hull," his mother said, "you make a very fair maiden indeed. And Henry, 'tis been much too long since we've done this."

He agreed. This tradition—singing songs in the parlor with his mother and sister—had always made the less pleasant aspects of their family life more bearable. Even more so when his brother did not sidle into the room to mock them.

"Will you play another, Jo?" his mother asked.

Josephine thought for a moment, then played the first few bars of a simple nursery song. Henry smiled. It was a tune that he had helped Josephine compose when she was very small, as a present for their mother's feast day.

"My mother cradled me as a babe," Josephine began, singing sweetly, if not well. "And sang lullabies to sooth my cries."

She paused and gestured for him to join her in harmony.

She was gentle to me when I was afraid
Oh mama, my dearest, my dear"

His mother, beside him, dabbed at her eyes and reached out to hold his hand.

"Oh Henry," she said quietly. "I'm so glad you've come home."

He leaned over and kissed her soft, full cheek. Out of the corner of his eye, he saw a flash of blue.

Alice, running from the room.

Josephine stopped playing abruptly. "Oh dear. Is something wrong?"

Yes, something certainly was wrong. With him. He was an *insensitive lout.*

"Her mother is ailing quite severely," he said, already moving to follow her. "I should have realized the song would upset her. Excuse me."

He rushed out of the room and down the corridor. Alice was already on the staircase. He called her name.

She turned around, her eyes glistening.

"Forgive me—" she said in a husky voice. "I did not mean to disturb your family, only to—"

He climbed up to the landing where she stood and took her hand. "I'm sorry. I wasn't thinking."

She shook her head. "I'm being so foolish. It's just a song."

He moved closer, for he hated how she admonished herself for a natural thing like grief. He tipped up her chin and saw she was not crying. She would not let the tears that so clearly stood in her eyes emerge.

She was so tough, this strange, small person, who rose only to his breastbone.

"Alice, I'll get you home to her," he said. "I promise."

She closed her eyes and nodded, pressing her knuckle against her lips.

Wordlessly they stood in the dark hall. Wordlessly, he bore witness as she did not shed a tear. It was the kind of grief that was beyond tears. There was nothing he could say to help her.

Except, perhaps, a blessing.

"Alice," he said softly. "Pray with me."

"I told you," she said, her breath ragged. "I'm not the type to pray."

"Prayer is just being alone with your thoughts and God. You needn't be a type."

She said nothing but she stood there, searching his eyes.

"May I?" he asked.

She did not object, and so he took her hands in his and bowed his head.

"Dear Lord, please grant peace and comfort to Alice's mother. Please let her know her daughter shines with love for her, and is doing everything she can to return to her side. Please bless her with comfort and your grace. Let her know that she is loved and cherished. And bless us, Lord, with better weather, so we may reach her soon. Amen."

As he'd prayed, Alice had leaned closer to him, so that her head was nearly resting on his chest.

He held himself very still, worried she bowed so low because he'd upset her. But then, in a faint voice she said, "Amen."

Help this child, Lord, he beseeched. *Help her find solace. Help me get her home. Help me lead her back to you.*

And forgive me. Forgive me because despite the solemnity of this moment, despite the urgency of my prayer to you, despite the sadness of this woman you have put in my path only so I might shelter her and lead her toward your grace, her nearness stirs me.

"Thank you," she whispered. In the dimness of the landing, with only a single flickering lamp for light, he could not make out her expression.

"Get some sleep," he said, forcing himself to release her hand and move away. "With any luck, the snow will stop, and I can drive you on to Fleetwend in the morning."

She nodded. "Good night, Henry."

He watched her ascend the stairs and disappear down the corridor.

And as he watched her, in that blue dress, all he could think was that it was not the Olivia Bradley-Houghs of the world who were made of the stuff he hoped for in a wife.

(It was the Alice Hulls he wanted.)

CHAPTER 12

Alice closed the door to her room, reproaching herself for the scene she'd made. Henry clearly had enough to worry about without her adding hysterics to his family's midst.

But. She did *not* regret his hands on hers.

He had such good, strong, hands. Square and big and warm and applying just the right amount of pressure. Gentle despite his size. Tender, even.

And then there was the rest of his body.

She should not have leaned on him like that—out there on the staircase, where anyone could have seen them. But for a moment she'd forgotten who he was, and where they were.

He was just a man, and a kind one. And she had wanted to be in his arms.

A knock sounded at the door. She hoped it was him. If it was, perhaps she could ask him to pray with her again, if only to eke out a little more of the comfort of his lovely arms.

But it was Baxter.

"Help with your gown, madam?" she asked, sailing inside without waiting for an answer.

Alice was quite capable of undressing herself, but it was nice to have Baxter's efficient ministrations distracting her from sorrowful thoughts. It reminded her of helping her sisters dress on cold mornings at home in Fleetwend.

I'm coming, she tried to signal to them with her mind. *I will be there soon, and I will take care of you.*

Somehow.

The obvious answer was by marrying William Thatcher. William had been her father's apprentice and had taken over Papa's business making organs. Her mother considered him as good as a son, her sisters adored him, and he'd made it known that Alice, with her musical skill and knowledge of the organ trade, would make him the perfect wife.

But not unlike the country maiden in the song she'd sung tonight, she knew what that life would be like. And she didn't want it.

She'd let Henry think she had been upset purely over his sister's sweet tribute to maternal love. But the song would not have made her so upset had it not been for the other song that came before it. She'd played the maiden with aplomb because she felt like her. She'd always felt like her.

When Baxter left, Alice crawled into the enormous bed and closed her eyes. But sleep did not come. Her thoughts kept returning to the dreadful question of what she would do when she got home.

What she would find there.

Or wouldn't.

She didn't want to think of this. She wouldn't. She refused.

She got up and found the journal she'd been reading the night before. She opened it to a random page and soothed herself with dull passages detailing the diarist's life.

He had a small garden in the plot of land behind his rooming house, and he scrupulously recorded what he planted, and how his plants were growing. He was quite proud of his lettuces, it seemed, and irritable with his mange tout, which was plagued by an infestation of hungry green caterpillars upon whom he fervently wished death, and just as fervently apologized to God for hating. She laughed as, day by day, his blistering asides about the pests became more vitriolic, and his apologies to his maker less and less sincere.

It was clear he was deeply religious, for he wrote long passages that she only skimmed in which he wondered at the meaning of some verse of scripture, or wrote his thoughts on what she gathered were debates about the proper path to salvation he'd had with friends. Faith, he kept insisting to himself, was more important than good works, but good works were still intrinsically part of faith.

She was more interested in the many pages of rigorous household accounting. The man seemed to be paid a quite handsome sum of money, but he had no servants or horses. Instead, he saved toward some purpose whose sum grew larger each month, and gave the rest away to charity.

The more she read, the more she began to wonder about him. He was a frustrating figure, her diarist, always denying himself harmless luxuries—regular haircuts, a rich dessert—and always blaming himself for not welcoming this self-denial with greater joy.

Self-indulgence breeds the appetites and distracts from serving the Lord, he wrote in several places, underlining the words so forcefully that there were dents in the paper from his quill.

Eat the cake, she wanted to shout back at him. *Indulge in that extra hour of sleep on Sunday. Death can come at any time.*

At least his grim self-admonitions were effective in exhausting her. She yawned, her eyes finally growing heavy. But just as she was about to close the book, she caught sight of the word *breast.*

She nearly laughed out loud. *Oh no, my poor, serious diarist. Hast thou espied a comely woman?*

The passage began below an update on the garden (turnips growing splendidly; snails eating the lamb's lettuce; forgive me, I murdered them with poison). But then, most intriguingly, the diarist's careful letters became a bit more jagged, his ink a bit more sharply scratched into the paper, leaving little speckles here and there, like he was writing in a lather.

I am a nuisance to myself. This morning at fellowship, Lydia Byron passed by me as I was making my donation and I ... I almost can't bear to commit the words to paper. I touched her breast. It was not intentional, of course—an accident, which we both pretended did not happen, for it would be too outrageous to address such a thing in the house of the Lord—but I cannot expunge it from my mind. All day I have been gripped with the memory of that accidental burst of flesh—so soft beneath my hand. The memory of it provokes an unwelcome excitement that I am tempted to sinfully relieve, and the evidence of which necessitates the wearing of my coat indoors for decency, though it is hot today, and the heat adds to my affliction. God, grant me please the coolness of mind and strength of will to eradicate this memory from my body, for I am in hourly danger, so tempted to indulge myself in sinful memory.

Alice bit her lip. Poor diarist.

She hoped, for his sake, that he had succumbed to temptation and brought himself relief.

His description of desire, so tortured and reproachful, reminded her of the way she'd felt herself, in the years before she'd met Elena Brearley.

She'd also felt a sickly kind of guilt when, as a girl, she wanted things she was told she mustn't. Her mother was always catching her—with her father's organ student in the woods, or in the barn with the hired boy who kept their livestock, or in the graveyard on the hill behind their cottage with the baker's son, who always smelled like bread. Unlike when Alice wandered, or said bold things, or laughed at the wrong time, her mother did not chastise her for these lapses. Instead, she hustled her away, a look of fear in her eyes. *Nothing below the skirt or you'll wind up with a baby in your belly.*

It had been wonderful, when she arrived at Elena's, to match her yearnings to knowledge of the flesh. On Charlotte Street desire was not considered a shortcoming of one's character. She'd observed what ecstasies were possible, from the commonplace to the exotic. How touch could turn patrician men into writhing boys. How made-up fantasies could transform stone-faced women into purring felines. She'd learned from her mistress exactly how babies were begotten and how she could avoid one, without sacrificing her desire to be touched. Elena did not mind if she brought lovers to her garret room on nights she wasn't working, so long as they came up the back stairs and did not disturb the members. With these men, she traded favors. Learned how to channel longings into pleasure.

She hoped her diarist had met some woman and realized he needn't torture himself with guilt. She immediately set upon skimming the journal to see how he'd progressed. Toward the back, she caught sight of the words "crisis of lust."

She raised a brow. "Wicked of you, diarist."

I walked ten miles today, stricken by a dream in which I found myself reliving once again the crisis of lust that set me on this course of purification. In the dream, I lingered after worship, working on a hymn. Sarah came in with a rag and bucket, and was pleased to see me—crediting me with finding her the work as maid. She ran up and embraced me as I sat on the pianoforte bench. She was effusive and did not let go, hanging on me, and though I knew that I should move aside, I lingered overlong because, I will confess, it felt so good.

Her former trade being what it is, and her not long out of it, she is too free with favors, and she kissed me. I became paralyzed with shock, knowing I must get up but unable to move, which she took as enthusiasm. Her hand went to my manhood, which had plumped at her nearness in a way she could perceive.

"Let me comfort you," she said. "I am so grateful for all you've done for me."

In life, of course, I came to my senses in time, refused, and fled.

But in the dream, I let her do what I'd imagined on that day—what I'd truly wanted.

"Would you wash my feet?"

And in the dream she found her bucket and took down her hair, as in the Gospel of Luke, and most tenderly undressed me. She used her hair to wash me, as the whore did for Christ. Her hands crept higher, higher, toward my shame—

And then I woke up in the throes of pleasure, unable to prevent what had, in sleep, already progressed past the point of stopping.

Now, I am left to face that my excitement was not just from her tender touch, nor her comely face, but from the fact that my desire was based in scripture, that it was intensified because we were in church—that place that should be most separate from sin.

I cannot tell the reverend about this for he will think me depraved, so instead I write it here, to hold myself to account and ask forgiveness from the Lord.

This journal was becoming very diverting indeed. Now she understood why she had found it at the whipping house. It must belong to a member with religious fantasies, who had left it behind by mistake. She wondered if she'd answered the door for him, or assisted in one of his sessions. She wondered what he looked like—if he was handsome.

She decided to imagine he looked like Henry Evesham. A man of compelling proportions—tall and sturdy and inviting. Very much the kind of man she might enjoy watching explore his most forbidden urges. Or, at the very least, entertaining in her room, alone.

Did Henry *know* that he was so appealing? She wondered how he would react if she told him she desired him. If she put her hands on his and brought them to her skin.

She reached beneath her nightdress and closed her eyes and grazed her fingers over her breasts, then lower, to her cunt. She allowed her thoughts to wander over the plains of Henry's body.

He would be sweet. *A virgin.* Eager, but unsure of what to do. Cautious not to hurt her with his size. So gentle she would have to pull him down on top of her and show him exactly how indelicate a small girl could be.

She imagined how his face would change as she brought them both closer to release. How he would look at her with wondrous desperation. She came quickly, in moments, with a quiet gasp. And then, exhausted and spent and finally calm, she slept.

Just as suddenly, she woke.

She did not know the time—it was still dark.

Her heart was in her throat.

Mama. Mama.

Oh God, what would she do?

She tried to breathe, but she could not, for she was choked with black, stifling fear. Why would the world be so cruel as to take her mother, when it had already taken her father? And why *now,* when she needed more time?

What would she do?

The room was too small. She couldn't breathe. She was suffocating.

She threw off her blankets and stood, bare feet pressing

against the freezing floor. Out the window, the night was dark, endless, swirling with the snow.

Outside.

She must go outside, to breathe.

She fumbled in the dark to dress and tiptoed from the room, holding her boots so as not to wake the house. A lamp burned on a table in the corridor and she took it, creeping through the vast interior until she found the downstairs cloakroom. She crept into her ermine, put on her boots, and stepped outside the cloakroom door into the night.

She was in an empty kitchen yard. She panted, inhaling the freezing, humid winter air like sips of icy water.

In the distance, she saw the outline of the old priory in the moonlight, blanketed by snow.

She knew what it was she needed.

She ran.

CHAPTER 13

Henry awoke, as he did every morning, at four, to the shame of an unchaste state.

His manhood was stout and aloft. There was a telltale dampness between his stomach and his nightshirt, a sign that his sinful desires had leaked out in his sleep.

He'd lay awake for hours, tossing and turning as his body vibrated from his near-embrace with Alice. When he finally slept, he'd dreamt of her. Of her pulling open heavy doors in a dark house, describing an endless list of ways to sin. Of her oiled hands caressing him. Of a dove-eyed woman kneeling in a room that smelled like church. Of a girl in a blue dress sticking out her hip, waggling her finger, vowing she knew better than to marry him.

Is that where the strange notion had come from, which had struck him on the staircase? The preposterous idea that he wanted to marry a woman like Alice Hull?

Marriage was on his mind, of course. The plan Reverend Keeper had proposed to him—carving out a circuit of ministry in their connexion that would enable him to continue his charity work in London, while also expanding it to other cities, like

Manchester and Birmingham—came with a condition. Henry was to find a woman who shared his faith to join him as a helpmeet. It was not appropriate for a bachelor to minister to whores and fallen women, the minister had said; it would be too rife with temptation. Besides, Henry's sinful urges would abate if he had a proper, healthy outlet for his lust. The scripture was clear on this: *it was better to marry than to burn.*

But this did not explain why Henry's skin had prickled at the perverse, impossible, utterly strange notion of marrying a girl who was unsuitable in every single way.

(Because she is intelligent and brave and sometimes oddly sweet? Because you desire her? Because the heart and loins don't deal in what is possible?)

He rose from his bed and into the coldness of the bedroom and used the basin of water to clean himself, taking pains not to linger on his swollen manhood, where he might be tempted to enjoy his own ablutions.

He might be weak in mind, but he would not lower himself to being weak in body.

Bodily desire was given by God to be enjoyed by man and wife. To indulge it in any other circumstances was to invite a flood of other indulgences that rent a man from his devotions.

When he'd first begun to visit dens of fornication, he'd tried to greet the evidence of the trade—the nudity, the profane words, the sights and smells of sex—with objectivity and distance, like a naturalist who must visit the cave of a bear to understand its habits.

But objectivity was more difficult to muster when one was sleeping.

And women did not have the same effect on him as bears.

He'd taken to sleeping without a quilt or fire and his windows open, hoping his body would be too cold to manifest fleshly preoccupations in his slumber. But ever since the week before, when Alice had led him through the whipping house murmuring all sorts of wild things, no amount of frigid morning air was enough to slake the visions that haunted his sleep. The dreams left him as ashamed as they did sinfully, depravedly tumescent.

He dropped to the floor and began his morning exercise, which always served to calm his mind. He pushed his own weight up on his biceps over and over and over, until his muscles quivered. He rolled onto his back and lifted his abdomen up into his knees one hundred times. He went through his routine, torturing his muscles until he'd exhausted his arms and legs and belly.

The searing in his muscles exorcised his bodily temptations.

If it did not make him pure, it at least made him sore.

He examined his proportions in the looking glass as he dressed. He did not keep a mirror in his rooms in London, for it fostered vanity, but here he could not resist inspecting his reflection.

It was shocking to see exactly how broad he'd become.

His shoulders were wide and his arms were thick, with veins that stood out from his exertions. He was lean—his fasting kept him from carrying excess flesh atop his muscle—but he looked every inch the names his father and brother always sneered at him.

Lummox. Beast.

His size gave proof to their condemnations, however his conscious mind objected that the insults had no basis in reality, that this body had been given to him by God.

He watched his large hands tying his cravat around his neck and wished fervently that there were less of him to dress. It was foolish to entertain thoughts of Alice when a woman of her petite size would no doubt look at him in horror, worrying of being smothered.

It was too cold for a walk—he'd work instead. He spread his notes out on his desk. He'd already compiled all the findings from his interviews into orderly files, arranged by topic. He had evidence on the preponderance of prostitution, areas of the city most afflicted with it, data on pimps, culls, procurers, brothels, molly houses. He had suggestions from doctors on the prevalence and treatment of venereal disease, accounts from magistrates on the frequency of unlawful brothel-keeping and public solicitation. And mostly he had stories—so many stories—from those who plied the trade.

He'd expected, when he'd begun this work, that stricter laws and harsher punishments were what was needed to clean up London's streets. But the more he'd probed into the flesh trade, the less convinced he was that harsh punishments would meaningfully change the situation. More likely to help the most unpleasant aspects of it—sick and injured women, public fornication, the spate of illegitimacy heaping costs upon the councils—would be requiring licenses of brothels, issued in such a way as to reduce violence and procurement. The fees raised could be used to provide things like condoms and maternity hospitals that would keep prostitutes healthier, at less burden to the city and its charities.

But this would provoke outrage, and he could not say he didn't share it.

If he still wrote *Saints & Satyrs*, he'd have thundered against such measures himself.

This central dilemma was intransigent. No matter how clear the facts and figures, he could not resign himself to using his powers, such as they were, to advocate changes that would reduce the consequence of sin.

He looked out the window into the swirling snow and prayed to God.

Oh Lord, what is the more virtuous path? What should I do? Guide me.

He saw a flash of something in the kitchen yard.

He squinted.

Through the haze of falling snow, he could faintly make out the glow of a lamp. He pressed his face to the glass, and vaguely discerned the silhouette of a queenly cape. It was Alice, dashing toward the gate leading to the garden.

Where was she going?

Something must be horribly wrong.

He put his candle in a lamp and rushed downstairs and out the nearest door, not pausing to find a coat.

Alice was nowhere in sight by the time he made it to the gate. He followed her small footprints through the gardens, past the stables, and onward, toward the old priory.

Her tracks stopped at the door to the stone building. He stepped inside and raised his lamp.

"Alice?" he called.

There was a mighty boom, like the bursting of a pipe. Then a gusty, stentorian moan.

And then the priory surged with a wave of sound so forceful he felt it vibrate through the stone floors.

Organ music.

It was not a song he recognized—it sounded improvised, a ferocious counterpoint of dramatic falls and minor lifts surging into rhapsody, like the calling of a ghost.

A chill ran down his spine. "Alice?" he called again.

The organ overpowered his voice as he walked toward the chapel. The ancient stone walls echoed with its howls. He felt like he was walking through a storm of sound.

He pulled open the chapel door. In the back, above the choir nave, the brass pipes of the organ reflected moonlight shining through a stained-glass window. Alice was bent over the manual of the organ, her tiny body even smaller set against the instrument's mighty pipes. She moved fluidly as she played, like she and the instrument were merged into a single creature.

He moved closer, silent, transfixed by her hands moving rapidly over the keys, and the sorcery they were capable of stirring.

CHAPTER 14

Somehow Alice had known she would feel better here. Her body had been drawn to this place, sensing what she needed like she was a wounded animal.

She closed her eyes and gave herself over to the music, playing from touch and instinct, not caring how it sounded. She poured all of her sadness into the organ's keys, all of her fear, her outrage at this life and its crushing disappointments. She did not know what she played, only that she must.

She played for her mother, for her father, for her sisters. She played for Elena, and the hope she'd given her, and the life she wanted so badly to return to and knew she never would. She played for Henry Evesham and his rotten brother and cruel father. She played until she was not a small, sad woman but a mighty swell of sound, larger than she could ever hope to be, so powerful she made the stone walls shake.

"Alice!"

She froze and opened her eyes.

Henry Evesham was staring at her like she was possessed.

"What… " He looked from her hands on the manual to her eyes

and back to her hands, which were still suspended over the keys, not moving.

She held herself still, braced for the words to come, like a blow. Daring him to say them and knowing that he would and prepared to riot, to scream that he was wrong. *Don't make me stop. I'll die if you make me stop. I'll tear my hair and beat my breast.*

"That was …"

Sinful. Immodest. Immoral.

"… Astonishing," he whispered.

He did not look on her with judgment. He looked on her with wonder.

His face flickered in the lamplight, as he moved closer, and she saw his expression was soft with uncomplicated pleasure. She felt his presence like a touch.

She was grateful she was seated, or she might swoon.

"You are a remarkable player," he murmured. "One of the best I've ever heard. A natural."

She was not a natural. She'd been taught, drilled at scales since before her earliest memory, tutored for hours a day most of her life. She could not recall a time she could not play.

She forced herself to speak. "Oh, I'm not. I've played since I was very small."

He shook his head, his eyes gleaming. "You have a true gift, Alice."

She stared at him, wordless, unable to fully believe his face held admiration rather than outrage. She was so relieved he was not rebuking her she began to shiver.

She'd not known how much she missed this. Playing the organ felt, to her, the way that Henry described prayer. *To be alone with your thoughts and God.*

That is what Vicar Helmsley had taken from her, with his

sneering words: *'Tis a sin for a female like you to make music in the house of God. You should be ashamed.*

"You must be freezing," Henry said softly. He reached down and retrieved her cloak, which had fallen to the floor. He placed it over her shoulders and smoothed it down, rubbing warmth into her.

"Thank you," she whispered. The simple gesture touched her. She could not remember last time she'd felt so cared for.

"Would you play me something I might know?" he asked. "Perhaps a psalm?"

At the shy enthusiasm of his request, she suddenly felt nervous. It had been so many years since she'd played for an audience. Another age. Another life.

"The organ's out of tune," she said. "The pipes don't like the cold. But I shall try."

She turned back to the manual. She played slowly at first, trying to recall in her mind's eye the pages of Crowley's Psalter, well-worn in her father's workshop. She played the opening, hit a discordant tone, winced. But within a few bars her ear took over, working with the memory in her fingers and her foot. And then she found it—*truly* found it—and all at once the melody unfolded from her.

Henry laughed with recognition. "Psalm Twenty-Four."

It had been a performance piece when she'd toured the countryside with her father every summer, demonstrating his barrel organs at grand houses and small churches, hoping for a sale.

Henry hummed in pleasure, then began to sing the words, his lovely tenor voice in harmony with her notes.

The earth and all that it holdeth, do to the Lord belong:
The world and all that dwell therein as well the old as young.

For it is he that above all the seas hath it founded:
And that above the fresh waters hath the same prepared.

SHE WENT UP AN OCTAVE, IMPROVISING ON THE TUNE. SHOWING off.

She felt her father, beaming at her as she delighted a crowd. She felt her mother, absently mouthing the words as she made supper while Alice practiced playing.

And for a moment, making music with Henry Evesham in an abandoned priory in a snowstorm in the midst of the unraveling of her life, she felt at peace.

CHAPTER 15

When the final notes of the psalm stopped echoing through the old stone walls, Alice turned around to face him. In the light of his lamp her eyes locked on his, luminous. Henry smiled at her and she smiled back and for a moment they just stood there, mute and smiling, locked in a conspiracy of joy.

"Alice, you play as for a king. As for the Lord himself."

She laughed shyly. "Thank you. I enjoy it. It's been such a very long time I'm surprised that I remember how."

"How did you learn to play like that?"

"My father taught me. He was an organ maker," she said, her voice rough. "I took to music from a young age, and when I showed talent for it he took me on the road with him, to demonstrate for customers. It always felt like the most natural thing—the thing I liked best."

"Why did you stop?"

She smiled sadly. "When my father died we had to sell the instruments we had at home. There was nothing to play anymore. I had imagined I might replace my father as an organist at our church, but the vicar did not think it appropriate." She glanced at him, as if seeing if he agreed.

"I'm sorry," he said. "I can't imagine a greater compliment to divinity than the way you play. Did you consider teaching, or performing?"

She shrugged. "Mama didn't want me to play anymore—she thought it made me odd, too much in my own head, always wandering off humming tunes, ignoring my chores to test a composition, playing the same chords over and over in the house until I drove everyone mad. She sold the instruments and that was that."

Her voice was very small, very quiet.

"You must have been devastated."

She sighed. "It was a loss. But nothing was the same with Papa gone. We needed money so badly there wasn't time to dwell on where it came from. I found other work."

At the whipping house, she meant. He'd never given much thought to her past, but this story explained so much about her. Her dreamy quality, her lovely voice, her absent-minded humming. Her mix of homespun speech and flourishes that bespoke some form of education. She had alluded to her family's poverty, but he had not realized she'd fallen in the world. Lost her place in it.

Because one thing was certain: she looked, sitting before this organ, like herself. He wished that he could give the instrument to her. If it were not built into the wall, he would.

"Do you miss it?" he asked. To have such talent and no use for it seemed to him a tragedy.

Her expression turned grave and her gaze flashed dark and distant, as if she surveyed a burning city from a cliff. "I miss my father. And now, with my mother being sick … The music feels like part of that same loss."

He wanted to lean over and gather her up, this lonely girl.

He knew he mustn't. But perhaps he could offer something that might bring her pleasure.

"Alice, I wonder. Unless the snow stops and we can travel, I might ask a few old friends to the priory today, for fellowship. Would you play a hymn for us?" He paused, suddenly feeling shy himself. "I write them, you see ..."

She grinned at him. "I thought you might be musical. Last night when you sang—I could tell you have an ear for it."

It was an insult to her obvious gifts to equate them with his simple talents, but he was flattered she had noticed, for he harbored a vanity about his voice. "Nothing like you, Alice. But I enjoy it. Would you play?"

"Of course. But I thought you might mind my playing in a chapel. I'm surprised you would suggest it."

He did not quite follow her reasoning. Had he not been clear in his opinion that everyone was welcome in church? Did she still think he judged her?

He just firmly shook his head. "Alice, it would be an *honor* if you played for us."

Her smile widened, pure and happy. It made him smile too, deep inside his chest.

"Very well," she said. "It would be my pleasure. It's the least I can do after you have helped me."

He chewed the corner of his lip, for he did not particularly feel as though he *had* helped her.

Not yet.

Clearly, there was more that he should do, if she felt unwelcome playing music in a church. But that wasn't what she meant, and he'd promised not to proselytize.

"I feel badly that I have not been able to deliver you to your family as quickly as I hoped. I can't help but wonder if you had taken a sturdier vehicle, perhaps—"

She waved this away. "No. You aren't to blame." She gave him a look that was almost playful. "I imagine even a lofty Lord Lieutenant can't control the weather. Unless, of course, you have a prayer for that." She winked.

Her wink caused something to pop in his chest, like a button coming off a too-small pair of breeches.

"I *do* have a prayer for that," he returned, in a manner that, if he was honest, could only be described as flirtatious. "I have a prayer for most everything. I'm quite a prolific prayer."

She nodded gravely. "I've gathered, Henry Evesham."

"It simply hasn't been answered yet," he added, hoping to prolong the moment.

She snorted. "Are they ever?"

Oh, Alice.

He met her gaze head on. "*Yes.*"

She looked away. It was like a wall descended over her face whenever he spoke sincerely of his faith.

Don't give up. He felt the words deep inside himself, like the Lord was speaking to him.

So he lightened his tone. "We'll get there Alice. We will. I promise you."

She nodded, and a yawn stole out of her. He remembered it was not yet dawn.

"Shall we return to the house?" he asked her. "You should try to sleep."

"So should you."

"Oh no. I never sleep past four."

"Never?" she asked, as they made their way back through the old stone rooms and out into the snowy night.

He considered this. "Only if I have a fever."

She glanced at him over her shoulder, a strange expression knitting her features.

"What?" he asked.

She shook her head and looked away. "Sometimes you remind me of someone."

He wondered who.

He hoped it was someone she liked.

Outside, the night had turned gray with a presentiment of dawn. They walked in silence. He paused to unlatch the gate to the kitchen yard and moved aside so Alice could climb up the stone steps. She went slowly, careful of the ice, but just as she reached the top step a whoosh of breath went out of her and she slipped backward. He caught her arm and steadied her against his body. She felt—

(Don't think of it. Don't think of it.)

"Pardon me," she gasped.

"You're all right?"

She nodded and he moved away, putting space between them as quickly as he could. He climbed to the top step and reached down for her. "Here, take my hand so you don't slip."

Her hand slid into his. Neither of them were wearing gloves, and their flesh, pressed together, was so cold that he felt her palm as he might a piece of marble.

"There now," he said, gripping it. "Watch that second step."

He pulled her up to safety. "There you are."

She did not release his hand. They stood for a moment, neither of them moving, their breath coming out in little puffs of steam in the cold air.

"You've got snow in your hair," she said.

He shook his head. "Didn't think to wear a hat."

She let go of his hand and reached up to brush some snowflakes from his eyebrows. He lowered his head to let her. Her hand paused, moved lower, rested on his neck, below his ear. Her fingers were so cold that every quarter inch of flesh she touched produced a shiver in him.

But he didn't stop her. It felt so good he could not—would not—stop her.

She rose up on her toes and brushed his cheek with her lips.

"Thank you," she murmured. "For coming after me."

He stood still, frozen, shocked at the feathery warmth of her breath on his cold skin. Her eyes met his, a question in them now—one he didn't have the answer to.

(Yes. Yes.)

And then her lips moved toward his.

He stepped backward.

(Lunged away.)

His abrupt movement disrupted her balance again, and she toppled sideways. She caught herself on a snowy topiary, panting.

Oh, he was a donkey. An absolute *donkey*.

"I'm sorry," he gasped, his entire body feeling like it was burning in a vat of boiling water. "I …"

"No, no," she said lightly, standing straighter, her manner brisk. "I should not have—oh, devil-shining *bloody* hellfire."

She turned around and ran into the house, leaving him in the frozen garden, unsure whether he'd been blessed or cursed.

CHAPTER 16

W*here in* *eternal blazing Hades* was the *godforsaken bloody* staircase in this *preposterously large pile?*

In her rush to get away from Henry, Alice had snuffed out her lamp, leaving her fumbling through dark rooms with tears in her eyes and her heart in her throat.

Stairs. She'd found the stairs. Oh, thank merciful Jesus.

She dashed up them, half blind and tripping on her cloak, and slunk down the hallway in what she hoped was the direction of her bedchamber.

Oh, what had she just done? Had she really tried to kiss *Lord Lieutenant Henry Evesham*?

She'd forgotten, momentarily, who and what he was. She'd only felt the pull between them.

If only he hadn't lowered his head when she'd smoothed the snow from his brow. She knew hunger like she knew music. She had no doubt he'd wanted to feel her hands on him. But to *want* touch—even to need it—and to *welcome* it were two different things.

She doubted he'd ever look her in the eyes again, let alone find it in himself to drive her on to Fleetwend.

A door shuffled open just ahead of her, and a male voice cursed.

She froze.

The light of a candle moved toward her, and behind it, Jonathan Evesham stood, in a nightshirt and a sleeping cap. "Are you quite all right, Mrs. Hull?"

"Oh, yes, thank you," she stammered. "I was looking for the necessary and seem to have lost my way."

He lifted the candle. She felt the dim light shine over her damp hair, her ermine cape, her winter boots.

"In your furs?" She could not make out his face, but she could hear the sarcasm in his voice.

Oh, *bile of witches*. What would he think she'd been doing? Nothing that would reflect well on her reputation as a Methodist widow. She prayed Henry would not materialize behind her and make the appearance of the situation any worse.

"I was chilled," she explained, shivering for effect. "I've been a bit ill since my husband's passing. The shock."

"My sympathies on your loss," he said, without much hint of sympathy. "A recent one?"

"Yes," she said, clutching herself. "Christmastime. Could you point me to the necessary?"

He gestured at a doorway at the end of the hall. "Just there."

She stumbled ahead, but he cleared his throat. "Do you need light?"

"Oh, yes, thank you." She held out her lamp to him and he lifted up the glass and relit the candle with his own.

He moved aside so she could pass, but she felt him watching her intently as she walked down the corridor to the privy. She closed the door and leaned against the wall, cursing herself. She remained there for five minutes, in case Jonathan was waiting to see if she'd been lying.

When she stepped back into the hall it was empty. She rushed to her bedchamber and shut the door, shaking. She took off her boots and got under the covers, cloak and all. She closed her eyes and held herself. *Don't let it come to anything. Please. Please.*

She awoke, hours later, to knocking at her door. She rose, drowsily, and opened it.

Henry stood there, stiff and uncertain. She flinched, wondering if he'd entertained questions from his brother on her whereabouts in the night, or if he merely appeared shaken because she'd molested him.

He took in her state of dress, her rumpled hair, the pillow indentation on her cheek, and his shoulders softened. "Are you all right, Alice?" he asked in a low voice.

His concern made her feel worse. She wanted to tell him about his brother, but she could not risk someone hearing her if anyone else was about in the hall.

She glanced up at his eyes. "Yes. And you?"

A corner of his mouth twitched. That tiny, faint tremble, not so much a smile as the idea of one, heartened her.

"Well enough." He glanced at her eyes, then at his shoes.

Was he nervous? What was he thinking?

"I went out to visit a few friends who live on the estate, and they are gathering at the priory at two o'clock. If you would still like to play the organ, I'd be most appreciative."

She nodded with everything she had. "Yes, of course."

Meaning, *forgive me.*

Meaning, *I'm sorry, it was a mistake.*

He held out a book of music. "A hymnal for you. And there's a list of songs to play, tucked inside." He gestured at a piece of paper that stuck out between the pages.

She withdrew it from the book. He'd jotted out the names of five hymns, along with their pages in the book. His writing was orderly and neat.

It was writing that she *knew*.

She'd been reading it the night before.

Her diarist was *Henry Evesham*.

She gripped the door handle and prayed that it would hold her up. "Thank you," she said through a dry mouth.

He nodded, frowning like he wanted to ask her what was wrong. His face knit together in her mind's eye with the one so like it she'd been imagining for her long-suffering, self-denying, grumpy, amusing, tedious, lustful diarist, whose thoughts she'd become so intimately acquainted with.

"You're certain you're well?" he asked.

She nodded, because she couldn't speak.

He stepped back tentatively. "Meet me downstairs in the great room at half past one?"

She nodded again. He bowed, then retreated from her door.

She snapped it shut and leaned against it, reeling.

Two days ago, she'd hated Henry, and now she wanted to open the door, run down the hall, grab him by the shoulders, and tell him what she knew. He was taller than her by nearly two heads, but she wanted to cradle him like a child and tell him he was too hard on himself, that he needn't suffer so, that life didn't need to be so dreadful. She wanted to lead him to the kitchen and feed him cream cakes while giving him a back massage, and also to kick him in his shins for pretending to lack doubt, pretending to be above human desires, pretending not to see what the diarist so clearly saw.

But, oh God, if he knew she had his journal—

He'd be humiliated.

And the things he'd *think* of her. A wave of bile surged into her throat. She swallowed it, breathing through her nose. Stay calm. Stay bloody calm.

Perhaps she'd only imagined it. She went to the bedside table where she'd left the journal and opened it to a random page.

Today Reverend Keeper preached on marriage, and read from the Song of Solomon. It moved me, but not in a way that honors God nor my intentions.

It made me envious of the poet, and his dove-eyed woman.

One is not meant to read the Bible in a state of depravity but I did so. I went home and I read it and God forgive me, I burned.

Oh, Henry. It *was* his handwriting. But more than that, it was his character.

She remembered how stiff and stern he'd been when she'd given him his tour of the whipping house. She'd thought he'd been tense with condemnation.

She'd misread who that judgment had been aimed at.

Not at her.

At *himself.*

Slowly, she shut the book.

She could not tell him that she had this. It was kinder, surely, to return it to Elena, who could say it had been found in some forgotten corner by a servant.

She would not read it again. She tucked the book into her satchel and forced her attention to the songbook Henry'd given her, to the musical notations in the book of hymns.

But all she could think were two words.

I burned.

CHAPTER 17

Henry stood outside Alice's door, unable to shake the sense he'd ruined something.

She'd scarcely been able to *look* at him. The sight of him hurt her so severely she'd seemed like she might faint dead away.

He wanted to knock again.

Apologize.

Explain himself.

To say "I didn't mean to hurt you. I simply don't know what it would make me if I took your caress as freely as you offered it."

(A hypocrite.)

But he could not knock again, because she'd so very clearly wanted him to leave. And, of course, he did not need to say the words aloud to her for her to know that there could be nothing between them.

But he hated the thought that he had wounded her.

(He wished it could be different. He wished he could knock and apologize by giving her the kiss he'd dodged last night. He wanted to. Oh, how he wanted to.)

He trudged miserably down the stairs to his father's study,

where he'd been summoned with a letter on his breakfast tray demanding "an audience to discuss your upcoming marriage" on his father's formal stationery.

"Henry, there you are," his father greeted him brusquely. "You're late."

Henry glanced at the clock. It was one minute past the appointed hour. "My apologies, sir."

His father gestured at a hardback chair in front of his broad desk. "Have a seat."

Ah, so he planned to address Henry from behind his desk, like an employer, rather than, say, deigning to sit on the sofa near the fire with the son he had not seen in half a decade. Splendid.

(Honor. Thy. Father.)

"I won't waste time with niceties," his father said, folding his hands on top of his desk. "I asked you here because I'm ruined."

The muzzled thoughts in his head—guilt, Alice, want, pain, kissing—stopped swirling abruptly.

"Ruined, sir?"

His father leaned back in his chair, adjusted his silver wig and nodded curtly. "I had hoped to expand production—Jonathan is keen to enlarge the concern—and a few ventures proved riskier than we anticipated."

Henry's father was a cautious businessman and notoriously tight with money. Whatever this misadventure had been, it was almost certainly his brother's doing. And yet his father acted brisk and unconcerned. He'd shown more rage when Henry had declined the lamb at supper.

"There are," his father stated, "debts." He leveled his eyes at Henry, piercing him.

Henry said nothing, waiting to hear what this might have to do with him.

"If I cannot raise twenty thousand pounds by quarter's end, I shall have to sell the factory."

Henry blinked. That number was a fortune.

"Perhaps you can sell this house," he offered.

"Already mortgaged," his father said crisply. "I have two options. I can sell to Bradley-Hough, who will give me half what the concern is worth and stamp his name on my legacy. Or my son can marry his daughter. Who, you see, has a dowry double what I need."

His father rarely spoke to him so frankly. Some small, malnourished part of him awakened, flattered that he'd been asked to save the family business, even if it was at a cost to himself.

But even as the feeling stirred, he knew that it was pitiful.

He owed his father respect. Not this.

"Sir, I am troubled by your predicament," he said slowly. "But my circumstances are such that I highly doubt Miss Bradley-Hough would view me as a welcome suitor. I live in rented rooms, keep no servants—"

"Miss Bradley-Hough can afford to keep the both of you. She is the sole heir to her father's fortune, and has her dowry besides. And in return for lending me the capital, I'll pay you a handsome dividend, plus interest. You'll be a rich man, Henry. Richer than I ever was."

He had never wanted to be rich. He cared little for money.

"And what if you sell to Bradley-Hough instead? Will it cover your debts?"

His father looked, for a brief minute, old. "Just. But I shall lose the enterprise I've spent my entire life building up from nothing. You, who have had everything given to you, would not understand." His expression hardened. "And I shall know my son willed it."

Henry closed his eyes. This was not fair. He was grateful for his education at the fine public schools his father had insisted he attend, but he hadn't taken a penny from his family since he'd graduated Oxford. He had taken the position at *Saints & Satyrs* precisely because he knew his father would balk at supporting him after he'd refused to enter the clergy.

"Sir, I am not unsympathetic to your circumstances," he said slowly. "But I cannot promise to enter an unsuitable marriage."

Henry's father slammed his fist down on the desk. "Unsuitable! You act as though marriage to a fine woman who will make you a wealthy man is a burden. If you don't like the girl leave her in Bath and go about your ridiculous revivals. I am asking you to see sense, for once in your life. To do what this family requires of you."

"Marriage is a sacred vow, made before God," Henry said quietly. "I will not undertake it for venial reasons."

His father closed his eyes, like this sentence gave him stomach pains.

It troubled Henry, to be the cause of this. He understood what his father would lose.

Was this what the Lord meant, when he commanded 'honor thy father'? That if one's parent suffered, one suffered too, however little warmth there was between you?

Henry decided to provide what little mercy he was able. "I will speak to Miss Bradley-Hough. Should I find that she and I might be compatible, I will consider what you ask."

(We won't be compatible, however, and I will not do what you ask.)

His father opened his eyes and looked at him. They looked colder than the snowy day outside. "Approach the girl however you like, Henry. But if you don't leave this house betrothed to her, don't bother coming back. Ever."

Henry rose. Bowed. Left the room.

He walked to the great hall slowly, feeling drugged.

Alice and Josephine were waiting for him, ready to depart for the priory. He put his hand to his hair to smooth it, ran his tongue over his teeth. Tried to revive his faculties, which were dulled from lack of sleep, and Alice's nearness, and his father's severity, and what he'd just agreed to, however disingenuously.

Alice said nothing, keeping her eyes carefully on the floor. He desperately wished he knew what she thought of him.

"You look rather low," Josephine said to him cheerfully.

"Just came from a meeting with our father."

Jo winced. "Ah."

He wondered if his sister knew why he'd been summoned here. Were all of them in on it? Had the baby's christening simply been a pretext to get him home? Did his mother and sister also want him to marry Miss Bradley-Hough, to save their comfortable life in this grand house?

It was uncharitable to even think it, but he didn't know who he could trust.

The only person he trusted here was Alice.

He was silent on the walk to the priory. He half-listened to Josephine chatter to Alice about the preparations for her season. Apparently, no expense was being spared. He could not begrudge his sister her excitement over balls and dresses, but he wondered at his father spending such a fortune to present his daughter as a lady on money borrowed from God knew where.

"Ah, so many people out despite the snow!" Josephine said, looking at the crowd assembling in front of the priory. He smiled at the sight of his old friends, touched they had traveled through the snow to worship with him at short notice.

His spirits lifted instantly.

These people—many of them his father's tenants, who he'd

met at a revival when he'd been home from University—were some of the earliest fellow pilgrims in his journey toward a more evangelical faith. They were all older now. Some of them who'd once carried babies now stood with large broods of children. Some who'd come with husbands or wives now stood alone, their hair more gray, their faces lined.

All of them greeted him more happily than his own family had. And among them, he felt better than he had in days.

When everyone had settled onto the pews he walked up to the altar and glanced up at the organ. Alice was seated there, waiting for his signal.

"Ready?" he mouthed to her. She nodded.

He lifted his arms. "My brothers and sisters," he said, projecting his voice so that he could be heard even at the back of the chapel. "Though 'tis icy out of doors, my heart is warm with your fellowship and the light of God's love."

He smiled at the murmurs of "Amen" and opened his hymnal. "Join me in a hymn."

At his nod to Alice, the room swelled with music. She had not had time to practice, and could not know these songs, as most had been written by himself or his friends, but she played flawlessly. He smiled as the faces around him lit with surprise and joy. One by one, their voices rose and met his in harmony. He let the music lift his spirit up to God.

Among this chorus, he caught a beautiful alto, true and clear.

Alice's voice.

She improvised a harmony of her own, delighting the better singers in the crowd, who began to add their own flourishes to her tune. There was a soulfulness in the way she sang the hymn that made him certain she had been faithful once. He wondered when she had become estranged from God. And why.

He itched for her to share the peace he could see in his fellow worshiper's expressions. To remind her of God's love for her. That it was there, even when one's family's was less steadfast.

The parable of the prodigal was on his mind, and he opened the Bible and read the story from the Book of Luke, about the father welcoming home his son.

"As a child, I used to think this story was about reconciliation of the family," he told his friends. "It was not until I was older that I realized it was about faith. The truth is, one cannot always count on the people we love to welcome us home. But the infinite mercy of God is eternally renewable. No matter how we stray, how far we wander, how much we sin, he is always overjoyed to welcome us back into his grace."

Several of his friends nodded in the nearest pews, their eyes shining. Perhaps this moment was all he needed from this place. Not the admiration of his family, but a reconnection with that joyous, wondrous feeling that he'd first experienced here, among these people: the boundless, miraculous ecstasy when one felt—truly *felt*—the radiant love of God.

He closed his Bible and looked out at the dear, familiar faces. "You here know what I know," he continued. "Salvation cannot be taught. It must be asked for and accepted. It must be trusted, the way one trusts ours legs to hold us up after a fall. That is grace. It is the certainty in one's body and one's soul of the expansive measure of God's infinite forgiveness."

The room echoed with "Amens."

And though, in the emotion that had come over him, he had forgotten to give Alice her cue to play the closing hymn—the room swelled again with music.

CHAPTER 18

The strangest feeling overtook Alice as she listened to Henry preach. She felt rather moved.

To her, faith had never seemed distinct from church, and church had never seemed much more than a ritual requiring boredom and uncomfortable shoes. It was a list of obligations and an even longer list of things you could not do. Another joyless, restrictive code dictated from male authorities who offered little beyond demands that she must follow or face egregious consequences.

She had not considered that faith might fill you up, instead of limiting you. That God could lift, rather than confine. But as she watched Henry and his friends bow their heads in prayer, she could see the tranquility on their faces.

How moving, to watch Henry Evesham lead them to this state of peace.

She'd misunderstood what he believed—or perhaps just wrongly assumed she knew it, drawing inferences from his writings in *Saints & Satyrs*. The fiery, holier-than-thou tone of those essays and verses had almost nothing in common with the words he'd spoken here, to this small group. They were also different from the worries of the diarist, who longed to perfect himself and railed at himself for failing.

She wondered how often Henry allowed himself to be *this* man, who insisted sin could be forgiven, whose eyes filled with tears as he spoke of mercy.

But then, had she not seen glimpses of him? Had he not marveled at a woman playing music in an abandoned chapel? Whispered prayers to her through a wall? Bowed his head in the desire for her affection in a snowy garden, in the middle of the night?

Alice watched him saying farewell to his fellow worshipers. A group of children with their mother were among the final people to approach him. He bent down attentively, speaking to the littlest worshipers with solemnity and good humor. So kind. So gentle.

"He's good with children," Josephine remarked, walking up beside her. "He'll make a lovely father."

"No doubt," Alice agreed.

"We hope he'll marry soon. I don't suppose you know if he's courting anyone in London? Perhaps a member of your congregation?"

Josephine asked the question casually, but something about it struck Alice as odd. What could she say? Would he want her to repeat what he'd told her in the carriage? She knew so little about him, and yet so much. She knew his horror at the accidental touching of a woman's breast, his stirring at *The song of Solomon*. The way he tore the page underlining those telling words, *I burned*.

Evidently mistaking her fluster for hesitation, Josephine blushed. "I'm sorry, I should not press for gossip. Mama and I are always so desperate for news of Henry's life in London, since he writes of personal things so rarely. He knows Papa does not approve of him, and I suspect it makes him reluctant to tell us much about his life."

Oh, how she could relate to that. Her letters to her mother were a kind of symphony of saying nothing, of quotidian details that added up to a picture so opaque she may as well have sent a dirty window.

"I don't know if he intends to marry," Alice said, not wishing to reveal anything he'd rather they not know. "But I'm not aware of any courtship."

Josephine looked at her intently. "My father is hoping his visit might produce some happy news between himself and Miss Bradley-Hough."

Oh dear. Was that why Henry had been so uncomfortable when she'd almost kissed him? She had not considered he might have feelings for another. A fresh wave of mortification clenched through her.

Henry walked towards them, looking happy and refreshed. "Thank you for coming, ladies. And for playing, Alice. My friends were so pleased."

"It was a pleasure," Alice said, fully meeting his eye for the first time since the night before.

He held her gaze and smiled. She tried not to wonder what it meant.

"Shall we go back for supper?" he asked.

Outside, the snow had stopped. It was a calm, cold, winter evening, the ground blanketed in white.

"It's clearing," Henry observed, smiling at her again, as though the previous night had never happened. "If it holds I'll drive you home in the morning."

"Thank you," she said.

She did not know what else to say.

She was grateful when Josephine changed the subject to speak of local neighbors, and she could walk ahead in silence. At the house, Josephine asked if she wished to borrow another dress, and she declined.

"I am quite tired. I think I will skip the evening meal. Would you make my apologies to your mother?"

It was absurd of her, but she did not wish to watch Henry speaking to Miss Bradley-Hough, wondering if he planned to marry her. She felt sad enough as it was.

She set off for her rooms, longing for the escape of sleep.

"Mrs. Hull," Henry called, just as she reached the staircase. She stopped and turned. He was striding quickly to catch up with her.

He smiled when he reached her. "I just wanted to say to meet me in the breakfast room at seven. We'll take off early."

She nodded.

He looked like he might say more, then hesitated, and turned to go.

"I wanted to say how much I enjoyed that," she blurted to his back.

He turned around, his face a question. "Enjoyed what?"

Oh dear, she hoped he didn't think she meant the night before. The garden.

"Your fellowship," she said quickly. "Thank you for inviting me. It's been ages since I've been in church. I never knew that it could feel like that. So peaceful."

His entire face lit up. "I'm so very, very glad." He paused for a moment, bit his lip, which of course made him seem younger and sweeter and … he was likely about to be engaged and he was a minister and she was wicked and she had to look away.

"I hope you don't mind if I repeat myself," he continued, "but you'd truly be welcome at my congregation when you return to London."

She laughed, without thinking.

She instantly wished she hadn't, disliking the note of bitterness she could hear in her own voice. But she was unsure how to say that she would likely not be returning to London.

"Thank you. But as I've said, I'm long past saving."

Henry looked at her for a long moment without speaking. "Alice, God's mercy is not conditional. Your profession is no hindrance, if you wish to be saved."

She shook her head. "It has little to do with my profession."

He looked at her so softly, his green eyes like a caress. "Why don't you wish to go to church? What happened?"

She looked at the floor, ignoring the part of her that again wanted more, more. "Oh, everything and nothing. I won't bore you with the tale."

"It takes very much to bore *me,* Mrs. Hull. I'm quite dull by nature."

"You are very far from dull," she objected, finally returning his gaze. Her tone sounded a touch more sentimental than she had meant it to.

"I'm tired," she added quickly. "I will see you in the morning."

He nodded. "I will say my Prayer of Weather before bed and hope we can set back off tomorrow."

"Thank you," she said, but she walked up the stairs hoping his Prayer of Weather wouldn't work. She should be relieved that the weather had calmed, but the lack of snow only heightened her dread.

She wished the snow might fall indefinitely.

She wished she could stay here, trapped in this frozen place where her mother lived, where the problems in the house belonged to other people, where she could sip down Henry

Evesham's private words like claret, savoring the complexities of his luminous, dark soul.

It was restful, to pretend this was her life, this blank canvas suspended in a world with no future and no past.

It was treasonous to think it, but she never wanted to go home.

CHAPTER 19

Henry tried not to resent Miss Bradley-Hough for not being Alice at supper.

It was not Miss Bradley-Hough's fault that, after the short drive to Fleetwend in the morning, he would likely never see Alice again. Nor was it her fault that all he could think about was sneaking away and up to Alice's rooms to hold her hands and pray with her. (To hold her hands.)

But he must stay, for he felt his father's eyes on him, monitoring the currents of potential courtship like a sentry. Dutifully, Henry set out asking his companion questions about her life.

Miss Bradley-Hough was genuinely lovely. She described with charm and verve her sociable life in Bath, which sounded luxurious and pleasant, if lacking purpose. In turn, he told her of his work investigating vice and doing charity for prostitutes. She was so poised that she almost—almost—succeeded in hiding her alarm behind her gracious manners.

"Henry is nearly done with his duties to the Lords," his father interjected. "He will soon move on to other work."

Miss Bradley-Hough looked relieved on Henry's behalf. "You

must be ever so eager to leave such unpleasantness behind," she said with perfect sympathy.

"No," he said slowly. "I'll miss it. I quite like gathering facts, meeting such different people, writing my impressions."

In saying it, he realized it was true.

"But you will return to the church?" she pressed.

He hesitated. "My plans are as yet undetermined. I hope to expand my charity work to other cities. Make use of my findings. Whether that is through ministry or other means, I have yet to decide."

His father glowered at him.

Henry smiled at Miss Bradley-Hough as though he did not notice. "Whatever work I do, I hope to marry soon, to find a helpmeet eager to undertake it alongside me."

Miss Bradley-Hough nodded. "Yes, no doubt such work would be much eased by the help of a woman of noble character and profound faith." She paused, and smiled at him kindly. "I hope you find her very soon."

There was a moment of such perfect understanding between them that he could have kissed her.

Instead, he smiled back at her with equal warmth. "Indeed. So do I."

He glanced at his father, who was furiously carving at his meat, his cheeks nearly purple with anger. Well, he could rage all he liked, but he could not deny that it was clear Miss Bradley-Hough had no intention of marrying Henry.

As soon as supper was over, he excused himself to take a constitutional outside. He walked under the clear sky thinking of the pleasure of another drive with Alice. One last chance to talk to her. To convince her to come visit his meeting house in London. (To be alone with her, just the two of them, in a space so small he could feel her warmth and hear her breathe.)

He began to hum that jaunty tune Alice had hummed in the curricle, smiling to himself. He was still humming it when he went inside and stopped in the library, where he had left his Bible. Jonathan was lying on a sofa with a large glass of brandy sitting on his chest.

He inclined his head, like he wanted to hear Henry better, and let out a shout of laughter so forceful the brandy nearly toppled to the floor.

(Don't think unkind—) *Miserable drunkard.*

"Where did you learn *that* tune?" Jonathan asked, taking a sip between chortles.

Henry snatched his Bible off the table. "Just something Mrs. Hull was humming in the carriage to pass the time."

Jonathan snorted. "Ah, of course. I should have guessed."

Henry stopped and turned around, furious that Jonathan would speak of Alice in that knowing tone.

"What does that mean?" he asked sharply.

Jonathan stretched, looking immensely pleased with himself. "When did she lose her husband, your Mrs. Hull?"

Henry narrowed his eyes, still not following. "Last autumn, sadly."

Jonathan raised a brow. "Ah. I *see*."

"What, exactly, do you see?"

Jonathan took another sip. Smacked his lips. "Only that it is quite odd, *you* driving a woman like her alone. Bringing her here."

His brother's speech was slurred and he knew better than to engage with him, but Henry could not seem to hold back. "A woman like what?"

Jonathan made a lewd gesture. "You've always liked the little ones."

Henry relaxed. It was just Jonathan trying to rile him, and he would not ruin his evening by allowing himself to be drawn in by veiled accusations that were based in nothing more than his elder brother's lifelong desire to antagonize him. "A simple act of kindness, driving her. You *would* think it odd."

He turned his back on his brother and continued toward his bedchamber, humming the song louder as he walked away.

CHAPTER 20

Alice dragged herself to the breakfast room alone. The snow had stopped. She would be going home.

She felt like the entire world was drawn in gray. Even the fine spread of cakes and hothouse fruit set out on the breakfast buffet was not enough to cheer her. She took a single boiled egg. And then, since she was alone, she wrapped a few cakes in a napkin for her sisters and put them in her pocket.

Henry walked into the room as she sat down at the table. He flashed her a smile so big that for a moment she saw colors again. Had he ever looked at her so fondly before? Was it because he knew that after today he would be rid of her?

"We can drive on to Fleetwend now that the snow has stopped," he said cheerfully. "I'll ready the horses as soon as I break my fast."

She forced herself to smile. "Thank you." The bundle of cakes felt strangely heavy against her thigh, like the weight of her fate was crushing her.

Henry's father came into the room and immediately scowled

at the servant who was handing Henry a bowl of porridge. He grunted a greeting to Alice and then pointed at Henry's bowl.

"Where do you get that infernal mush? Surely we don't stock that in my kitchens."

"I brought some from my own home so that I need not inconvenience your household, sir," he said in a pleasant tone. Alice marveled that he was polite to his father even though the man was an ill-tempered tyrant who treated him worse than bones scavenged by wolves in a long-abandoned graveyard.

His father watched him chew, which Henry did slowly, deliberately, as though the man was not staring at him like every swallow was an insult.

"Fascinating, he remains so large when he is so ill-nourished," the elder Mr. Evesham drawled to Alice, helping himself to a plate of sausages. "Is it not, Mrs. Hull?"

Henry froze, looking like he'd been slapped.

Alice turned to Henry's father's, imagining her eyes were needles that could drill into his pupils. "I hope you will not think me too forward, Mr. Evesham, if I tell you that the Lord Lieutenant's great strength and height is considered very pleasing among the young ladies back home. It will embarrass him to hear this, but they find him very handsome and are always doing their best to catch his eye. I suspect he'll have his pick if he decides to marry."

Henry and his father looked at her with similar expressions of disbelief.

She shrugged and picked at her egg. Henry had been a friend to her. Even if he was engaged to a fine lady and she'd never see him again after today, she could be a friend to him. The kind of friend who ate what remained of her egg very, very slowly, so that he would not have to be alone with his rat pecker of a father.

Mr. Evesham recovered himself. "Speaking of marriage," he

said to his son, "I'll do what I can to repair what damage you did with Miss Bradley-Hough at supper" his father said. "You'll have to give up this foolish notion of ministering to whores, of course."

Henry looked up from his porridge.

"Foolish, sir?" he asked, keeping his tone neutral.

"Her father wants her wed within the year. She's his only heir. If you'll simply do what I've so helpfully arranged, you'll be a rich man, Henry. Olivia will gladly have you, whatever she says. Her father's given me his word."

"We'll discuss it upon my return," Henry said in a tone that made clear the discussion would go badly.

So he *wasn't* engaged. And very obviously did not want to be. A smile bloomed on her face, and she put her napkin to her mouth so neither man would see her grinning like a fool. Suddenly the morning was bright and she was hungry. She waved to the servant and took three fat, fragrant sausages from his silver tray.

Delicious.

Mr. Evesham had wrinkled his prodigious brows at his son, making them look like distressed caterpillars writhing around in salt. "Your return from where?" he demanded. "You can't possibly mean to travel in this weather."

"The weather is perfectly suitable for travel. Bright, sunny, and the roads will be empty because of the snow. We'll make excellent time. Mrs. Hull will be with her mother before luncheon and I'll be back by supper."

He directed his attention to Alice. "Mrs. Hull, I will go prepare the horses for our journey. Ring for a footman to help you carry your things downstairs. We'll depart at eight."

She nodded and took a bite of sausage, enjoying the fat exploding on her tongue.

"Henry, the snow will pick back up," his father said. "Leave now and you'll be stranded."

"We'll take the risk. Mrs. Hull's mother is ill and there's not a cloud in the sky."

Henry's father slammed his knife and fork down on the table, rattling the glasses. "Henry, don't be foolish. The weather is going to turn. I feel it in my wrist."

"I'm not foolish," Henry snapped, stretching to his full height. "Nor am I willing to further delay Mrs. Hull's journey over the paganish superstitions of your wrist."

"Well I shan't be coming after you when you find yourself trapped in a storm, you fool-headed boy."

"I should imagine not," Henry said. "Good day, sir."

He marched from the room before his father could say another word. Alice snatched the last of her sausages off her plate and scurried off behind him.

"What a right *prick*," she muttered, when she caught up.

And despite her cursing, he laughed.

But she could tell he was still upset as they drove away from Bowery Priory a quarter hour later. Henry appeared to invest great effort into seeming unperturbed, fixing a smile on his face and holding it there so stiffly she thought his mouth must hurt. But his fingers gave him away. He twisted them around the reins like he was trying to strangle the leather.

"Are you all right?" she ventured.

"I'm very well," he murmured. "'Tis a lovely day for a drive."

"I meant about your father."

He sighed. "I'm sorry. He is coarse to speak so bluntly before guests."

"He is a rotten cur to speak to *you* that way, never mind the guests."

Henry glanced at her with pained amusement. "What shall I do without you to do my cursing for me, Alice Hull?"

"Tell the bastard off yourself!"

He laughed, shaking his head. "Thank you for your words in my defense." He paused, and she realized he was blushing. "About … the ladies. I should not encourage lying but I won't pretend I did not welcome that particular untruth."

Oh, Henry Evesham, you dear, stupid man. "If what I said was not precisely true in the particulars, it is surely true in general, Henry. I saw the way the young women looked upon you when you were preaching yesterday. Religious admiration cannot account for that much sighing."

He blushed, and she liked it immensely. Now that she knew he was the man from the journal, the poor fellow who found such fault with himself, she wanted to spoil him with praise. And now that she knew he was not promised to another woman, she felt quite entitled to do exactly as she liked.

"You are very handsome, Henry. I am quite an expert in these things, you know."

He flushed even darker. She wished to run her fingers through the hair that fell over his ears—she knew, from the journal, he visited the barber sparingly as an economy—but instead, she told him something else she wished for him to hear before they parted.

"And your father is a brute."

His eyes darted over to the trees, to the horizon, looking anywhere but at her. "Don't say that, Alice."

"He is cruel to you for his own amusement. And he's wrong. You deserve better than to suffer abuse from a man like that. You are kind."

His eyes finally glanced at hers, and she saw tears shining in them.

It made her chest constrict.

"Oh, Henry," she said. She took his hand and squeezed it. She expected him to pull away.

But he didn't.

"It's humiliating to me that you witnessed his temper, Alice, but I am grateful for your kindness. I don't know how I can possibly return it."

"You already have. Hate to make you big with flattery, but you have been a perfect hero as far as I'm concerned."

He squeezed her hand and grinned. "A perfect hero. 'Tis unspeakably vain of me, but I rather like that."

And then, as if realizing he was flirting with her while holding her hand, he dropped it and his face went rigid.

He was so unpracticed at such games that he was adorable. Still, she doubted it would get him very far with women less odd than herself. She resolved to do what she could to give him lessons. Her own small thank you for his service, so that the poor man could find a wife.

Besides, she enjoyed flirting with him, and she didn't know when she would next have the opportunity to enjoy herself.

She inclined her head demurely, gave him an inviting, womanly smile. "You've spent days driving in all weather in an attempt to get me home. And you've been such a comfort in my low moments." She softened her voice, remembering his face when he'd prayed with her in the staircase. "A girl could get accustomed to having you about."

He winced, but she could tell he liked it.

He turned to her shyly and said, "Alice, if you flatter me like this I may decide to keep you as my captive rather than driving you home."

Please. I'd like nothing better.

"It's not flattery. It's *true*. Without you I would not have a hope of saying goodbye to my mother."

All at once, her flirtatious mood deserted her. She had not meant to say those words—they had come out accidentally. It was the first time she'd acknowledged aloud that this was what awaited her in Fleetwend: her dear, difficult mother, dying. The person who loved her with a ferocity that was like a compass, showing her what was north. Gone.

For all their disagreements, she could not imagine life without that love. It was like a furnace that blazed and blazed but never ran out of coal. Even if she could not feel its warmth on her skin, she'd always known it would be there when she came back to it.

In a way, it made her brave. For she knew that the strength of that love was enough to overcome whatever Alice might do to cause her mother disappointment.

It was so fierce, she had taken it for granted.

"Don't fret, Alice," Henry said softly, misreading her sudden silence. "We'll be there soon. Two hours at the most."

"I've not been good to her, Henry," she whispered. "I've treated her as a nuisance."

He looked at her with a deep sympathy in his eyes. "Don't condemn yourself. It's clear how much you love her. And you have this drive to think of what you'd like to say to her. I have seen many a parishioner who misses the opportunity to say farewell."

"I don't condemn myself," she confessed. She said the words that had been troubling her for days: "In a way, I feel I am not nearly sad enough. I am angry this has happened. For myself. I don't want to go home."

It was a shocking sentiment. The words felt bitter in her mouth. She could not bring herself to look at him, knowing what he would think of her for airing such thoughts.

He reached out and touched her hand. "It's more common than you might imagine, to feel angry." His tone was gentle, and not the least bit judgmental. "I've been at many funerals, many bedsides. There is no right or wrong way to feel in the face of loss."

Surely, her way—blistering pity for herself and resentment at what her life would be—was not the right one. Henry would almost certainly be appalled if he could see inside her heart.

She was glad she did not possess a journal he might find.

"I think I might be a truly bad person, Henry," she confessed. "*Truly*."

He wrinkled his brow. "Why?"

She liked him so much for that simple question. For not dismissing her concern, but probing it. It would be such a relief to pour out the dark, black thoughts that were ricocheting in her mind. To tell him of her dread at the narrowing of her future. The dreams she'd dared to have and must abandon.

But they were not dreams he would support. Would he not counsel her to do as she'd already decided? To abandon the frivolities of the heart in favor of duty, family, devotion? If he knew the nature of the things she wanted, it would blacken his opinion of her, and at this moment, she was grateful for his friendship.

It was easier to let him think she was merely grieving an imminent loss.

And she was.

It was only that what she stood to lose was far more than he imagined.

She tried to formulate a vague response that would not reveal more than she had already said, but something cold bit her cheek, and then her eyelash, and then her hand.

"Damnation!" she cried.

Henry winced, but did not comment on her cursing. "I'm sorry. I said too much. You haven't asked for my counsel."

"It's not that, Henry," she said. "It's snowing."

He looked up at the sky, which was grayer, but still cloudless. "No it isn't. Don't jest."

"I'm not jesting."

He held out his hand. She watched a single snowflake float lazily down and melt atop his glove, staining a dark patch onto the leather.

"See?" she moaned.

"Just a few flurries, with any luck," he said. "Nothing to fret over." But his jaw was tense, and he resumed his agitated worrying of the reins.

As they drove on, the sky became more ominous, and the flecks of ice became more regular, until they fell in fat, wet flakes.

Within a quarter hour, the flakes became a storm. The wind picked up, blowing up snow from the fallen drifts along the road. At first it was pretty, swirling about in the air, mingling with the fresh snow falling from the sky. But as the wind became more forceful, they could scarcely see five feet ahead of them. Henry's driving slowed from a clip to a trot to a crawl.

He bowed his head.

When he looked up, there was a blackness in his eyes she had never seen in them before. "He was right."

"Pardon?"

"My father. He was right."

He looked so chagrined she wanted to insist that it wasn't true, though there was no denying that on this small point the man had been correct.

"We need to seek shelter," Henry said, in a tone that made her want to press him to her breast. It held a touch of resignation, and a touch shame. It was like his father was here, perched between them in the gig, gloating.

"I'll stop at the next house we encounter."

She had to summon the fortitude to inform him that this would not be possible.

"We aren't near any houses," she said carefully. They were close enough to her village that she knew exactly where they were. The road here ran alongside a river that marked the boundaries of several large estates, with nothing but forest and farmland for miles. At their current pace, it could be hours before they found a dwelling. And turning off the carriage road in search of a path through the forest would be futile, for the dainty, single-axle curricle would not survive the rough roads in such limited visibility.

"There is an old mill along the stream up ahead. We can take shelter there until the snow stops."

Henry leaned forward, squinting, and they drove on and on, at an ever-slower pace. She could feel the wheels skittering on the frozen ground beneath them and prayed they would not break.

Finally, when her eyelashes felt as if they were frozen into icicles and even Henry had begun to shiver from the cold, she saw the faint outline of a water wheel.

"There," she said, pointing in the distance. "The mill."

Henry stopped at the side of the road.

They stumbled about in the snowbank that had formed over the hedgerow until she found a low gap where there must be a footpath. She kicked at it until she'd dislodged the heavy snow to find the latch.

No smoke came from the chimney and no lights flickered in the windows of the mill.

"It's empty," she called to Henry. She went back to help him unharness the horses.

He led the pair of mares through the gate, coaxing them in a soft voice toward a small shed that leaned against the millhouse. While he tied them up, she retrieved their satchels from the curricle, and tried to let herself inside. But the door was locked. She trudged around to see if there was another entrance, but there was only a window beside the doorway, which did not budge when she tried to open it.

"The door's locked and the window's frozen shut," she grunted.

Henry came up behind her and tried rattling the glass loose. But even with his superior strength, it did not move.

She looked at him anxiously, a wail rising in her throat at the increasing likelihood that they would be spending the foreseeable future huddled in the shed with the horses.

"Stand back," he said. He removed his cravat and wrapped it around his gloved hand. And then he made a fist and sent it flying through the window.

An eruption of glass and snow burst all around them. He repeated the gesture once, twice, three times more, like he was pummeling a man to death. Each time, she could not help crying out, picturing his flesh tearing through the fractured glass.

He beat back the jagged panes with his elbow, grunting with effort, and if she was not mistaken, rage. He beat back the glass until there was just enough room for a small man to climb through the window.

Henry was not a small man.

"Wait, let me," she cried, as he hoisted himself up and began to jam his broad shoulders through the jagged space.

"Nonsense, you'll be injured," he said, gritting his teeth with the effort of wrestling his way inside.

For a moment, he disappeared.

And then he stood in the open door, his red hair askew around his head, the sleeve of his coat torn, and a rivulet of blood falling from his hairline.

"Welcome, my lady," he said with a deep, courtly bow.

She did not find this amusing, given he was bleeding. "Henry, you're hurt."

"Hit my head," he confirmed. "Nothing terrible. Not as bad as my *hand*."

He lifted his right hand up. Despite the cravat, his glove was shredded from the glass.

"Oh no," she said. "Are you cut?"

"Luckily, if I am, I'm too cold to feel it." He winked at her.

Apparently, this is what it took for Henry Evesham to develop a playful air: a deadly ice storm and a flesh wound.

Despite the cold and her dread at what awaited them, she laughed.

He laughed too, dropping his shoulders and leaning against the door. "It seems we invite perilous luck when we venture out together."

"We are indeed quite doomed."

But now that she knew he was not hurt, and they would not freeze, she could not repress a glimmer of gladness at their fate.

Perhaps they would tour the English countryside forever, courting disaster, making each other smile at the oddest things. She could imagine worse existences.

Like marrying William Thatcher.

She brushed off the thought and stepped inside to look about the mill house. There was a hearth at the rear of the snug room, and, *thank fate for this one small miracle*: a basket of twigs and a pile of wood. If they could get a fire lit, perhaps they would not freeze.

"I have a fire steel in my satchel," Henry said. He tried to fumble through the leather bag to retrieve it with his uninjured hand, but seemed to flounder, for he was right-handed.

"Let me," she said. She found the tool in his bag and crouched in front of the hearth, arranging twigs into a pyramid and lighting a flame. She blew on it until the tiny flame had grown into a small, feeble blaze. Henry knelt beside her, shivering.

All she wanted was to touch him.

"We must do something about your hand," she said decisively. "Here, let me remove your gloves so I can see the wounds."

CHAPTER 21

Henry held himself still as Alice attempted to peel the leather from his hands, pausing now and then to pick out tiny shards of glass. Normally he would be rigid with nerves at a woman touching him so intimately. But he was growing so used to Alice's nearness that he sometimes failed to mark the sin of it when his hands found hers. And besides, the cuts smarted so fiercely that he could think of little beyond pain.

(Liar.)

Alice accidentally nudged a tiny shard of glass deeper into his palm and he sucked in his breath and snatched his hand away from her, tucking it to his chest.

"I'll just leave them on," he said.

She looked at him with a mix of frustration and affection, like he was a disobedient child. "No you bloody won't, you goat." She gently pulled his hands back to her lap. "Wounds left unattended breed sickness. I wish I had some brandy to give you for the pain."

"I wouldn't drink it if you did," he muttered, to distract himself.

"I know," she sighed. "You are a tiresome, saintly man."

She said this with a wry smile that lightened his mood. Her manner made him feel well nursed in a way he was not accustomed to. It was like a balm after the harsh raillery from his father. His father who must be even now looking at the window and smiling, rubbing his ever-knowing wrist in vindication.

The thought made Henry want to smash another window.

"Don't move," Alice told him, rising.

She fetched an old pot attached to the wall with a nail and stepped outside. When she'd returned, the pot was filled with snow. She set it next to the weak fire, then returned to the business of slowly, painstakingly, freeing his hands from his gloves.

When she was done, she held both of his hands in hers, turning them over to observe his injuries. His left hand had only a scrape or two, but the right one was pocked with little cuts and smeared with blood.

"My father will be so smug." He had not meant to say that aloud, but Alice looked up at him with a malevolent glint in her eyes.

"Your father is a plague-bepissed weasel whose opinion matters naught."

"Alice!" he cried, unable to avoid laughing at the sheer fluency of her expletives, however he felt obligated to disapprove of them.

"What? You told me I must be honest," she said piously, albeit with a grin.

She went to the fire and retrieved the pot. The snow had melted into icy slush.

"Plunge," she instructed, looking at his hands. He obeyed her, dunking his stinging flesh into the cold water.

When he lifted them out, she used the sleeve of her dress to clean away the remaining smears of blood.

His thoughts flashed to that night in the meeting house, the maid offering to wash him. To the dream he'd had of Alice, performing a similar act.

Despite the chill in his raw hands, and the innocence of Alice tending to his injuries, he flushed.

He shouldn't let her do this, if he was going to corrupt her Christian-natured gesture with sinful longings. He pulled away from her. "You'll ruin your gown," he said, by not entirely convincing way of explanation.

"Better than your hand," she said, snatching the hand back. She leaned over him to dab carefully at the worst cut. She was so close, he could smell her hair. He wanted to lean in and bury his face in it. Pick her up and put her on his lap and absorb that smell into his skin.

Evidently deeming him well enough to survive, or perhaps sensing that if she lingered he might pounce on her and never let her go, she stood. "There you are."

She walked over to the hearth and added two large logs to the fire, grumbling as she tried to coax the feeble embers to light the wood.

"Can I help you?" he asked.

"Come here and blow on those a bit," she said. Her accent, amidst the cold and the stress of their situation, sounded more like a countrywoman. He found it charming, because he knew it meant she wasn't being careful.

He knelt down to blow on the embers, praying to God they would light, for he had never been this cold in all his life.

Alice took the pan outside and came back with clean snow. "To melt for the horses," she explained.

His heart squeezed for the poor horses. He was a fool for dragging them out into an ice storm, a bigger fool for dragging Alice. And the worst of it was, his father had been *right.* If they lived through this nightmare—and God willing, they would—he dreaded his eventual return home. His father's glee at having been proven smarter than his feckless son would sting more than Henry's shredded hand.

When the snow had melted in the pot he reached for it, hoping to spare Alice another trip outside. She swatted him away.

"Don't even think about using them bedeviled hands, Henry Evesham," she said. "Not after I worked so hard to save them."

So he sat, feeling useless and yet strangely … anticipatory.

His brother's words came to him unbidden. *You always did like the small ones.*

Is that what this was? Is that why he felt so curiously light despite being trapped in the snow and in acute pain?

(Yes. Phrasing it as a question will not excuse your intellectual dishonesty.)

When Alice returned, she was covered in snow from the top of her head to the hem of her dress. She looked like a frozen winter fairy.

"What?" she asked, narrowing her eyes at the smile on his face.

"You look …" (Enchanting.)

"Frozen as a witch's cunny?" she provided.

"Alice!"

She grinned as she removed a handkerchief from her pocket, which she opened to reveal the contents of a plate of cakes he'd last seen at breakfast.

"I took them," she admitted sheepishly. "I thought my sisters would like to try a taste of something so fine."

He smiled. "That was kind of you."

"Now he approves of theft," she said mordantly to the walls. "I've thoroughly corrupted him." She offered him a cake. "Will you have a nip of devil's sugar or will you be starving tonight, Reverend?"

He rolled his eyes at her, snatched the cake with his good hand, and took a bite. He closed his eyes as the sugar hit his tongue.

He loved sweets. He truly did.

"Praise God," he murmured.

She reached out and brushed away a bit of sugar from his bottom lip. His entire body seized at her touch. She glanced down, pretending not to notice that he'd gasped.

But oddly, she was smiling.

Together, they ate the cakes as they watched the last of the light die out through the windows.

A mouse scurried past them, startling their peaceful silence. Henry jumped and rose to chase it away.

"Oh, leave him," Alice said, leaning back contentedly. "I love mice."

He gaped at her. "You *love* mice?"

She smiled sweetly at the scurrying rodent. "Yes. They are so small and curious and clever."

"Until they chew through the walls and leave droppings in the cupboards."

"You sound like my mother," she groaned. "When I was a girl, I lured one into a box with cheese and tried to keep it in my room. Mama smacked me so hard I saw stars when she found it. Marched it right outside and fed it to a barn cat, she did."

She told the story like it was funny, but it struck him as gruesome. "That sounds upsetting for a child."

She grinned. "Bah. I was fourteen."

He smiled, picturing a nearly grown girl still whimsical enough in spirit to wish to keep a rodent as a pet. "Shall I catch you one to look after now?"

She laughed. "No, but thank you for the gallant offer. I'm sure the mouse found it none too inspiring living in that box in my closet. Wild creatures are better off free."

She stood and rummaged in her bag, then came back to their nook in front of the fire holding a pile of rumpled garments. Her teeth were chattering. Perhaps she intended to don extra layers to ward off the cold.

Instead, she spread them out on the floor into a makeshift pallet. "There. We can sleep here. It won't be comfortable but it will be better than lying on the cold floor."

We? She could not think he intended to share a bed with her, makeshift or otherwise.

"You rest. I'll sit by the fire and tend it overnight."

"It's warmer here. And there's room for two."

Not with any decency between them, there wasn't. "I'm not yet tired. You sleep. You've been working hard, while I've just sat here."

She did not argue, just closed her eyes.

He made himself watch the fire, because it would be very embarrassing if she caught him gazing at her. He wished there was enough light to read, for he had his Bible in his satchel and he could use a bracing dose of scripture. But the fire was too small to illuminate anything beyond the circle by the hearth. So instead, he tended the fire, refusing to look at Alice, who he could hear gently snoring. When the flame became low he looked in the basket of logs and was alarmed to discover that there were only a few left. He prowled around the dark room searching for more wood, but found nothing.

He burnt what little there was left, but with the wind howling through the broken window it put off little heat.

The mill was freezing even with the fire. Without it, it would be unbearable.

Alice stirred. "Henry?" she asked sleepily. "I'm so cold. Build the fire up."

"We're out of wood," he admitted.

"Then come here before it gets any colder. We'll freeze."

"I can't share a bed with you Alice. It's not right."

He heard an expulsion of air emerge from her that sounded like a mix of sleep nonsense and curses.

She leaned over and poked his knee. "Henry. Evesham," she said, through chattering teeth. "I will not freeze to death over some foolish notion of decency."

"I suspect you will not freeze to death," he corrected. "You will merely be very, very cold."

"Henry," she hissed. *"Come. Here."*

He trudged over to the pallet and knelt on it beside her. It was wrong but he was so, so cold and so, so tired.

"Take off your coat and use it as a blanket," she said. "It's warmer that way."

He removed it, shivering at the onslaught of the chill.

Alice lifted up the edge of her own cloak. "Here, come join me for warmth. We'll share."

He wanted to weep at how soft and warm her ermine looked, how her body must be just as soft and warm beneath it.

Which meant he must resist.

"I'm sorry, Alice," he said, drawing his coat over his own body and turning away from her. He closed his eyes.

But sleep did not come to him. He was so cold that his fingers and toes ached, so cold that the coldness felt like a pain spread out inside his body. Beside him, Alice's teeth were chattering noisily. Every time a gust of snowy wind blew in from the window, she shivered violently and swore.

Was she right? Was he allowing decorum to get in the way of the larger Christian duty towards protecting life and health? Perhaps he was, or perhaps he was just too cold to care.

(The latter.)

"God forgive me," he muttered. "Come here, Alice Hull."

He lifted up his coat and she scurried under it, lodging herself under his arm.

Such soft, plush, warmth, her body. She curved against him the way a snail fit to its shell, perfectly spooned within the contours of his larger frame. He draped her cloak over the layer of wool, and since they were already long past the point of decency, drew her to him with all his strength to help warm her.

She burrowed herself into him as tightly as she could. "You could have done this an hour ago, you wretched man."

"Don't remind me of my failed convictions or I might change my mind."

(He would not change his mind. Having her in his arms was far, far better than freezing alone on the floor.)

He closed his eyes and she shifted sleepily against him.

But he still did not fall asleep. For now that he was not so cold he was in pain, the pleasure of her next to him did not feel purely comforting.

It felt dangerous.

All he could feel or think or see was her—the rising and falling of her chest as she breathed, the occasional shivers that went through her when the wind picked up through the broken window. The smell of woodsmoke that wafted from her hair.

He was no longer tired.

His exhaustion, he realized with rising dread, had been replaced with a more troublesome sensation: the stirring of his groin.

Cretin.

He tried to edge away from Alice, to put some modicum of distance between them, but she groaned in protest and snuggled back.

With horror, he felt his cock thickening.

You gutter-bred, Devil-cursed wretch, he imagined her saying if she noticed.

How could he produce such a state amidst this bitter cold?

He edged away again, praying she was too lost to slumber to feel the hardness that exposed his shame. But every time he moved away, she grumbled and shivered and restored the distance.

The fourth or fifth time he tried to move aside, she reached behind her and clamped his leg down over her haunches with her bony little fingers. Surprising strength she had, for such a tiny person.

"Henry," she said wearily. "I know you have a cockstand. I don't care. It's the natural reaction when a young man lies with a woman, particularly a young man who perhaps is not accustomed to such practice. I am very cold, and I would much rather feel your cock poking me than freeze to death."

He did not know what to say.

Some part of him was relieved that she had simply addressed the problem. Some other part of him wanted to climb out of the nest they'd made and run into the cold and freeze to death in a snowdrift.

He held himself stiff, barely daring to breathe, for in truth his breath was coming more quickly due to the surging of his desire and he did not want her to perceive how bad a state he was truly in.

He prayed for his cock to go down like he had never prayed for anything before.

Instead, the bugger surged to life, pulsing about inside his breeches, leaking. The trail it left was wet against his belly—a cold reproach.

The third time it twitched against her he could not stand to ignore it in silence.

"I'm sorry," he whispered, scarcely getting the words out around his acute embarrassment. "I don't mean to it's just … happening."

"Henry," she sighed, squeezing his shoulder, which did not help at all. "Nothing you wish to tell me about cocks would surprise me. I spend my days wiping their leavings from the floors. I've seen them swell at all manner of things. Don't worry. Just hold me and try not to freeze."

But he couldn't, for his wretched, hungry organ was pulsing rudely at the pressure of her hand innocently patting his back, and the notion of her familiarity with the state that he was in.

She laughed softly and shifted her buttocks to better accommodate the space so insistently claimed by his erection, which made him groan involuntarily.

He was going to die of embarrassment or lust, he did not know which.

She sighed with what sounded curiously like sympathy. "If you need to attend to yourself to be comfortable I don't mind. I won't watch."

He stopped breathing. Was she suggesting—

"No!" he said in a strangled voice.

She inhaled, as if in understanding. "Aye, I suppose you'd need your hand for that."

Before he could sputter a response, she moved her own hand to his stomach, touching him lightly over his shirt. "I could satisfy you, if it would help," she said in a voice that was more amiable than seductive. "Perhaps then you could sleep?"

His brain disappeared in a puff of smoke, filling his head with ash. He was nothing but the throbbing beneath his hips, the nerves that rippled at the light pressure of her fingers on the cotton between their skin.

He lurched backward. "Have mercy, Alice," he sputtered out,

"not to speak of such things." He'd be cursed with remembering this agony for months. Years.

"Just thinking of your comfort," she said in a frank tone, as though the situation was entirely unremarkable.

"Alice! Please, don't speak of this. I am celibate. I told you that."

She went quiet, allowing him to focus more intently on his exquisite humiliation.

"You mean you don't even touch *yourself?"* she whispered, after a long pause.

"No!"

"Never?"

"Do you?" he parried miserably, to end this conversation, wanting to disappear.

She laughed softly. "Nightly."

His question had not been serious. He was not even aware women did such things. His cock lurched violently at this idea, and to his horror a sound left his throat that was something like a moan.

"Oh, you poor man," she chuckled. "No wonder your cock is flopping around like a dying weevil. You must be in agony. How have you not gone mad?"

"Please let's not discuss this," he said, for his cock was indeed now in such a state that if she moved any closer to him it might erupt, and if that were to happen he would never, ever be able to look at her again.

(And yet an evil, treacherous part of him *wanted* to discuss this. A vulgar, sinful part of him *delighted* in the idea of Alice Hull doing such a thing—touching herself. He wanted to know how and when she did it and what she thought about and—)

He wanted her so much. So bloody much.

"Very well, Reverend," she said. "But I hate to see you suffer on my account."

"Of course I would not dishonor you like that," he croaked in the rough, shattered remains of his voice. "Or myself."

"Dishonor? I think when someone wishes to give or receive such a favor, it can be quite an honor."

"What do you mean?" he asked, genuinely baffled.

"I mean it's flattering, to be wanted. Or tended to, when one is in a state of need. It's the closest thing we common folk get to being royalty. There's no reason to fear such things, Henry."

"You ... do this. Exchange ... favors?"

"Mmm," she said, in sleepy affirmation. "There's plenty of lovely favors that don't lead to trouble for a girl. I could tell you about them, if you want."

He shifted about and pressed his cock into the floor, to keep himself sane.

"A bit of touching, tender, between the legs," she provided, her voice slightly breathy. "Kissing those wanting parts. It can't be too grave a sin, I'd think. Just harmless fun that leaves one feeling like a princess."

Her voice was so husky that he wondered if she was touching herself as she said this. At the thought, his thighs began to tremble. Oh no. *Oh no.* A low moan burst from his throat as, without so much as a touch from either of their hands, his seed began to flow. "God forgive me," he whispered, his hand over his mouth.

He shook, unable to stop the emission, unable to silence his shaking breath.

He was coming and she was right beside him, her shoulder beneath his arm, and surely, surely she must know.

"You know, Henry," she said in a tender, sleepy voice. "I used to think lust was a plague. I used to lie awake with it night after night, wondering what was wrong with me. But I've come to see there's no affliction in relieving it. It always makes me feel so much better."

She knew he had just erupted right beside her, *touching her*, and she was telling him not worry about it. He said nothing, furtively wiping away the emission with his shirt as best he could, hating himself for the fact that he did, in fact, feel better, now that the agony had ended.

"Anyway, Henry Evesham," she whispered. "I shall not corrupt you further with my wicked tongue. But I might have enjoyed the chance."

He did not answer her, for he was reciting prayers in his own head.

Asking his savior why it was that if Alice Hull confessing her most private secrets to him was devilry, it had felt so much like grace.

CHAPTER 22

"Alice."

Alice awoke on a cold, hard floor to a bright morning and Henry Evesham murmuring her name. She groaned, and kept her eyes shut tight against the light. She felt Henry move nearer, crouching over her.

Touch me.

His fingers brushed her shoulder. *Yes.*

"Alice?"

She fluttered open her eyes, just enough to see his face, and lifted up her arms. *Get down here and make me warm.*

But he moved away without acknowledging her invitation, moving about like nothing at all was different between them.

Like nothing had been whispered, nothing stoked, the night before.

She felt all at once unpleasantly awake.

"Time to rise," Henry chattered, rummaging about. "Are you hungry? I found a dry log in the shed for a fire. I'm going to make porridge."

She sat up and wiped her eyes. He made a triumphant noise and turned around, brandishing a single silver spoon.

"There is only one. But better than eating with our hands."

She hunched inside her cloak, breathing into her palms for warmth, as he poured oats into a pot of melting snow and stirred his concoction over the tiny blaze. When it was cooked, he came and presented her the pot, filled with beige mush, and the single spoon. "For the lady."

He sat down opposite her. She dug the spoon into the porridge and took a bite. She tried not to wince. It was very hot and very bland.

"Delicious," she said, trying to force the flavorless mush down her throat.

Henry chuckled at the look on her face. "Normally I make it with milk and a bit of salt."

"No wonder you decline spiced buns and kippers, with tasty fare like this at the ready."

She forced down another bite, then pushed the pot across the floor to him. "All yours. Thank you."

He took a bite and winced. "Not my finest, effort I'll admit."

"Better than starvation," she allowed. "But only slightly."

He ate a few more bites, then pushed the pot away and looked into her eyes.

"Alice, I'm sorry for last night."

Ah, so he *was* going to acknowledge it.

She shook her head. "There is nothing to apologize for."

"Oh, I think there is," he sighed. "You are … That is, around you, I feel… ," he looked at her, then down at his hands. "Quite a bit too much for my own good, it seems."

The yearning in his eyes made her want to cry. Made her want to take him in her arms.

But he was not professing the kind of sentiment that invited *more* affection. He spoke in a tone that made clear his desire for her was an unwanted temptation to which he had succumbed.

She understood. She did not wish to want *him* either. The chasm that ran between their ways of thinking was too deep to ever be breached in any satisfying way. She wanted a man who wanted her affection and her lust. Not a lover whose judgment—of her or of himself—she had to fear when morning came.

Still, she wanted him to know he had not been alone. She was not remotely innocent. Every word she'd said to him in the dark had been deliberate. Every intake of his breath, every tremor of his body, she had felt like it was hers.

"Henry, if I spoke too boldly to you last night, then I'm sorry, too. I was caught up in the moment, and perhaps I imagined … You see, you make me feel quite a bit as well."

She hoped he understood, in his modest way, that what she really meant was: *I wanted you. My body does not reveal its want as unmistakably as yours does but if it did, you would understand that even now, I am alive with it.*

She sensed he did understand, for his mouth opened, and then shut. A fierce red flushed at the center of each cheek, and he looked down at his lap. "It was not your fault, given my excitement. I've been … wrestling with things, desires, and I …" He lowered his voice. "I am flattered that you felt the same."

I know all about it, Henry, she wanted to say. *How it feels to burn.* The only difference between them was that she no longer believed in the merits of burning. Life was short and often brutal. To suffer willfully—to deprive oneself of easy, harmless pleasures—struck her as a waste of breath.

She reached across the table and took his uninjured hand. "No shame in it, Henry Evesham, to be alive. To want things."

"Thank you," he said softly. "If things were different … well, you are lovely, Alice."

Oh, she would miss him. She would miss him so much that the sadness of it almost left her breathless.

Get accustomed to it. There are many things you long for you will have to live without.

She stood up quickly. "I'll gather my things so we can go. "

She set about picking up the gowns she'd slept on and rolling them up, so she didn't have to look at him. When she turned around he had retrieved her satchel and held it open for her to stuff the gowns back into it.

"One minute," she said, trying to jam them into a smaller ball so that they'd fit.

His eyes shifted down inside the bag, and his expression changed. She followed his gaze, and realized what he was looking at.

A book bound in brown leather.

Her heart dropped to her toes. The only thing she could think to do was to pretend she hadn't noticed what he'd seen, and hope he'd assume he was mistaken. But he reached inside her bag and grabbed the book.

"Henry," she said quickly, but he had opened the book to confirm his suspicions and was now staring at his own writing.

He looked up at her, stricken. "Alice, what—" He shook his head, like he was searching for words.

She had no earthly idea of what to say. How could she possibly explain? "I didn't," she sputtered. "You see—I—that is—"

"You have my journal," he stated, like he was trying to make himself understand that this was true. "*You have my journal.*"

"I picked it up by mistake," she said feebly. "I didn't even know it was yours. I only realized yesterday."

"Have you *read* this?" he asked, holding it up with his good hand, which was shaking.

"No!" she said. But that was not true.

"Yes," she admitted, more softly.

He regarded her like she was a snake.

"I was going to give it back. I was just trying to think how to explain why I came to have it, and—"

"You should have returned it the instant you found it, unread," he shouted. "This is private. This is personal. Aren't your people the ones always going on about trust? Discretion?"

She didn't know what to say. He was exactly right. She *should* have done so. But it would have made them both uncomfortable and made her look like a thief or a blackmailer, and she had not wanted to fall in his esteem. She'd decided returning the book to Elena's would be the most elegant way around the whole mess.

He looked up at her, his cheeks on fire. "Is this why you offered to touch me last night? Because you know about my—"

"No!" she cried. "I wanted you before I read it."

He froze. She realized she'd just said directly the thing they'd talked around with such tortured vagueness. She decided to tell the truth.

"When I realized it was yours, it just made me want you more."

He put the book in his own satchel, looking disgusted. "Come," he said tersely. "Let's go."

CHAPTER 23

Henry drove slowly but determinedly down the road, occasionally stopping to remove tree branches that had fallen in the storm, ignoring Alice's protests about his hand.

He invited the pain. He welcomed anything that might distract him from his thoughts.

From her presence beside him.

From the drive, which should have taken less than an hour, but took two.

During those two hours, he did not say a single word to Alice. The closer they got to Fleetwend, the more miserable he felt. The sharpness of his anger had settled into something more like a weight around his heart.

It hurt him, that she'd done this. It *hurt*.

They passed a sign noting her village was two miles away. Oddly, the snowstorm had not reached this far inland. There was no ice on the ground at all.

"The turn is just up the road on the right," Alice said quietly.

"Alice, how much of my journal did you read?" The question was abrupt, but he knew he would never see her again after this ride was over, and he would never know the answer if he did not ask her now. There were certain passages that made him sting with embarrassment, passages that could ruin him. He did not *want* to know; he had to.

She looked at him sadly. "Not very much, Henry. But enough."

Enough. He nodded, taut with such shame he felt like his bones were made of his father's most delicate, breakable porcelain.

"Enough," she repeated softly, "to know that you are a wonderful person. And I wish you could see it for yourself."

The porcelain shattered into one thousand tiny, painful pieces.

He said nothing. He did not trust himself to speak.

"When Mistress Brearley first invited you to the whipping house, I was angry," Alice said quietly. "I told her she put us all at risk, and she insisted that I was wrong about you. She believed you genuinely wanted to do good, to help, and would do the right thing if given the chance."

Alice paused, for her voice was shaky. She took a deep breath. "And now that I know you, Henry, I see she was right. I'm sorry that I read your journal. I'm sorry I didn't give it back when I realized it was yours. But I'm not sorry that I know your thoughts. Because they made me understand why it was I liked you, even when I thought I shouldn't."

Tears had welled up in his eyes and he angrily blinked them away. Why did these words mean so much to him? Why was it that when he should be furious with Alice, his strongest emotion was sadness that this was how their time together would end?

He wished he hadn't seen that journal in her bag.

He made the turn toward her village, breathing slowly in an effort to collect himself before he had to use his voice to say goodbye. When they reached the small square at the center of town she looked over at him. "You can let me out here."

He glanced around at the square, which was deserted. "Where is your home?"

"Oh, no, just stop here in the square. I don't want to inconvenience you in case the weather turns again. I'll walk the rest of the way."

He looked at her with displeasure. "Why?"

There was a strange expression on her face. Like she was nervous. She seemed to be trying to think of a response, and it made him angry.

"Driving you a few more minutes to your door is no extra burden when I've spent the better part of a week trying to see you safely home. Please, direct me to your house."

She fidgeted with the collar of her cloak. "Just follow this road straight ahead," she finally said. "You'll see a church on a hilltop. Our cottage is in the valley just below it."

He nodded, wondering why she, who had blithely read about all his fears and fantasies, acted like telling him where she *lived* was a difficult confession.

He soon saw the church in the distance. They were only a few minutes away.

"When we arrive," Alice said very quietly, "I must ask—that is, I do not consider myself dishonest, though I could see how you would think otherwise—but no one here knows the truth about my life in London."

He turned his head sharply. "What?"

She sighed. "They all believe I'm a housekeeper for a widowed relation of my father's. I didn't wish to burden them with worry—"

He nodded curtly.

She shrank in her side of the carriage. Clearly, it did not escape either of them that she who espoused the nobility of her work should keep it secret, in the precise manner of someone who was ashamed. He wondered if she had been, all this time, more like him than she was willing to admit. Both of them trying to live by certain convictions. Both wavering in practice.

Were he feeling more generous toward her, it might make him sad to know she, who believed so passionately in living freely without judgment, had kept this from her dying parent. But he was determined not to continue the bad habit of indulging soft emotions for Alice Hull.

"I will not say otherwise," he said tersely. "I don't wish to make trouble for you."

He turned off the road to a small cottage tucked into a valley, with a ramshackle barn and a single field that did not appear to be in active use. The roof was in need of rethatching, and the entire dwelling listed to one side. The house itself was small—it could not be more than four rooms. Despite its disrepair, the home was in a pretty place, with a forest bordering its field, and a view of the large, handsome church above it on the hill.

The front door of the house opened as they neared, and two girls came running toward them. One of them was about Alice's height, and the other was a child. At the sight of them, Alice's face broke into a smile.

"Liza! Sally!"

As soon as he stopped the curricle she jumped down and rushed to her sisters. The three of them nearly fell on top of each other, clutching each other's shoulders so tightly it was like they were one being.

As angry as he was at Alice, he could not help but be touched by the obvious emotion in this embrace.

"How tall you've grown, Liza," Alice exclaimed, stepping back to admire the bigger girl. She turned to the younger one. "And you, Sally, are the very image of Papa. Except quite a bit prettier."

The younger girl laughed, but the older one was beside herself.

"Where have you *been*, Ally? We were so worried something dreadful happened to you."

Alice took her sister by the shoulders and looked into her eye. "Eliza, I will *never* leave you to fend for yourself alone. I got caught in the blasted snow, but I've been racing here for days."

"What *snow?*" the girl protested. "It hasn't snowed all winter."

Henry glanced out at the surrounding countryside. It was cold and damp, but there was not even frost on the trees. He could not make sense of it.

"How is Mama?" Alice murmured, taking the older girl's hands.

Alice's sisters exchanged a worried look. The older one swallowed. "She's hanging on, resting. She'll be so happy that you've come home."

"Of course I've come home," Alice said, drawing both girls back into her embrace. Her eyes fell on Henry over their heads. There was something haunted in them, but the hoarseness he had heard in her voice when she'd run to them was gone.

She was being strong for them.

He wondered when, or if, she ever let herself be weak.

"Girls," she said. "This is Mr. Evesham. A friend of my mistress, who was kind enough to drive me here."

He bowed to the girls. "It's a pleasure to meet you, albeit in such somber circumstances."

The girls curtsied to him.

He turned back to Alice. "I shall be going now. I will pray for your mother's health."

"Wait," she said. Her voice was urgent, almost shrill. He paused.

She came and touched his hand. "You should come inside and warm up first," she said softly, looking into his eyes with something like a plea. "Give the horses some hay and water and a bit of rest."

Her voice was steady but her eyes were desperate. If she had not wanted him to see her home, now, for some reason, she did not wish for him to leave it.

"I've just made luncheon, Mr. Evesham," the older sister, Eliza, said. "We'd be pleased if you could join us."

He did not wish to linger here, feeling as angry as he did. But Alice had a point about the horses.

"That's very kind. If I could just put my team in your barn."

Once the mares were seen to, he followed the girls inside the house. The cottage was clean, but small and close. There was a haze about the air, as though the smoke of the coal fire could not escape through the chimney, and instead lingered in the house. He was practical with his hands—a necessity of looking after the Meeting House in exchange for his board. He itched to go about offering to repair things, though he bit the impulse back, sensitive that he might embarrass the family if he implied their home was less than shipshape.

He could see from the spare selection of tattered and beaten furnishings, and the bare shelves that passed for a pantry—a sack of apples, a few onions, a bag of flour that appeared nearly empty—that money must be very scarce.

He felt a momentary pang that he had shamed Alice for her work, when her family clearly needed every pence that they could get. It must have seemed cruel and arrogant of him, especially when she'd seen his father's ridiculous wealth.

Whatever bitterness was between them, she had been right. He must not lose sight of this when he set out to write his recommendations to the Lords.

"I'm going to go in and look on Mama," Alice said.

"No, don't," Eliza said quickly. "She's just fallen asleep and it's so difficult for her to rest with her breathing. I'll take you in to see her after lunch, and we'll give her a bit of broth. She'll be so happy to see you."

Alice looked perturbed by this. "I'll just go in quietly—"

Sally came over and took Alice's hand and led her to a seat at the table. "Mama needs to rest. The physician said it's very important."

"And I made your favorite, Ally," Eliza said. "Soup." She winked at Alice, as if this were a joke.

"How I've missed your soup," Alice groaned. "A rare, exotic delicacy."

Sally glanced up at Henry. "Liza can make a soup out of anything," she whispered, wrinkling her nose. "Carrot tops. Old shoes. Rocks."

"Actually," Eliza pronounced, ruffling Sally's hair, "we're dining like kings today. Mr. Hovis slaughtered his cow, and brought us a lovely side of beef." She passed Henry a bowl of broth studded with chunks of meat.

Alice looked horrified. "Oh, Eliza, Mr. Evesham does not—"

But Henry caught her eye and subtly shook his head. "I'm ravenous, Miss Eliza. And this smells delicious. It just so happens that beef stew is my favorite. Second only to old shoe soup, of course," he added, with a wink at Sally.

Alice looked at him gratefully and he smiled at her, trying to communicate with his eyes that she need not add him to her considerable list of worries. Whatever tension remained between them, he would not embarrass her family.

"Tell us of your life in town, Ally," Sally said around a mouthful of bread.

"Chew before you speak, m'dear," Alice corrected.

Sally giggled and made a show of chewing. After she'd swallowed, she repeated the question, assuming a broad version of an aristocratic accent. "Do tell us of your life in town, Miss Hull."

Henry chuckled at her cheek but stopped when he noticed Alice glancing at him nervously, as if she was afraid that he would challenge any fact that she asserted. He leaned over toward her little sister. "Miss Hull is a cherished member of the household in which she's employed. Mrs. Brearley tells me Alice is the finest housekeeper she has ever had."

Her sisters both beamed at her with obvious pride.

"Mama talks of you to everyone who'll listen," Eliza said. "'My daughter, the London miss, sending us fine gifts from town.' She took your cherry cordials into the market and gave them to everyone with a mouth. Even poor Mr. Dunn, who hasn't any teeth to chew them with."

Alice laughed, but was visibly shrinking under this praise. "I'm sorry I could only send cherries," she said. "I missed you at Christmas."

"Well, we missed you too, but William said you managed to have quite a bit of cheer at the markets in London. He told us all about the lights and the carolers. Said you gave him memories he'll treasure all his life."

The warmth with which Eliza said this made Henry wonder who this William was. Was Alice attached to this man? Mustn't she be, for him to visit her in London and take her to a Christmas market?

Did *he* know about her true employment? Had he received her … favors?

(Envy. Utter, despicable envy. He'd need to pray for an entire day after this. A month.)

Alice just smiled wanly and shoved bread into her mouth, refusing to look at Henry.

"How are you acquainted with Alice's mistress, Mr. Evesham?"

Eliza asked. "We're mighty curious about her. Mama says she's a grand lady."

Henry was not yet over the disorientation of imagining Alice being courted, or—(stop!)—and fumbled to form words.

Alice swallowed down her bread in a lump to beat him to it. "Mr. Evesham was a dear friend of Mrs. Brearley's late husband, the sea captain."

He found himself nodding along. "Yes. A fine man. A sea captain."

"Are you a sailor?" Sally asked, looking thrilled at this possibility.

"I'm afraid nothing as exciting as that. I am a minister by training, and run a charity." He did not mention his work for the Lords, lest it lead to other questions about the precise nature of his work, which might cause the family to worry that Alice was consorting with disreputable people.

"You're a minister?" Eliza asked, looking oddly at Alice, who was inspecting her soup.

"I am."

He had finished his soup, and he should be on his way. But he hesitated. He did not know why he wished to prolong his stay here, except he had a kind of ache around his heart, because the words Alice had said to him kept running through his head.

Enough to know that you're a wonderful person.

He had never felt such a jarring mix of affection and yearning and pique for any human being in his entire lifetime as he felt for Alice Hull. Perhaps it was only the difficulty of the weather, the odd direction their journey had taken, the high emotions of their circumstances. But he felt the way he had as a man at university, when his head had been in turmoil as he felt himself moving inexorably toward a reckoning he could feel but not yet understand.

What that internal miasma had been, in retrospect, was the first stirrings of his salvation. His heart opening to God.

What was opening in him now?

"I'd be happy to say a prayer for your mother before I leave, if you would like," he offered. He should have offered before. He'd been too caught up in his own anger to exercise compassion.

Eliza twisted her mouth, glancing sideways at Alice. "Oh, we can't ask that of you."

"'Twould be no trouble. It's the least I could do after this delicious lunch."

Eliza frowned. "Well you see, Mr. Evesham, Mama's not in good graces with the Church. She stopped attending after Alice's dispute with the vicar."

Alice's eyes went wide. "Mama stopped attending?"

Eliza nodded. "Never went back after Papa's funeral."

Alice looked like someone had punched her in the stomach.

"May I ask what happened?" Henry asked.

"'Twas nothing," Alice said in a low voice, her face distraught. "Just a disagreement."

"The vicar would not let Ally play the organ at our father's funeral," Eliza said. "He said that it was a desecration for a woman of her character to play music in church and that our father was a philistine for letting her go around performing. Mother sat through the funeral service for Papa's sake, God rest his soul, but never entered the place again. Alice didn't even attend the rites. But I think Mama misses it. She prays on her own."

Alice looked down at her lap, blinking away tears.

He could not swallow back his outrage. Of all the things he'd imagined that might have rent Alice from her faith, a *vicar* was not a possibility he'd considered.

"And this man, your vicar, has done nothing to welcome your mother back to the church? Not even in her recent illness?"

Eliza looked uncomfortable. “No … Ally told him he was a pox-blistered son of Beelzebub. After that I think he decided we were not worthy of his efforts. Besides, he rarely comes to town, and there’s no curate.”

This made him angrier still. To hold the emotions of a grieving daughter against her was contrary to the spirit of ministry. And to occupy a curacy without fulfilling the religious needs of the community was just as bad—exactly the kind of pestilential behavior that had made him begin to question his desire to assume a higher office in the Church of England during his brief year as a curate.

“A rotten practice, vicars holding curacies themselves,” he seethed aloud. “If the man had any decency, he would at least attend the sick, whatever his relations in the past. I’m sorry your mother’s been neglected in her faith, particularly in her time of need.”

Alice, who he knew had valiantly held back tears for days, suddenly let out a wail.

CHAPTER 24

"Oh, Ally!" Eliza cried, jumping up and wrapping her arms around Alice. "Don't cry over the vicar!"

But she was not crying over the vicar. She was crying because her mother had never returned to church, which was the social center of their village, and had always been her greatest comfort. That she had persisted in this quiet act of loyalty to a daughter who would not even deign to come home for Christmas.

And now, her mother lay in the next room, dying, and Alice had not even gone in to hold her hand.

She had listened to her sisters' warnings not to because some small, scared part of her hoped that if she delayed actually seeing her mother suffering and ill, this truth she could not truly reckon with—her hale, vibrant, forceful mother, dying—would not be real. But now she could not wait.

All the emotion she had held back on the journey was escaping her in great wracking sobs.

She stood up, unable to stop the tears. "Oh, poor Mama. I'm sorry Liza, but I have to see her."

Eliza jumped up and moved in front of her, appearing frightened. "No, Alice, not yet. You must wait just a bit longer while she rests. The doctor said—"

"What does it matter if she's dying? I need to see her. And Henry can say a prayer with her. I know it would mean a great deal."

"Of course," Henry murmured. He'd risen to his feet. "Anything I can do for her."

"Ally, not yet," her sister insisted, putting a hand on her shoulder to stop her.

She stepped around Eliza and rushed to her mother's room and opened the door, bracing herself for darkness, for the smells of illness, for dreadful rattling breaths.

But the curtains were open, letting in a grayish winter light.

The bed was neatly made with her mother's wedding quit.

And there was no one in it.

"Mama?" She turned and crossed the hall to the other bedchamber, wondering if she was sleeping in the girls' bed for some reason. But that room was also neat and empty.

Oh, God. Oh, God.

She hadn't made it here in time.

"Where is she?" she screamed, running back into the kitchen. "She isn't here."

Eliza and Sally just stood still, as if they'd been enchanted.

And she knew.

She knew.

Her mother had died and they hadn't wanted to tell her in front of Henry. They'd been waiting for him to leave.

She was going to be sick all over the floor.

"She's dead," she gasped, weaving on her feet. "Isn't she? Isn't she?"

Henry ran to her, and her sisters were behind him, shrieking.

"No, Ally, don't cry!" Eliza said desperately. "She's just—"

Sally rushed over to the front door and threw it open.

"Ally don't cry, don't cry," her little sister said. "Come look, she isn't dead, she's just outside."

Outside? What was a dying woman doing outside in the freezing winter air?

Alice ran to the door. A horse cart was pulling down the pathway from the road to the cottage, carrying something large and wooden on its bed, covered by a tarp.

A coffin.

But no, a coffin would not be so tall. She squinted to make out the driver.

It was William Thatcher. And sitting beside him, looking just as hale as ever, her plump cheeks rosy with good health, was Alice's mother.

Very much alive.

And waving.

"What?" Alice gasped. She turned to look at her sisters.

Sally Ann was beaming like the King himself was in that cart. Eliza just looked faint.

"Liza," Alice hissed. "You told me Mama was sick. *Dying*. She looks fine."

Eliza instantly began to cry. "I'm sorry. She *was* a bit ill. She told me to exaggerate as she wanted to be sure you would come home."

"You lied? You lied to me about our mother *dying*?"

"Don't be angry!" Sally said. "Mam's been helping William plan a surprise for you, that's all."

Alice turned her head back to the approaching horse cart. Rain had begun to fall while they were eating, and the air had a thick and humid quality. The bright day had gone surly.

Her mother was smiling at her merrily from the approaching

cart, and William Thatcher was smiling too. Between them on the seat was a large bouquet of hothouse roses.

Alice began to feel a very different form of dread.

She put her hand to her chest, because her breath was coming so rapidly she felt like she might faint.

The cart stopped before the house. Sally Ann rushed forward to take the reins from William and tie his horse to the post.

Alice's mother stepped down and opened her arms. "Ally! My girl! You're home! You're finally home."

Alice stood still and accepted her mother's embrace, unable to make herself move or speak or blink.

"William here has been planning a surprise for you," her mother whispered, her voice buoyant with excitement. She squeezed Alice's shoulders.

William walked up slowly, shyly, holding the bouquet. When he reached her he bowed low, and offered her the roses.

"Alice, it's been no secret for some time that I want you for my wife. I hope that you will do me the honor of accepting my hand."

Alice looked at the roses, so red. At William, so blond. At her mother, so jolly.

"Take the roses," her mother prodded, clapping her hands in delight.

Stunned, Alice could think of nothing to do but obey. She took them from William's hands, and he turned around and gestured at his cart.

"I know how you love music, Ally, so as a token of my affection I have spent the last year making you a wedding gift." He grinned, then walked over to the carriage and pulled up a corner of the burlap tarp. It was a barrel organ—a pretty one—all brass and gleaming hand-worked wood.

"I managed to track down the one your father owned, the one

he taught you on. It was in bad shape, but I salvaged his original ivories. The keys are grooved from his own fingers."

Alice put her hand over her mouth.

Her father had always said William was a gifted craftsman. And this organ, she could see, was truly a piece of artistry. That he had made her an instrument using the keys of her father's own organ was such a touching gesture that it genuinely took her breath away.

It would all be so moving, *were it not the bait in a trap her entire family had conspired to set for her.*

"She's touched," her mother declared, mistaking her fury for sentimentality. "Can hardly speak. It will do her good, I think, to play again."

William smiled at Alice fondly, his blue eyes twinkling. "You always were Mr. Hull's best shop window, Ally. And now you'll be mine."

Shop window.

She heard a noise behind her that echoed how she felt: a strangled gasp. She turned and saw that it had come from Henry, who's eyes darted and met hers, horrified.

"Well don't just stand there gaping, Ally," her mother chuckled. "Answer him."

She looked at William, standing with his hand on the instrument he'd made her using the skills he'd learned from the man who'd loved her more than anyone ever had.

She felt like she'd been lifted up to the sky, and was observing the scene take place from heaven. And what she saw down there, in her mother's driveway, was not a picture of herself being presented with her future.

It was a portrait of her about to say farewell to her past.

"No, William. I can't marry you. I'm sorry."

"Ally!" her mother yelped. She gripped Alice's shoulder painfully. "What are you doing?" she hissed.

Alice ripped her arm away.

William was a kind man, one she'd been friendly with since childhood. One who saw past her reputation as a loose-skirted, bad-mannered girl to her talent. She knew the life she'd have with him. Comfortable, secure, familiar.

But she did not want familiar. She did not want to be wanted for her *talent*.

She wanted a man who wanted her the way Henry Evesham wanted her. Someone who burned for her.

"Don't be a fool," her mother was whispering. "This is just as we've all planned. Just what your father wanted."

"No, this isn't what I planned. In fact, I haven't been honest with you. With any of you." She took a long, deep breath. "The place I work in London—it's a whipping house. A private club where people come to indulge in unusual desires."

She glanced at her mother to make sure she understood.

Her mother's eyes went wide. "Alice! Don't speak of such—"

"No, it's time we all speak honestly. I look after the establishment, and sometimes help my mistress with the members of her club. I've been training to take on more duties. To become a governess, like my mistress."

William let out a soft breath. "Ally. You don't have to do that. I have the money to look after you all—"

She shook her head. "William, you are so kind to do what my father asked of you. But you see, I have never felt so much at home as I do in London. I have seen things that would shock you and I covet every sight. If I were to return here to marry you, I'd always pine for something else. And I won't do that to either of us. I simply can't."

William stared at her, shocked and silent.

And then something flat and cold smacked her along the cheek.

Her mother's open hand.

She wobbled on her feet, for the blow had hit her so hard she nearly lost her balance.

And then she picked up her skirts and ran.

She didn't know where she was going.

But she knew her future would not—must not—end in Fleetwend.

CHAPTER 25

No one moved as Alice dashed off toward the hillside.

Henry waited for this man, William, to chase after her—but he just looked in puzzlement at Mrs. Hull, seeming baffled that his proposal had been met with rejection. Henry wanted to shake him. *You called her a shop window. A shop window! Do you even know her? What I would give for such a—*

"Odd, ungrateful girl," Mrs. Hull muttered, in a tone rich with self-pity. "Always has been a trouble to me."

Henry could not remain silent. "Madam, your daughter has travelled for five days in miserable weather in order to reach you, afraid she would not make it back in time. I have listened to her sobbing through the walls at night in grief, thinking you were dying. I have prayed with her for your health and for your soul. Whatever you think of her, she loves you. It was very unkind to make her think you were ailing when you might have simply told the truth."

"And who are you?" the woman sniffed. "Someone from that wicked place she's working at?"

"I'm a friend of Alice's. And I think she deserves better than such trickery."

"Trickery! An 'andsome 'usband and an organ—most girls'd love such trickery as that I reckon."

"We only meant it as a surprise, not a trick," the suitor, William, said, aggrieved. "I hoped to do something nice for her. Her pa asked me to look after his girls when he passed on, and it took me longer than I hoped to get myself settled."

A great boom of thunder struck, and a violent thread of lightning cracked in the sky.

"Will, the organ!" Mrs. Hull cried. "Never mind about Ally. You must move the cart into the barn before it's ruined."

Henry looked at her unable to believe that an instrument could be of greater concern than the feelings of her daughter.

"But Alice ... ," William protested weakly. Henry swallowed down a surge of irrational, unattractive jealousy at this man uttering her name.

Mrs. Hull waved her hand. "She's probably gone up to the graveyard to complain to her father's ghost or some such nonsense. You know how she indulges in dramatics."

"I'll go after her," Henry said.

He ran toward her up the muddy hillside. By the time he managed to clamber to the top, he was soaked and filthy and panting.

Alice knelt before a headstone. She pressed her forehead to it, as though the slab of granite might embrace her back.

The sight of her broke his heart.

"Alice," he said quietly.

She did not look up nor cease her sobbing.

He'd wondered at her composure this last week, her ability to remain calm despite their trials on the road and the obvious weight of her sadness. She'd been so good at keeping it at bay he'd nearly forgotten about it at times.

But here, cradling a rock, her shoulders quaking, rain plastering her hair onto her neck—here was the truth of what she'd carried, silently and strong.

"Alice," he repeated, aching for her.

She must be aware of him, yet she was fixed in her posture of bereavement, lost to her grief. Harsh, guttural sobs heaved out of her, like they were being pulled from her against her will.

Feeling helpless, he knelt beside her. "Alice, love, come here," he breathed.

He put his hands on either of her shoulders and she froze under his touch. Slowly, she turned around to look at him. And then she flung herself at him and resumed her sobbing, this time burying her head on his shoulder.

He wrapped his arms around her and held her as she wept.

He'd always disliked his stature. He'd always felt too big. But in this moment, he was grateful for his size. He was big enough to hold her grief.

Over Alice's trembling shoulders, he read the words etched onto the headstone.

Joseph Louis Hull

Beloved father and husband. Maker of music.

"Oh, Alice," he murmured, stroking the back of her hair, the way his mother used to do for him when he had nightmares. He no longer cared if she knew his faults and his embarrassments, or that she'd been untruthful. He only wanted to ease her pain.

"Henry, I was going to come here and give up *everything.* I've been mourning for myself, and for them, and for her, all bloody week. And then, oh God, I thought she was *dead.*"

He wrapped his arms around her tighter. "You're a good girl, Alice. So good."

She laughed through her tears. "You don't think that of me, Henry. I know you don't. You think I'm wicked."

No. He didn't.

He had seen enough of her character to know that whatever flaws she might possess, they existed with a fundamental decency and bravery that was unmistakable.

"That's not true. I've been with you for almost a week, day and night, and have seen very little except you trying to do the right thing. Advocating for reform. Defending me from my own family. Fretting over horses. Over mice." He held her tighter, running his thumbs down her back to massage some warmth into her.

"You're just being nice because I'm crying," she warbled.

"Oh, Alice, love," he murmured. "No, I'm not. I just wonder. For all you look after others, who's looking after you?"

She sobbed harder, clutching at his coat. He rubbed circles on her back and said a silent prayer to God.

Show me how to give her solace. Help me ease her anguish.

A bolt of lightning cracked once more, and the church lit up, its spires glittering in the light.

Yes. Of course.

He tilted up Alice's chin and gently rubbed the tears from her face with his thumbs, which were larger than her nose.

"Come inside the church with me, out of this rain."

Shakily, she nodded. He wrapped an arm around her and dashed with her through the freezing rain to the deserted church. It was empty. Their footsteps echoed to the buttresses a hundred feet above their heads.

The vast, cold expanse of the empty stone room was awesome, but not comforting. He guided Alice beyond the nave to the apse, where, as he'd suspected, there were candles to light for the ailing.

"Alice, will you help me light a candle? For a blessing?"

She didn't speak, just twisted her fingers together until her wrists wrenched.

He took two candles anyway and lit them off one that was already burning, then set them in brass sticks.

He took her hands in his and closed his eyes. "Dear Lord," he said. "Please bless this dear, good woman who works so hard to see to the happiness and wellbeing of others. And who needs a bit of care herself."

He paused, and looked up, because if Alice did not wish for him to continue praying he would stop. But she was quiet, and her eyes were closed, and her hands had ceased their wringing, so he went on.

"And Lord, bless her family. May they see the good in her. May they love her the way you do, without condition."

Alice began to cry again, but she continued to hold the posture of prayer, listening. "Lord, thank you for putting me in her path, for I am better for knowing her."

She held herself still, and he squeezed her hands as tight as he could without hurting her. "Lord, please let Alice know that she is safe in your everlasting grace and love, and can be comforted and redeemed in it. Let her know that your light shines on her as it does all your children, and that if she wishes for it she need only—"

He could not continue, because Alice suddenly yanked her hand away and placed her fingers over his mouth.

"Stop, Henry," she said in a ravaged voice. "Don't say it. Don't say it."

He gripped her hand and kissed it. "But it's true. There is nothing more steadfast than God's love for you."

"God's love is not what I need," she said in desperate voice.

"What do you need?" He asked her. "Anything."

And then he knew.

Music.

Music was her comfort. Music was her prayer.

He took her hand. "Where's the organ? Will you play me something?"

She looked at him, fear on her face. "But, I'm not allowed. The vicar forbade it."

He shrugged. "No one's here but us. And God. And I cannot fathom the Lord would not welcome it."

She gripped his hand and walked with him back through the church to a staircase. He followed her up and past a landing to a balcony, where the mighty pipes of a handsome instrument ran up the back walls of the church.

"My father played it," she whispered. "I never have."

Tentatively, she sat down on the bench and put her hands on the keys. She played a single note, as if waiting to see if she would be struck down by God. It vibrated in the empty cathedral, long and plangent.

"Play," he whispered.

She adjusted a knob, then returned her hands to the manual and spread her fingers. And then the church began to moan. To cry. To vent pure sadness from its metal lungs.

The notes she played were not a hymn, nor any song that he could recognize. The melody was mournful, haunting—and then, delicate. It sounded like grief rising towards hope. It sounded like prayer.

It was the most beautiful thing he'd ever heard.

Her hands stopped. Neither of them breathed. She looked up at him, her dove's eyes shining.

A tear fell to his cheek, and he didn't bother to wipe it away. He leaned down and brushed his lips against hers.

She was still. Absolutely still.

And then her lips moved beneath his, so light and fluttery it made his stomach drop.

"Alice," he said raggedly, melting onto the bench beside her, pulling her toward him. He pressed his forehead to hers, desperately unsure of what to do. He was all tension, every ligament in his body alive and pulled in two directions—to move away, to hold her closer. To run, to stay.

(To kiss her again.)

To kiss her again.

He pressed his lips closer to hers and pulled her close against his body.

A noise came out of her, like a gasp for air after she'd been under water. She kissed him differently this time, less carefully, like she needed him for sustenance.

Oh, how good that felt. How good to be needed in such a way.

And then she stopped, like she'd been pulled back by someone's hand. Her eyes were fierce. "Tell me if I imagine it," she said. "You must *tell* me if I imagine it."

Her voice was anguished, and all he could do was answer truthfully. "I want you," he whispered. "You."

Her lips were back on his then, and her face was wet, either with rain or tears, and he pulled her onto his lap and let her know, with every muscle that he had, that he wanted this embrace. *He wanted it.*

His body felt like it would overflow from recognition. *This, this. Yes, this.*

He collapsed upon the organ bench and she clambered up onto

his lap, her body pressing into his, his into hers. It was so much, so new, that he scarcely knew where she ended and he began, only that neither of them could seem to get enough of the other's breath or heat, that he felt like he was plunging, tumbling deep into the earth. And then she was rocking, moving her hips in a way that made the hollow between her thighs press back and forth against his cock, and they were clothed but he somehow felt her heat, that it matched his own, that every pang that rocked through him answered in her—

"Who's there?" a masculine voice bellowed from the church below them.

They froze. Footsteps boomed across the floor.

Henry met Alice's eye, about to speak, but she shook her head.

Slowly, she slid off his body, arranged her dress, and leaned over the railing of the balcony.

"You know who it is, Vicar," she called, her voice ringing out and echoing through the church. "It's Alice Hull."

CHAPTER 26

He was waiting for her at the bottom of the stairs, his expression sour.

She curtsied low, ironically. "Vicar Helmsley. How very unexpected to see you here at your own church."

"Miss Hull," he sneered, looking at her muddy gown, her dripping hair, her swollen lips. "I heard the organ playing. Not you, I hope. I thought I made it clear that you are not to play in this church."

"You did, sir. At my own father's funeral."

She would not apologize for playing now. It had reminded her of something sacred she had lost. Something this man, this *vicar*, had stolen from her.

She might never have known what that loss had cost her if it were not for Henry.

It was the deepest, realest, purest part of her, this music. More her birthright than a pipe organ fit with her father's ivories. She didn't need her father's instrument to remember him; he lived every time she played.

At the sound of Henry's footsteps coming down the stairs, the vicar gave her a knowing look. "Ah, Miss Hull has company. I should have suspected. Who is he this time?"

His face changed as Henry reached the landing, derision melting into outright shock. "I know you," he said in a strangled voice. "You're—"

"Lord Lieutenant Henry Evesham," Alice supplied.

"—Charles Evesham's boy," the vicar finished

"Indeed, sir," Henry said. He put his hand on Alice's shoulder, as if his touch could protect her from the scorn in the vicar's voice. "Reverend Helmsley is a friend of my father," he explained.

"Who would no doubt be appalled at your being here with a girl of Miss Hull's character. And who evidently insists on disrespecting our rules."

"Miss Hull came here to pray, and played at my request. We meant no disrespect. And I would ask you not to speak of her that way."

"Anyone who knows how Miss Hull comported herself as a girl would find the description more charitable than she deserves. Unsurprising, I must say, to find her in the company of a man who spends his time with whores."

"What exactly are you implying, sir?" Henry asked sharply.

"He's implying he once caught me with his son's hand between my legs in the vestry," Alice said serenely. "How is dear Richard? I remember him most fondly."

She winked as the vicar sputtered.

"Leave here," he finally got out.

"Gladly. But if you have any decency, sir, you'll pay my mother a visit and invite her to return to worship here. She is a woman of great faith, no thanks to you. Good day."

She took Henry's hand and sailed out of the church without sparing the vicar another look.

"Pleasant fellow," Henry muttered.

"I hope he doesn't cause trouble with your father."

"Yes," Henry drawled. "Not *now*, when things are going so well between us."

She burst out laughing. It felt wonderful to laugh, after the awfulness of every aspect of this rotten day. "Oh, Henry. We are cursed, I think."

Henry snorted, which made her laugh harder still. Her mirth became contagious, and soon they were both helplessly chortling in the churchyard.

Henry offered her his arm. "Let's leave before the good vicar comes to accuse of us of further heresies."

She took it, and together they trudged back down the hill. It was harder climbing down than going up. They had to shuffle to keep from tumbling face first down the steep incline, and every step left them splattered with droplets of wet muck.

"Bother!" Henry said, stumbling over a patch of mud. He went veering wildly, his heel skating over the slippery slope. She reached out and caught him by his sleeve to steady him, but succeeded only in sending him toppling downhill on his arse.

"No!" she cried, leaping to catch him.

But of course, she did not catch him. She slipped onto her own backside and went sliding in his trail.

They landed in a muddy heap outside her mother's henhouse.

A curious rooster flapped over to her, and pecked her hair exploratorily.

"Scabby, putrid bollocks," Alice cursed, wiping mud and feathers off her face with her sleeve.

Henry groaned. "Are you all right?" he asked, without bothering to rise from the puddle he was splayed in. She looked at him, and down at herself, and over at the chickens, and collapsed into laughter again.

"Oh, Henry Evesham," she sighed. "What a pair we make."

"I think," he said, wiping ineffectively at his hair, "that I have chicken shit in my—"

"Don't say it," she giggled. "I shall cry."

He shook his head, grinning despite everything. "I must say, Alice, I will remember this week all my life."

She smiled at him fondly. "What will I do without you?"

"Oh, you are not rid of me yet," he said decisively. He stood up and offered her a filthy hand to help her to her feet. "You are going to come with me, and I am going to get you very far away from here."

She raised her brow at him, such affection blossoming in her bosom that she felt warm despite the raindrops falling in her eyes. "Is that wise, Reverend? To undertake another of our fateful trips?"

"I have abandoned myself to the providence of the Lord. And I'm *not* leaving you here."

She sensed that Henry had reached the limits of his own patience with the world. She rather liked this devil-may-care side of him.

"There's a coaching inn at Ennesbough where the mail coach stops," she said. "If you take me there, I'll can return to London on my own in the morning."

Her sister Eliza walked out of the house holding a milking pail, saw them, and came running.

"Ally, you're filthy! Where have you been?"

"Church," she said merrily.

Confusion and concern flashed in her little sister's eyes, chastening Alice's good humor.

"I lit a candle for Papa," she explained, trying to ease the worry from her sister's face.

But her sister winced. "Vicar Helmsley is in town this week. I hope you didn't—"

"I did. He's as awful as I remember."

Eliza just sighed. "Come in and wash up. Mr. Evesham too. I've been heating water on the stove."

Alice shook her head. "I don't wish to see Mama."

"She's not here," her sister said in a tone of perfect misery. "She went to the public house with William. Said you'd driven her to drink."

Alice turned to Henry. "Shall we wash up before we go on?"

"Go on?" Eliza cried. "You're not leaving. You just arrived."

She looked at her sister sadly. "If I stay, Mama will hector me until I lose my temper. I will return some other time, under happier circumstances."

Her sister's lip trembled. "Ally, I'm sorry I lied to you. I felt awful about it but Mama was convinced you'd be so thrilled by the surprise it wouldn't matter. I should have known better."

Alice put her arm around her sister's shoulders. "I'm sorry too, Liza, Come, let's get water for Mr. Evesham."

Liza sent Sally out to carry a warm pot of water and a cloth to the barn so Henry could clean up as best he could. She warmed more water for Alice over the fire, and gave her a gown to wear in place of Alice's filthy one. Alice let her sister brush out and pin up her hair.

"Thank you for looking after me," she said, kissing Liza's cheek. "You were always the best of us. I'm sure you've had your work cut out for you, looking after Mama and Sally."

Liza squeezed her tight. "I've missed you. I was so worried when you didn't come. Was there really snow?"

"Yes. Oh, Liza, I promise, I was on my way the very hour I got your letter. I will always come if you need me. Always. No matter what."

Liza stepped back, her face rigid with concern. "Ally, are you *certain* you won't marry William? I know you're angry at Mama for the trick, but I'm worried for you."

She kissed her sister's cheek. "Please don't worry. I will write to you when I return to London. We'll always take care of each other. I promise."

Her sister did not look reassured.

She knew what Eliza was thinking: that life for an unwed girl alone was perilous. That bad things happened to girls like that. Their mother had raised them to believe that marriage was the only means to guard their futures, never imagining that there might be another path for them.

If someone was to imagine such a thing, it would have to be Alice.

CHAPTER 27

As soon as they were on the road Alice closed her eyes and began humming a sad song.

He didn't know this one. He didn't try to harmonize. Her head drooped as they drove on, until it rested on his shoulder. Soon enough, she was asleep.

He tried very hard not to feel bereft that he would likely never experience the comforting weight of her touching him again.

He felt more like a shipwreck than a man—like shards of splintered wood casting about a roiling sea.

He tried to formulate a prayer to steady himself, but nothing came, and it was terrifying, for he could not recall the last time he had lacked words to offer God.

Once, during a revival in Yorkshire, he'd helped a farmer tie a rope between his cottage and the barn before a snowstorm. When the blizzard came, the farmer explained, he would follow the rope to feed his animals, even if he could not see a foot in front of him.

Henry had often used the story as a metaphor. Whenever you are plagued with uncertainty, he had preached so many times, you can find your way back to God through prayer. Prayer was the rope.

But on this awful day, he felt like he had dropped the rope in the middle of the storm, and lost it. He was casting about blindly, fumbling in a haze for something he knew must be close at hand, but that he couldn't grasp.

All he had were questions. Most pressingly, what had made him kiss Alice in the church? And what was she to him? And if the answer was nothing—*must* be nothing—why had he abandoned his principles, his faith, his decency, pawing her in a consecrated place with no thought other than the way she made him feel?

And why, when he was guilty of this, when he had failed himself so deeply, was it not shame that lingered queasy and churning in his gut, but this voracious, restless, hunger, chanting *more, more, more*?

(He was not being disingenuous. He truly didn't know. It terrified him, because he really, truly, didn't know.)

He steered the horses into the inn's stable yard. The sudden loss of motion roused Alice. "Oh, pardon me," she said, moving away from him.

Don't ever ask pardon for that, he wanted to object. His shoulder felt lonely without her head on it. He had to restrain himself from pulling her back into the crook of his arm, and pleading. *Just a little longer.*

Instead, he shifted, so as not to crowd her. "I didn't want to wake you. You looked so peaceful asleep."

She yawned. "It's been an exhausting day."

"An exhausting week."

Alice nodded, glancing up at the sky, which was low and dark and wet. "You won't drive on in this, will you? I don't want you getting stranded again."

(He had not planned to stay, but now that she had raised the possibility, it was decided.)

He shook his head. "No. I'll stay at the inn and return to my father's in the morning."

(One more night with her. One more.)

She smiled at him. "Good. I hate eating alone."

Inside, there was a crowd of people milling at the innkeeper's desk. The innkeeper looked harried, handing out keys to a large travel party who, Henry gathered, were on their way to a horse race.

"My sister and I would like two rooms for the night, please," he said, when it was finally his turn.

"No vacancies," the man said, too exhausted to even seem apologetic.

At Henry's stricken face he reconsidered. "Well, there's a small room off the attic. It's for servants but has a bed big enough for one, if t'other of you don't mind the floor."

Henry stared at him in disbelief. Why was it that whenever he set out with Alice, everything went wrong?

Looking at Henry's face, Alice burst into laughter.

The innkeeper squinted at her. "Is something wrong, miss?"

She put a hand over her mouth, and shook her head, her eyes sparkling with mirth.

"My apologies, sir," Henry said to the offended man. "It's only we've encountered a great deal of inconvenience on this journey, and my sister is amused by our poor fortune. We'll make do with whatever room you have. Thank you."

He took the key that was offered and shepherded Alice toward the stairs.

"I'm sorry," she said, still chuckling. "It's just … Oh, Henry. Your face. What a misfortunate pair we are."

He imagined his face looked even more chagrined when he

opened the door to their room to find it was no larger than a pantry.

If he was to sleep on the floor, he was not sure where. Perhaps half under the cot, half in the drawers of the cupboard.

"You stay here and take the room for yourself," he said immediately. "I'll go on and find other lodgings."

"Nonsense," she said. "You may not find anywhere for miles, and it's already dark. You can have the bed and I'll take the floor."

"Of course not. I can't have you sleeping on the floor."

She looked at him up and down. "Well *you* will never fit," she laughed.

He felt his cheeks flame. In this tiny room, he could physically feel the imposition of his ungainly stature. He felt enormous, hulking.

Alice winced. "Oh, no—I only meant that with your height there's scarcely any room for you. Not that I don't like your size."

He felt even worse at her cognizance of his discomfort.

"Henry," she said with a frank stare that made him uncomfortable in an entirely different way. "Can you really have any doubt that I find you attractive? I think you're perhaps the most appealing man I've ever had the misfortune of being stranded with. It's narrow in this room. That's all I meant."

Her concern for his feelings touched him. As did her avowal that she liked the way he looked.

But that did nothing to solve the predicament about the bed.

He heard Alice's stomach make a noise of hunger.

"Let's have supper," he said, relieved at the reprieve. "I'll leave you to freshen up. Meet me in the dining room."

He went downstairs and paced, unsure of how this had happened once again. It was like God was pushing them together. But why, when their proximity only ever seemed to lead to sin? Could he survive another night in such close quarters? Would he embarrass himself again, with the memory of her kiss so fresh on his body?

"There you are," Alice called.

She smiled at him, and he felt like he was breaking open. An involuntary grin gashed across his face, as quick as a heartbeat. He saw her notice and look at him more closely.

He lifted up a hand in greeting and pretended like he did not have to brace his knees to keep them from buckling at the sight of her.

Evidently he was not effective, for her brow knit in concern as soon as she came near enough to see his face.

"Are you all right, Henry? You look ill."

Did she really not know the effect she had on him? Could she not see that he felt like he'd been cut open? That he needed her to sew his heart back up? That even if she did it wouldn't work, because he was different now, in a way he could not understand, but only feel?

"Just hungry. Shall we sit down to eat?"

They found a quiet table near the fireplace, and a waitress brought them bread and took down their orders for supper.

As soon as she was gone, Alice frowned at him. "You seem perturbed."

He sighed. "You are kind to worry after me given the trouble with your family. I hope you aren't too terribly upset."

"Will it sound too odd if I admit I count myself relieved?"

"Of course you are," he murmured, feeling foolish. "Whatever your mother may be guilty of, 'tis certainly preferable to losing her. I apologize."

"Yes, but that isn't what I meant. I was going to do it, you see. I think I really was."

"Do what?"

"Marry William."

Henry's shirt felt too tight at the thought of Alice marrying William, or anyone at all. (Except for … Henry.)

(Which, of course, was absurd, as that could never be.)

(Unless … But no, *no,* what was he thinking?)

But William! *William.* Alice Hull—who played music like she played for God himself, who frightened men double her in size, who kissed him like she wanted to sear herself inside his body—deserved better than the likes of *William,* who considered her *a shop window* and an *inherited one* at that.

"You care for him?" he forced himself to ask.

He went weak with relief when she sputtered out a mouthful of ale at the very notion of it.

"No. William's a kind man, but I have more of a spark with Vicar Helmsley, if I'm honest. I considered it because we would not have been able to keep the house without my mother's widow's income, and I can't very well bring Liza and Sally to Charlotte Street. I've been so sad thinking about the life I would have, married to him. So in a way, I am glad this happened. Because now my family know everything, and I'm free to do whatever I like."

She slathered a piece of bread with butter and bit into it.

"And what will you do?" he asked.

"I'll go back to Elena's and finish my training."

"Training?"

She nodded, chewing. "She wants me to specialize in discipline, but I don't know. I might prefer the chapel." She smiled wolfishly.

"The chapel?" he asked.

"Yes, the chapel. You recall—the one you ran away from?"

She clearly thought he was now ready to laugh at this, but he was not. He did not know what he wanted. To know more. To steal her ale and drink it down in a single gulp. To go outside and drive into the blinding rain, and away from this terrible feeling of wanting and loathing himself for wanting.

He coughed. "What is it that you would do in this ... chapel?"

"It's a bit like you wrote in your journal. Some members are excited by stern nuns, or lusty vicars. Others like the atmosphere itself. The sin of it."

He felt like his cravat was actually trying to choke him. He knew she had read about his fantasies. He had not known she was training to *fulfill them herself.*

"Alice, I should not have asked. We mustn't speak of this in public."

She gave him a very feminine smile. "Very well, Henry," she said primly. "Perhaps when I've done my training you can pay me a visit and we can speak of it in private."

Now his breeches were choking him. He nearly fell on the serving girl in gratitude when she arrived with their plates, if only because it meant Alice would eat instead of tormenting him.

She did, heartily, in that way he'd become so fond of—fawning over each thing on her plate. As he picked meagerly at his own roast turnips and stewed beets, she looked meaningfully into his eyes.

"Don't you ever get hungry, Henry?"

He frowned, surprised by the question, since she knew his diet.

"Vegetables and grains are very filling and nutritious, and I supplement them with milk and eggs."

"But don't you ever get *hungry*?" she repeated. "For more than you allow yourself?"

He put down his fork delicately, then looked up at her. "Alice, I'm always hungry for more than I allow myself."

She flushed.

He realized she thought he was referencing what happened in the church.

(He was.)

She stared at him, as if coming to some resolve. "Then just for tonight, we must order you something delicious."

She flagged the serving girl and asked for something sweet. He protested, but when an apple tart studded with currants and dusted with cinnamon arrived, she added extra cream and dug a fork into the center, taking the best part.

He liked the girlish way she licked cream off her fork, closing her eyes in delectation.

She caught him smiling. "I thought you disapproved of rich foods."

"I do. For myself. But you deserve them."

"And why is it that I deserve them but you do not?"

"Because I am a sensualist by nature, which goes against my principles. Even a small bit of indulgence and I find myself unchecked and sinning profligately. And so I must impose great discipline to live up to my ideals."

This time, he was *certain* he was talking about what happened in the church.

Her face made clear that she knew it too.

"Alice, I'm so sorry."

She stared at him, a tiny sliver of her tongue resting on a tine of her fork.

"Forgive me, for how I acted," he continued babbling. "I wanted you, and it was rash, and I hope I didn't—"

She looked into his eyes. "The only thing that I regret, Henry, is that we had to stop."

She speared the fork into the dessert again and prepared a perfect bite, with fragrant tender apples, succulent currants, swirls of caramel sauce, and a dollop of cream so sweet he could smell its freshness across the table. She held it out to him.

"Take a bite," she ordered.

"Alice..."

"I promise I won't let you have more than you can bear."

Something came over him, and instead of taking the utensil, he leaned in, opened his mouth, and ate from her outstretched fork.

He closed his eyes in ecstasy.

It had been so long since he'd consumed food of this richness—sugar and spice, warmth and fat, a hint of salt—all the things that made life delicious.

When he opened his eyes, she was staring at him, looking as hungry as he felt.

"Apple tart was always my favorite," he confessed.

"Have a little more," she whispered.

He wanted her to feed him, but he noticed an odd look from the innkeeper across the room and came to his senses. Instead, he took the fork from her, and fed himself just one more bite.

It was decadent, satisfying. It made him happy.

She smiled at him, pulled the dessert back across the table, and ate the last two bites.

"See," she said. "You're not in hell. Just a man who ate a bit of tart."

He suspected they were no longer talking about tarts. "Are you evangelizing, Alice?"

"I just think you would do well, Henry, to accept that you cannot be sustained by prayer and deprivation. Everyone needs pleasure and joy. I know you get great fulfillment from your faith, but I wish you would not be so strict with yourself about all the lovely parts to life. Did God not create our bodies and our hearts for us to use them?"

"I wish it were that simple."

She looked at him so sadly that he had to look away.

"I'm sure nothing is simple," she said softly, "but I do believe you can be a good man without denying yourself everything. You *are* one, in fact."

"Stop," he whispered.

"Oh, Henry, I'm only saying—"

"Stop," he repeated, louder.

He could not stand to listen to this because his self-denial was a part of who he was.

And until now, he could live with it.

There was only one thing he would regret denying himself, and she was sitting across the table. And he could not look at her any longer without saying something maudlin.

(Or worse: permanent.)

He rose abruptly to remove the temptation, and his knees hit the top of the table painfully. He hissed, and watched a pitcher of cream overturn. A rivulet dripped onto the floor, a waste of sweetness.

Alice stared up at him like she knew exactly why he was leaving, and like she had expected him to do just that, and like it caused her pain.

"I'm sorry," he said. "I'm going out for air. I'll collect a blanket from the innkeeper when I come back and try not to wake you. I might be late."

CHAPTER 28

He cared for her.

She knew it from the way he ate that tart. From the way he had looked up at her, quick and unguarded, and said *I'm always hungry for more than I allow myself.*

She cared for him too.

She'd known it when he'd touched her in the church, so full of desire, and yet more gently than any man ever had before. She'd known it when his face had broken open when she'd told him he was good.

They cared for one another, and they wanted one another, and it would not change a thing.

He would never act upon it. She was just another sinful thing that he'd deny himself.

And it was a shame, for were it not for the central difference that stood unshakably between their ways of thinking, she could do far more than care for a man like Henry Evesham. She could love a man like that. A man who was so much more generous when it came to her than he was to himself. A man who tried so hard to be disciplined, despite wanting so badly the things he had forbidden himself.

But it didn't matter whether she cared for, or loved, or wanted him because that single central difference between the way they saw the world may as well have been a continent. A mountain range. An ocean.

She had once asked Henry not to preach to her, and she would extend him the same courtesy. She would not try to convince him that his way of life—his deepest beliefs—were wrong.

She would not ask him to give them up for her.

The kindest thing, to him and to her, was not to give him any further hint of how she felt. To not let him see how he'd somehow nestled in her heart. To not tell him how deeply she desired him. For she was at a juncture in her life where she could not afford to be a sentimental creature. She must be a practical one. She must not focus on the heartache, but the lesson:

Henry Evesham was an educated man, from a wealthy family, with a great deal of responsibility and power. He *could* choose to have more than he would claim.

Having spent her life unable to claim anything by a simple act of will, to have such opportunity and not use it seemed a tragic waste.

She *would not* make the same choice.

Watching him eat a single bite of tart like a starving man—watching him look at her with hungry eyes as she offered him herself, and choose to run away instead of take it—she knew she must save herself from the same fate.

She would leave no uneaten scraps of tart upon the table.

She would return to London and take whatever risks she needed to build a life she would look back upon without regret.

She would not ask Henry Evesham to choose her. She would choose herself.

The freedom of this choice made her feel so weightless that she closed her eyes and laughed aloud in the silent, tiny room. She spun around and collapsed onto the bed, languid and light, imagining all the wonderful things that were ahead of her. She could work on Charlotte Street, write music, read books, take lovers.

Perhaps she would find someone who treated her as Henry did —or at least looked at her like Henry did—except, of course, without his air of being tortured by wanting what he saw. Someone who possessed his gentleness and his desire for her, but who would come to her without guilt or regret.

She ran her hands over her breasts and down her belly imagining they were that man's hands.

Her body, which had been nothing so much as a repository for her sorrow and worry this past week, suddenly felt alive in all its particles.

She undressed to her chemise and luxuriated in the feeling of her own touch.

Oh, she needed this.

Henry Evesham's body against hers had made her a festival of needs.

She closed her eyes and remembered the smell of the church. Beeswax polish on old wooden pews, the faint memory of smoke in the air from the candles he'd lit.

Henry, trembling and unsure and straining towards her.

His skin still cold and damp from the rain.

His body strong and sturdy, like he was made of oak.

She imagined Henry making love to her with unchecked abandon and it made her shiver. She hiked up her skirt and ran her fingers across her hips, then lower, toward her cunt, slick against her fingertips.

Oh, Henry. Henry.

She remembered the desperate sound that had emerged from his throat when he'd finally kissed her. The bulge of his cock, and how it had felt as she'd rubbed herself against it.

She wanted that feeling again.

She glanced around the room, looking for something that might feel the way he had felt before they'd been interrupted. There were four short, knobbed posts at each corner of the bed frame. Yes, that could do. She raised herself above one, so that the curved wood hit her right at the parting of her cunny. She held herself open and steadied herself against it, bracing her hand against the wall for balance.

Oh, yes. That was it.

She closed her eyes and rocked, wishing it was him beneath her. Them, together in this small dark room, frantic once again with their desire for each other.

She gave herself over to the fantasy, adding to the friction with her fingers. She wanted to moan with the pleasure, but she did not want to alert any passersby in the hallway to her activities within. The need to be silent made her arousal sharper and she gasped as the promise of an orgasm welled up inside her. She threw back her head and put her hand over her cunt, imagining Henry's lips curving around a fork, desperate to go over the edge.

The first tremor took her and she gasped and bucked against the bedpost. As pleasure claimed her she couldn't help but cry out into the darkness. She clasped her hand over her mouth and opened her eyes and the dimness in the room was broken by a flash of light from the hallway.

"Alice? Are you awake—"

She froze.

Henry Evesham stared at her, agape.

"What are you—" Henry asked in a strangled whisper. But it

was rather obvious, as she was mounted on the bedpost with her hand clutched to her cunt.

"Oh God," she cried, frantically rearranging herself and her limbs and her shift. In her haste to cover up her lower half she pulled her shift askew, exposing most of her breasts.

Henry stood silent and still in the shaft of light from the corridor, half inside the room, half out, looking as if he'd had a stroke.

In desperation she grabbed his arm and pulled him inside and shut the door behind him.

Which left her topless, holding him by his cravat in a tiny room that smelled of her desire.

"I thought you would be longer," she said, turning around and fumbling to cover up, trying to still her ragged breath. "I thought you would be longer. You usually walk for miles. You said you would be late."

"I came back for my satchel—I ... no. No."

Something in his voice made her pause. She stopped fumbling and turned back around to look at him.

"That's not why I came back," he said more quietly.

Slowly he reached out to her shoulder. Gently, ever so gently, he drew up the sleeve of her shift to cover up her breasts.

In her state, the feeling of the soft lawn falling against her nipples made her gasp. He noticed. She saw his eyes fall from her face down to her chest, to the peaks of her hard nipples beneath the sheer fabric. His lips parted.

"Why did you come back?" she asked him.

His gaze rested on her collarbone.

With his hand still lingering on her shoulder, he drew nearer, and placed a kiss in the shallow of her neck.

She stood completely still, unsure of what was happening.

He finally looked into her eyes. "I came, Alice, because I needed to say this plainly, or I am false."

Heat radiated from his skin, and he was trembling.

"I want you to be mine," he whispered. "So much I'm sick with it."

CHAPTER 29

He'd said it. Out loud.

It made him so weak with happiness that he took Alice in his arms and crushed her mouth to his and kissed her like she was all the things he'd ever given up.

"Henry," she gasped out, pushing her palm against his sternum. "Henry, wait."

He stopped, but he didn't want to wait. He was starved for softness and pleasure and abandonment and all the things that were here in this small, dark room.

But mostly he was starved for Alice.

"What is it?" he gasped, wanting to consume her. Wanting to sink his teeth into her flesh, his nose into her hair, his cock into her—

"Henry, you must be certain," she whispered, even as she lifted up his shirt and caressed his bare skin.

"Oh," he whispered, at the lightness of her touch. "*Oh.*"

She melted against him like a pat of butter on hot toast. He kissed her at her beating pulse. Her fingertips dug into his hair, his scalp.

"*Certain,*" she gasped out, sentences as lost to her as words were lost to him.

But he had to find them, he had to say this, because the answer was yes, he was certain, so certain, no parenthetical.

"Alice, I'm sure. Be mine. Be mine."

She lifted her shift over her head and dropped it to the floor and stood completely nude before him. Her breasts were like pale teacups capped with small, pretty nipples the color of a berry.

He leaned in and took one in his mouth, marveling at its firmness, at its heat. He was shocked at himself, but she did not seem to be. She sank back on the bed and pulled him down on top of her and he put his hands upon her breasts and found her mouth and kissed her like a starving brute.

Her hand clamped over his straining breeches and fumbled with buttons and then they were on his manhood and he hissed, for no hands save his own had ever touched that part of him.

"What shall I do, Alice?" he somehow managed to get out.

She took his hands and drew them to the dark whorl of hair where her thighs met. Her womanhood.

"Touch me," she said, closing her eyes.

Tentatively he ventured a finger to the cleft. He felt wetness. Delicate, soft skin. Impossibly slick, molten heat. He coated his fingers in it, in awe of how, like him, she dripped with need.

He had a vague sense of how a woman found pleasure, owing to his time in brothels, but he was unsure of the precise mechanics of it. Anytime the conversation had become too specific, he'd always left the room to pray. Now he wished he had listened to their vulgar chatter, for he might have had some hope of pleasing her.

But she seemed to know enough for both of them. She took his hand and placed it where she wanted it. "Stroke me there," she murmured, widening her thighs apart.

It felt sacramental, to touch her in this hidden place. He let her guide his fingers, showing him how to touch her. She trembled in his arms.

His touch had made her tremble.

He felt like he was falling, sinking, dying. He wanted to bathe in her. To put his mouth to her cunt and drink her.

She reached up for his lips and kissed him. She still tasted like the apple tart. He spread his fingers through her warmth and swirled her desire all across her flesh, hoping to make her tremble again. "Is this right?" he whispered. "How does it feel?"

"It feels like you, Henry," she whispered.

"Is that good?"

"Yes. Oh, yes, I love your hands." Her voice was soft and breathy. She was rubbing her womanhood against his palm, rocking her hips, mewling a bit at each new brush of herself against his fingers, and it was making him so hard he thought he might die from lust.

She put one hand over his, guiding him again. "Inside me," she whispered. His fingers met a silky, narrow passage and suddenly he understood what it might feel like to be joined with her. Why men might risk disease and ignominy and hell to sink themselves into such hot, sweet lovely places. Why they might be mad enough to do it on the street.

He knew about burning. But this was different. This was immolation.

"You feel like heaven itself," he whispered. Her lips fell on his neck and her gasps quickened, and then she was sucking on him, biting him, thrusting her hips in frantic time as his fingers slid against her, in and out, and his thumb caressed the swollen flesh that made her cry out when he touched it. She was almost dancing, undulating against his body, using him for pleasure.

"Use me," he whispered. "Oh, yes, please, use me."

She threw back her head and made a sound that was half his name, half rapture. Her flesh pulsed with pleasure beneath his hand, and his groin throbbed in time with it.

She sank back, collapsing onto him as though he was a fainting couch. "Oh, your body feels so good, after all this time of wanting it."

"You've wanted this?" he asked, tracing his fingers over her soft skin, marveling in the delicacy of another person's body. He felt it must be some other, better man experiencing the beauty of her breasts in the moonlight, the impossible sweetness of her navel, the harrowing vulnerability of the little mole over her ribcage—for he did not deserve this.

She was perfect. He had never seen such a lovely sight in all his life.

She snuggled back against him, letting him hold her, explore her, kiss her. Before, she'd been taut as a spring, but now she was limpid and sultry.

"Will you undress for me?" she whispered. "I want to feel your skin."

He pulled off his shirt and breeches and dropped them on the floor. No woman had ever looked on his nude form, and he was certain she would not like it—all that bulk from his exercise regime, the red hair along his chest that went fiery around his manhood, the rude way his cock jutted toward the ceiling, a long thread of his excited moisture dripping. It was an insult to her that this was all he had to give, when she was such a delicacy.

And yet, she smiled as her eyes raked up and down his body. She looked at him like she had the apple tart. It made him emotional, that anyone—that *she*—would look at him like that.

It felt like being loved.

She reached out, beckoning him closer. "You are a treasure. Get in this bed so I can feel you."

He slid beneath the sheets and she took him in her arms and his cock began to pulse in that ungentlemanly way he had so dreaded in the mill. But now, he was not embarrassed. He wanted her to feel it. He wanted to drag it against her. He wanted her to feel the magnitude of his desire for her.

She gripped the head of his cock in her small fist. "Henry," she uttered breathily, running her hand up and down its length.

He groaned. He loved the way it felt but he still flinched at her knowing the dimensions of it, which had earned him mockery in his school days.

"I'm sorry, I know it's coarse."

"Coarse?" She laughed softly. "My dear, on Charlotte Street you could command a pretty penny for such coarse stature."

She continued running her hands over it, in a way that made him almost want to cry.

"You don't mind?," he asked, sucking in his breath as she increased the pressure of her wanderings.

"I am grateful to the Lord who made you," she whispered, gripping him more firmly, and he felt his eyes might fall from the sockets from the sensation.

She ran her finger over the wet knob, smearing his lust around his cockhead. "Does it always weep so much?"

"Sometimes, Alice, I just look at you and it begins to happen. It was happening that day in the whipping house. When you gave me the tour. I was worried I might …"

He could not complete the thought, because she smeared the hot drips all around his organ with her thumb, coating him in his own desire. It felt so good he could not stop himself from moaning, from moving his hips in time with her strokes.

"You're dying for this, aren't you?" she asked in a tender voice.

"Yes," he whispered, exulting in the feeling. He bucked

forward, his body chasing the sensation, wanting more and more and more.

"Me too. I was imagining this in the mill," Alice whispered. "I could feel how big you were and how much you wanted me and I was in agony. I wanted to roll over and take you in my mouth."

"In your *mouth?"* he breathed. He knew that this was done but had never imagined it might be done to *him*. And yet now that she had said it all he could think about was the way she might look between his legs, licking the excitement from his erection.

"Would you like that?" she murmured. Her mouth was behind his ear, and her warm breath sent a shiver through him.

"Please," he said into her shoulder. "Please."

She shifted and knelt over him, placing her lips level with his swollen manhood. She breathed lightly on the tip, then licked away his ooze with her tongue.

He was so shocked by the heat of her mouth that he could not even pause to wonder if this was some especially grievous sin. The sensation made him think in scripture.

Draw me after you; let us run. The king has brought me into his chambers.

It felt rapturous, like prayer.

She paused. "Is that all right, Henry?"

He tried to say yes but it came out as more of a strangled, pleading cry, and at the desperation in it she returned her mouth to his erection and began to stroke his bollocks with her fingers as she sucked and swirled him with her tongue.

His hips jutted forward to get more of that wet heat, and he was horrified at his own cheek, but before he could apologize she took him deep into the back of her throat, and he couldn't think, he couldn't move, he couldn't breathe.

He began to spill.

The throes of it were so intense he could do nothing but shake as wave after wave wracked through him. He expected Alice to dodge out of the way of the streams of his emission but instead, to his shock, she kept him in her mouth and drank his seed.

"There now," she said, when he'd come back to himself, and she'd wiped off her mouth and come to snuggle next to him in bed. "Doesn't that feel better?"

"I feel like I'm floating," he whispered. "Like I'm in heaven, and you're there with me."

She kissed his ear. "I'm so glad you came to me. I've wanted this. I've wanted you. I never thought you might … I'm grateful."

He drew her against him, tucking her in the crook of his body, so he could hold her with his arms and mouth and toes. "I'm grateful too."

And he was. He was. Utterly and without hesitation, he was grateful.

If a sin could awaken a new destiny such as this, he would gladly ask God to forgive him.

But he would ask later, because in this moment, as he held her in the moonlight, he could only repeat, in his mind, a verse he loved from the Song of Solomon:

Behold, you are beautiful, my love;
Behold, you are beautiful;
Your eyes are doves.

CHAPTER 30

Alice awoke to the sensation of wearing Henry Evesham like a cloak. His body was even better than an ermine.

She gazed at him, admiring the way his chest and legs were dotted with auburn freckles and coppery hair. She had never been with a man who was shaped like him. His thighs were rounded and powerful, his arms were nearly as thick as her waist.

Being near him made her feel carnal, like she was closer to a creature than to a human being. She wanted to stay here in this bed forever, until she knew his body better than she knew her own, and had had it every way she could imagine.

His hand shifted from her ribs to her belly and she heard a hitch in his breathing—he was waking up.

She didn't want him to.

The sooner he arose, the sooner they would have to part. She doubted they would see much of each other after this day. She had read too much of his journal to be able to pretend to herself that he would not come to regret this.

But she didn't. She wished she could have a hundred mornings just like this one.

There were so many ways to burn.

He stirred against her back, and his cock grazed against her buttocks, hard and hot to the touch. It sent a wave of pure, animal desire rippling through her. She twitched her rear against him to feel more of it. He sighed, and she felt moisture smear against her skin. She put her fingers to her pussy, because the way he oozed with lust even in his sleep was unlike any other man she'd been with.

It drove her mad to be wanted in a way that simply could not be contained—and yet *was* contained, and contained so gently that you would never know the force of it unless he let you.

He had let her have this. Have him.

He made a sound of pleasure and moved his hands to cup her breasts. Oh, to know the pleasure of his body one more time.

"You are so beautiful," he whispered. "I can't stop looking at you."

She pressed herself back against his cock. "I love the way you feel."

He began to thrust slowly against the shallows of her back as he ran his thumbs over her nipples, wresting little cries from her each time he squeezed them just enough to spark. His hot breath along her neck made stars light behind her eyes. He gripped her ribs possessively, sliding his hands down either side of her torso until they held her hips. He pushed her closer to him, so she was laying on his cock. His hand came and flirted with hers, asking silent permission to replace her fingers in her pussy with his own.

She opened her legs for him and he made a sound almost like a sob.

"This is the loveliest thing I've ever touched," he whispered. "I want to kiss you there."

She wanted that too. Very much.

"Lay back," she murmured to him, "and you shall have your wish."

He reclined on the pillow, looking nervous and eager and flushed. She climbed up the length of his body, pausing to stroke his straining cock.

He leaned his head back and hissed. "Every time you do that, I worry I will die."

"Henry, I assure you—you've barely even lived."

She crawled up over his long, beautifully muscled torso, enjoying how he watched her, like he was witnessing a miracle. She knelt above him, so that her quim was just above his lips. His eyes darted up to hers, like he could not believe that this was happening, and had to check that she was real.

"I can …?" he breathed. "That, is you don't mind, if I …?"

She gave him a beatific smile. "Please. Take all the time you like."

He looked at her quim in something like astonishment. Tentatively, he began by exploring her, using his fingers to touch her gently, like he might break her. He glanced nervously at her face every time he ventured somewhere new, to see whether she liked it.

She definitely liked it.

It felt lovely, but even more than the sensation, she liked the wondrous way he looked at her. His absolute pleasure every time she sucked in her breath, or widened her thighs, or let out a little cry. He became more sure of himself with each shiver of her enjoyment.

And then, when she was so wet, and so frustrated, that she was about to lower herself over his mouth and beg him to use his tongue, he put his hands over her thighs and lifted her up and kissed her, very, very delicately, exactly where she wanted him to.

She put her hands flat against the wall and moaned. He drew

her closer, holding her like she weighed no more than a pillow, and nuzzled her pussy with his lips. And then his tongue began to roam and swirl, and *then* he discovered that she enjoyed a gentle suckle, and *then* he realized that if he lifted her up and down against his clever mouth in a rhythm, it made her shake and mewl.

And that was the end of Alice Hull. It was not Henry who would die in this bed, it was her.

She bore down against his lovely, lovely tongue and became a beam of sunlight, and then shattered into stars. The peaks kept building, each one stronger than the last. With every tremble that coursed through her Henry moaned, like he could feel her pleasure, like he exulted in it.

She had not imagined he might be capable of such freedom with himself.

It made her so happy.

It made her think they were not so different after all.

She closed her eyes and released herself to this moment. To being swathed in sunlight and his mouth, consumed in his desire, melting with her own. To panting and writhing and moaning like animals with no thoughts of anything beside the way they made each other burn.

She collapsed, slid down him, put her head onto his sweaty chest. His belly was sticky, and she realized he'd come already, from nothing more than his excitement at making her lose her bloody mind. The sweetness of it, the purity of his desire and his newness with it, made her heart ache.

"I'm sorry," he said, "I've made a mess."

"Oh, Henry. After that, you need never apologize to me again."

She reached for his discarded shirt from the floor and used it to clean his seed, nibbling at his nipples as she did so. "There you are. All better."

He turned her around to face him and smiled sweetly into her eyes. "Good morning."

She smiled back, and her heart ached worse and worse.

He straightened her hair, running his fingers down her head as gently as if she were a child, and she saw how he would make some woman a devoted husband. The kind who, in the most private hours, would funnel his passion into the bedchamber, sharing this secret part of himself generously.

It made her so sad that she would not be the one he shared it with that she had to look away.

Don't mourn. Be grateful that you got to have a little of him.

"Thank you," she said. "I can't think of a lovelier way to say goodbye."

His hands paused in her hair. "What do you mean," he said slowly, "'by 'goodbye?'"

She smiled sadly, not wanting to hurt him by seeming eager to part ways, but refusing to live in the delusion that this morning was more than anything but a lovely interlude before a permanent farewell.

"Well, I have to catch the mail coach, and I doubt we'll see much of each other in London, since you'll have filed your report."

"Alice," he said, drawing up on one arm. He smiled into her eyes. "We'll marry, of course."

She laughed. Not only was he sensuous, he was amusing, delivering the joke with such sincerity that for a moment she wondered if he was not joking at all.

"Wouldn't that be an irony? But not likely, unless I have converted you to a life of sin and you wish for a position at the whipping house."

He did not laugh. His face contorted. First into bemusement, and then to surprise, and then to hurt.

"I'm not jesting, Alice," he said quietly. "I'm proposing."

Proposing?

No, surely not.

If he meant this as a kind of game, she didn't want to play. If it was some guilty attempt to undo the sin—she could not encourage it.

She kissed his cheek and shimmied out of bed. "You are a sweet, lovely, silly man. Here, get dressed."

He ignored the shirt she held out. "I am not being silly in the slightest. We must marry. Surely you see that."

"That's not possible, and you know it," she murmured. She kept her tone light, but her pulse was beginning to speed up with the growing understanding that he was entirely seriously, and had been all along.

"It is," he said immediately, his face becoming flushed. "Of course it is. Besides, we must. We coupled."

He said this flatly, like what he suggested was not at all impossible or absurd.

"Henry, coupling does not obviate matrimony. Besides, you did not join with me. There is no risk of a baby."

"I'm not talking about risk," he said roughly. He inhaled deeply, like he was trying to remain composed. "Alice, I want you to be mine. I *told* you that."

"I thought you meant for the night," she answered honestly.

"I meant for the rest of our lives."

Her heart began to pound. She knew that he cared for her, but that did not change the reality of their circumstances. This was far too rash and ill-considered.

And what about what *she* wanted? He hadn't even asked.

"I ... Henry, you're a minister and I am training to be a whipping governess. Marriage between us is not possible. You must realize this."

He straightened. The last vestiges of her lover's impossibly sweet face hardened into the wiser-than-thou visage of her old foe, the Lord Lieutenant.

"I do know it will not be without complication," he said, his speech becoming rather arrogant and clipped. "But my ministry will serve fallen women, and you can use your knowledge of the trade to run our charitable efforts. And you can lead the choir, play the organ in church." He smiled at her, nodding. "It's quite logical."

Quite logical. Almost as touching as *you'll make me a fine shop window.* What a run of romantic declarations she was having.

She shook her head. "'Tis not logical at all. You were moved by what we shared. And it was lovely. But in your heart you know you cannot marry me. Don't make things difficult."

She looked away, began gathering her possessions. He stood up and caught her hands. "Don't fiddle with those," he chided. "I'm trying to have a conversation."

"No, you are trying to browbeat me into marrying you. Which I will not, for even if we were to ignore my circumstances and yours, we don't *agree* on anything."

She saw him consider this, hesitate, and then dismiss it. She saw him rearrange his face into something like sweetness, to cajole her. "Alice, we're not so different. We can make a life together. We'll have a family of our own. I've always longed to be a father. I shall look forward to the effort of trying to become one. I very much enjoyed our night together. And our morning … I shall never forget our morning so long as I live."

He smiled at her shyly, sincerely, and he was the full picture of the kind of man Henry Evesham might grow into. A caring, compassionate reformer with an abiding faith in God and a drive toward doing what he felt was right, no matter the odds against him. A man who would take his public responsibilities in stride and welcome private ones with tender affection.

A man who engaged in ideas, kept intelligent and interesting circles, loved music as much as she did.

For a moment, she longed to say yes to this fantasy he spun.

But he was ignoring the truth of the situation. Of *her.* And it made her angry that he put the burden of acknowledging reality solely on her shoulders.

"And how will you explain who you are marrying to your friends in Parliament? Your friends in church?"

He shook his head. "No one ever needs to know about your past."

She threw back her head in frustration. "Helmsley knows. Others will learn of it. Have you considered the difficulty of that? The shock it will cause? The damage to your own reputation? You know how eager people are to shame those they think are guilty of low morals. You've been one of them yourself. If we hide it, it would haunt us. And I don't want to hide who I am. I've done that long enough with my family and 'tis a very anxious life. I'm happy to be free of it. I'll not do it again."

The Lord Lieutenant dismissed these concerns with a swishing of his wrist, like he had the power to shove them in a bin. "I understand your fear, Alice, but I've prayed on it, and I am confident your past does not matter if you ask God for absolution. You will repent and be saved. And should others learn your history, your redemption will serve as a powerful demonstration of God's mercy."

Repent?

She squared her shoulders and glared into his eyes. "But I'm not sorry."

He closed his eyes. "Alice, I know how good you are. I see your spirit. You only need have faith—"

A single word coursed through her: *no.*

Whether she had faith was her concern. She would not make it the condition on which she was accepted. Married. Loved.

"You cannot mold me into the woman you want out of convenience, Henry. The fact you like to touch my cunny doesn't change who and what I am."

He softened. "I *know* who you are. You are brave and compassionate and sensitive and kind. I adore your spirit, I revel in your beauty." He paused, blushing. "And your, erm, cunny."

"And what of the fact that I don't go to church and barely know how to pray? That I don't share your views on sin?"

"I see how the spirit moves through you when you play music, Alice. I know that God loves and welcomes you, and that he is there when you are ready to open yourself to him."

He was sincere now. Fully sincere. And that was so much worse.

"And what of my sins, Henry? I've had lovers since I was a girl. So many I could scarcely recall their names if I tried. I've assisted on sessions on Charlotte Street. Witnessed lovemaking and torture. Supplied the instruments myself. Done it all without a second thought and not a regret to my name."

Each sentence she uttered seemed to hit him like a physical blow. He stared at her, his jaw pulsing with emotion. She did not enjoy hurting him, but she had to make him hear it, for both their sakes. "I wanted these things the same way I wanted you. And I'm not sorry. Not the slightest bit. Not for any of it."

"Why are you telling me this?" he rasped out.

A tear fell from the corner of his eye, and he wiped it away angrily, but another one came after it. She reached out and took his face in her hands and kissed the trail it made beneath his eye.

"Henry Evesham, I love how good you are. I love how kind you are, how much you care about doing the right thing, and helping people. I love watching you pray, and preach. And it would be an outrageous sin to pretend that being with me would not deprive you of the life you want to have. You're a Lord Lieutenant, and a Methodist, and a good man. And you deserve to have the life you wish for. It hurts me, to have to give you up. But I can't ask you to change the core of who you are for me."

She paused, wiping away her own tears. "And I deserve that too. I do. I cannot marry a man who will always be ashamed of my past, or wish it were different. I can't simply repent and become this woman that you want, because I'm not sorry. And living with a man who thinks I should be ... It's too much to ask."

He sucked in a breath like he'd been punched, but he did not answer.

Because there *was* no answer.

That was her point.

She kissed him tenderly on both cheeks.

"Thank you, you dear man, for all you've done for me. I will never forget you, Henry Evesham. I have great faith in what you will become—all the good you'll do. But now I'm going to take the mail coach home."

He stared at her like he might sink onto his knees and take her ankles and cling to her as a set of shackles.

"Please don't go," he whispered. "I know we are meant to be together. Why else would God have led me to Charlotte Street just as you needed to travel in the same direction I was headed? Why else would we have been felled by snow on our journey, when there is no sign of freezing weather outside our path? Why would we be forced into such close quarters over and over? It's providential, Alice. It must be."

She picked up her satchel. "It's coincidental. Please don't argue. Let's part as friends."

"Friends!" He cried. "Alice I *love* you."

He didn't though. Not all of her.

God might forgive her transgressions. But *Henry* wouldn't.

And she would not stand by and allow either of them to sacrifice their nature as the price of love.

"If that's true, Henry," she whispered, unable to look at him. "Then let me go."

She walked into the corridor and shut the door behind her and dug her fingernails into the palm of her hand, trying to quash down the tremendous sense of loss that engulfed her.

If she let herself, she could so easily put aside her principles and her instincts for the fantasy of a life with Henry Evesham.

But she'd only just begun to live for Alice Hull.

She was not prepared to give it up.

CHAPTER 31

Henry sat on the cot that smelled vividly of sin and stared at the door as the sound of Alice's footsteps faded.

He itched to get up and chase after her, but he willed his feet to stay planted on the floor.

He didn't know if he could walk even if he tried.

But he could get on his knees and pray.

This time, his words to God came easily and urgently.

He prayed for forgiveness. He prayed for clarity. He prayed for strength.

He prayed that someday this might hurt less.

That someday he might forget her.

Finally, he collected what remained of his things and went to pay the innkeeper.

At the sight of Henry, the man's face soured. "I hope you and your *sister* had a pleasant night," he sneered.

"Yes, thank you," Henry said, reaching in his pocket for his coin purse.

"No need. Your *sister* paid when she left, asking after the post chaise."

He winced that Alice had felt the need to pay their fee. "I see. Thank you."

The man stared at him in outright contempt. "Why would your *sister* have need of a post chaise?"

Henry paused, stunned at the force of the man's anger. "Sir, I beg your pardon—"

"For shame," the innkeeper shouted, beating his fist down onto his desk. "Do not darken my door again. We do not trade to whores in this establishment."

Henry went very, very still. "How dare you say such a thing?"

"How dare *I?*" the innkeeper snarled. "This is a decent place, sir. I heard the ungodly racket coming from your room. God should strike you down for bringing the likes of that trollop here. Leave, before I toss you out myself."

He reached across the desk and put his hands on the innkeeper's shoulders. He was gentle, careful not to injure him, for he knew the force of his size, the measure of his calm, would do as much to shock and affront the man as slapping him.

"I will own my own transgressions, sir," he said evenly. "But when you speak of any woman that way, the only person you shame is yourself."

The innkeeper spat viciously in his face.

Henry dropped his shoulders and stepped back. He took his handkerchief from his pocket and mopped the man's spittle from his cheeks. He walked to the door, feeling the eyes of the breakfasting strangers in the public room looking upon him with open curiosity and judgment.

A woman glared at him, moving toward her husband like he might reach out and grope her.

"Hope the tart was worth it, lad," an old man chortled, slapping him on his back as he passed.

Alice was right. It did hurt, to feel the condemnation of this crowd.

But it did not match the pain of leaving this inn without her. Perhaps that is what she'd meant by private morality. It was not society's rebuke that flayed him. It was hers.

But what did that make him? What did it mean that he had coupled, passionately and flagrantly and more than once, with a woman to whom he was not married? What did it mean that he would rather be exposed, to lose his position, than to give her up?

He was anguished for failing God, for failing to live up to his ideals, for believing himself to have been above such lapses. But he was not sorry he had lain with Alice. Nor that he had fallen in love with her. He was only sorry that he had not seen earlier that she was right.

If Alice accepted God as her savior, it would bring him tremendous joy. But that was her decision. If he wanted her, he had to love her without condition. He could not sit in judgment of her, or of himself for choosing her.

He drove back to Bowery Priory lost in thought, pondering what to do. When he arrived, the footman informed him that his father wished to see him as soon as he was home.

To gloat, no doubt.

He went upstairs to change his clothes and shave. He was shirtless and covered in shaving soap when someone pounded on his bedchamber door so forcefully that he nearly cut himself with the straight razor.

"Yes?" he called.

The door flung open and his father strode into the room, looking at Henry's half-dressed body with such an expression of revulsion that it made Henry want to dart behind the dressing screen. He forced himself not to flinch, to whisk away the whiskers from his neck as though he did not notice.

"May I help you, sir?" he asked, glancing at his father's reflection in the mirror.

"I told you to come speak to me immediately."

"I was planning to do so as soon as I made myself presentable, sir."

His father pounded on the wall in anger. "Stop that shaving and look at me."

Slowly, Henry turned around. His father's face was red and he was gripping a folded letter. He was so furious he seemed like his feet might levitate an inch off the floor.

"This came to me this morning from Vicar Helmsley," he shouted, waving the letter. "Would you care to guess what it says?"

Henry leaned back against the wall, bracing himself, as his father put on a pair of spectacles, cleared his throat, and began to read aloud.

"It brings me no pleasure to tell you that I discovered your son Henry in a rather curious pose with a woman of loose morals in my church this afternoon. Alice Hull, the chit in question, was known to consort sinfully with a number of men before going to London in a state of disgrace several years ago. Knowing you would be discomfited by this, I visited her family to ask after her relationship with your son, and discovered her mother in a state of extreme distress because Miss Hull had informed her she has been earning her living in a whipping house in London."

His father paused. "A *whipping house in London*," he repeated.

"Sir—"

"Oh no, you will let me finish. It goes on: 'To my horror,' the Reverend writes, 'Mrs. Hull informed me that her daughter left in Henry's company following this announcement. I will, of course, keep this matter between us, but I would advise you to speak to your son quickly, lest this bring dishonor upon your family. No doubt the boy has been seduced and lost his head to this jezebel. The sooner he is brought into line the lest he risks damaging his prospects permanently, and yours.'"

He stared at Henry, his face so pink with fury beneath his silver wig that he looked like a frosted cake. "I can only gather that this is the same 'Mrs. Hull' you brought into this home, to share a roof with your sister and Miss Bradley-Hough, who would both be ruined by the very rumor of *speaking to* a whore?"

"Miss Hull is not a whore," Henry said flatly.

"You, my son, are lying. Jonathan warned me that he'd found her wandering around the house in the middle of the night looking for your rooms, and heard you humming some vulgar song about her quim. I chose not to believe this could be possible. Far be it from me to defend you, Henry, but I thought *my son the minister* bringing *a whore* into his own father's house was simply beyond the realms of possibility."

"Alice Hull is a housekeeper at an establishment that—"

"Whatever she is, she's not a Methodist widow on her way to see her dying mother. You lied to me."

Henry inhaled deeply. "I did lie to you. For that, I ask God's forgiveness, and yours. But Miss Hull is a woman of good character, whatever her reputation."

His father shook his head and held up a hand. "Enough. I don't want to discuss such filth. The point, Henry, is that this letter I am holding is enough to destroy you. Vicar Helmsley is on track to become a bishop, and his word carries weight with the types who butter your bread. You will not find work as any kind of reverend if it is known you've been ferrying a harlot halfway across the kingdom, doing God knows what with her in a church."

Henry said nothing. He could not deny that what his father said was true.

"Here is what you are going to do," his father said tightly. "You are going to finish shaving and dress yourself half decently and try not to look like a farmhand. And you are going to find Miss Bradley-Hough and ask her to marry you. You are going to assure her that you have decided to leave the ministry to return to the family business as soon as you have concluded your duties to the Lords, and look forward to a charmed life with her in Bath. And if you do that, Henry, I will throw this letter in the fire. You can continue with your revivals and whatnots as long as I get the money to secure the business."

Henry looked down at the floor.

For an excruciating minute, the room was silent except for the sound of his father's labored breathing.

And then Henry began to laugh.

"No," he said simply, collapsing into a chair. "No."

His father stamped his foot. "Enough! Enough! This is not a negotiation. You will do as I ask or I will ruin you."

"Then ruin me," he said, because Alice Hull's words were echoing in his mind: *I'm not sorry.*

He was not sorry either. Not really. And whether his father went through with this threat or merely said it to coerce him, he did not care.

Alice had said if he wanted a woman like her, he'd have to be a different kind of man, and prepare himself for a different kind of life. She'd said *she* could not ask him to do this.

But he could choose it.

As he watched his father curse and rage and stomp about, he barely listened. All he saw, watching this display, was how naive his arguments must have seemed to Alice. This was exactly what she'd been afraid of. And it would only be the first of many such reactions.

He'd asked her for something that was not possible. He'd done it out of hope, and faith in the Lord's providence, and perhaps blind optimism.

But hope and faith and optimism could smooth a life, not make one.

The man he'd been could not marry Alice Hull and expect the world to reorder itself to suit his whims.

After all, however fervently Henry wanted to wallop his father or Vicar Helmsley or the innkeeper, they behaved exactly the way Henry might if he were in the same position. Had he not done just this many times before—railed at sinners for their hypocrisy and lack of decency?

Embarrassed them before a crowd?

And would he not face outrage and calls for an explanation were it known that the author of *Saints & Satyrs* had married a woman he'd found in a brothel?

He'd be a laughingstock. She'd be a target.

If he were to subject either of them to that, it must be because he'd thought the arguments through and truly believed them. Made certain within himself that shame would not come back to haunt him, and corrupt what he felt for her with guilt.

Only then, could he truly ask her to be with him.

She was not the one who had to change. He was.

His father was standing quietly, seething. "This is not an idle threat, Henry. I am giving you one final chance to save yourself."

"I'm going back to London. You may do whatever you feel you must, with my blessing."

His father spun on his heel and strode out the door.

Henry finished shaving, dressed himself, and gathered his possessions. He found his mother and sister in the parlor and explained he had had a disagreement with his father and would have to leave.

Both their faces turned pale. His mother cleared her throat.

"Your father indicated he expected you to have some happy news about Miss Bradley-Hough," she said tentatively.

"It seems he's been under a misapprehension."

"Perhaps you will stay for the christening," his mother ventured. She bit her lip. "You know he has a temper, Henry, but I'm certain that if—"

Henry went up and put his arms around his mother. "I love you, Mama. I wish that it were different."

She squeezed him so hard she hurt his ribs. When she released him, his sister came to him and took his arm. "I'll see you out," she said.

She walked beside him to the stables. "Is this about Mrs. Hull?" she asked in a low voice. "I overheard Papa and Jonathan—"

"Yes," he said simply, not wanting to hear whatever filth had been said.

"She loves you, doesn't she." She said it as a statement, not a question.

He stopped walking. "Pardon?"

Josephine smiled. "I thought there was something between you when she dressed down Jonathan at supper. But then, when I saw her watching you in church, I was certain. I tried to make her gossip about you, just to be sure she was kind, and she wouldn't."

His sister stood up on her toes and kissed his cheek. "I suspect Papa won't let me write to you. But know that Mama and I think of you, and we want so much for you to be happy."

Oh, was he going to cry again? Such kindness after the emotions of this day was more than his aching heart could endure.

"Jo," he said hoarsely. "I know it isn't easy for you here, and I fear it will get worse, given Papa's finances. If you should ever need anything at all—money, a home—just find a way to get a letter to me."

His sister nodded. "I love you, Henry."

"And I you, dear girl."

He drove the horses as far as he could until dark, his mind lost to prayer.

With every mile he drove, he felt more certain of himself. He knew what he must do.

And he was glad of it.

At sunset he found an inn, took a room, declined a meal, and opened the windows of his chamber to let in the cold air from outside. He lit a fire and the lamps and sat down at his desk and removed the draft of his report to the House of Lords.

He took out a fresh quill and began to work from the single premise that he had meditated on all day:

To be a man of faith is to live in constant tension between the love of the spirit that lies in the heart—grace—and the impulse toward sin—nature. To know God is not to eradicate nature but to live in this tension, striving for grace. That fight is the work of faith. It is also the work of character. To know God is to strive towards the highest ideals, despite the sin within us. To burn for them.

I burn for two things: I burn for grace, and I burn for the natural pleasures of the world that God has made. My faith resides between these impulses, and will never be perfected. But sin can exist where it does not reign in isolation. Virtue, too, can exist where purification is not whole and perfect.

To wish for perfection is to wish for Godliness, which is to lack humility. For men are not divine. We are creatures, striving. Never certain, but ever capable of faith.

Love is where the spirit of God and the nature of man meet. Tenderness, compassion, care, affection, kindness—here is where the best of the carnal meets the highest promise of the spiritual.

In love, we can burn doubly.

These words felt true.

He believed them.

And in them was the answer that had eluded him for months as he circled his dilemma with his report to the House of Lords: a way to reconcile his faith and his intellect in fulfillment of his duty.

Carnal law and spiritual law need not follow the same rules. For spiritual law is between man and God. But carnal law is earthly, a covenant between men. We can shape carnal law in line with spiritual law, but we cannot enforce faith, nor is it our responsibility to do so.

God will oversee his own righteousness.

On earth, man must do his best to make the world just as best he can. We should rule in the compassionate spirit of Christ, without over-reaching to claim for ourselves the powers that are and should be held only by God.

The rest of his report flowed easily from this principle. He spent the night enumerating his recommendations.

When his manuscript was done, the sun was rising, and he'd never been more proud of something he had written.

Nor as certain that his words would alter the course of the rest of his life.

He did not know if there was hope for himself and Alice.

He knew that he had hurt her, with his arrogance.

But he hoped that she would read this document and see in it the lessons she had tried so hard to teach him. He hoped she would know it was, in its way, a love letter. That beneath every word there was a simple prayer: *come back to me.*

He stepped out into the morning and drove back to London, bracing for what such a thing would cost him.

CHAPTER 32

The mail coach stopped in every town along the carriage road from Somerset to London, creeping at a crawl that made Alice want to pull out her own hair for sheer amusement.

She'd found a seat inside the carriage, but it was almost worse than outside, filled with the chatter and smells of six-odd passengers all sitting nearly in one another's laps. She was tired of hearing their chewing, their talking, their coughs, their wind. Her backside throbbed from sitting and her calves vibrated with the desire to walk and her jaw ached from grinding her teeth to keep from thinking about Henry, and why she felt so empty at the thought of losing him.

And then it began to rain.

The passengers sitting on the outside bench demanded to be let in, and crouched on the floor. The windows had no glass and drops of water dripped inside until everyone was miserably damp.

"We'll stop at the next town," the driver called, thumping on the roof.

Alice could not wait. She would rather walk the remaining

miles in the rain than sit pressed among these people, feeling trapped inside her anxious mind.

She drummed her fingers on her knee impatiently, willing the coach to move more quickly despite the pain that hit her arse with every bump.

Thunder rumbled in the distance and the rain became an almighty squall. She thought of how Henry would give her a long-suffering look if he were here and make some joke about their impossible luck with weather.

But Henry was no doubt back at Bowery Priory by now, safe and warm, regretting ever knowing her.

The thunder boomed like it was on top of them. A young woman beside Alice yelped in fear. Alice patted her knee. "There, there, just a spot of rain. It will pass quickly—"

Suddenly, the boom was all around them. They were inside the thunder, and it was a searing flash of light, launching them into the air. Pain went through Alice, fast and hot. All around her, she heard screaming.

She slammed onto a surface, blind, gasping sulfurous air.

As soon as she smelled the smoke, she was choking on it. Her head was ringing and her body tingled and she scrambled in the darkness, coughing, wild with the pain, not knowing where the floor was, trying to find light, to draw a breath. Her arm was trapped against something, and when she tried to free it she found it was barely connected to her shoulder. She wailed.

She was going to die.

She was in a carriage and it was burning and she was going to die.

Save me, she pleaded to her father's ghost. To the night. To Henry Evesham's God.

And then hands were on her ankles pulling her roughly over wood and she screamed because her arm came free in a way that was worse than being pinned and she was thrown onto the cold, wet earth.

She gasped, certain no more breath would ever come to her, that this must be the moment when she passed on to the other side.

But the air was cold in her burning throat. Rain fell violently down onto her face.

She'd never heard of rain in heaven nor in hell, which meant she must still be alive. Blessedly, miraculously alive.

Hazily, she watched a man run back to the coach to pull others from the flames. He was tall and thickly built and in the violet, smoky haze she almost thought that he was Henry, sent by divine providence to save her.

But he wasn't. He was just the coachman.

He pulled all eight bodies out. Injured, but alive.

She put her face into the dirt and sobbed, because she'd been so frightened. So certain she would die. So close to having done so.

And all she wanted, now that she wasn't dead, was Henry bloody Evesham.

She wanted him to pick her up and take her home and wash her off and kiss her and put her in bed and curl around her like a cloak. She wanted to tell him that she'd been wrong, that life was tenuous and fragile and that if they could find each other despite the odds, then maybe …

Maybe she'd been too quick to say what was impossible.

She lay on the road, alone with her thoughts and God, and she prayed to the Lord for another chance.

And then everything went black.

She awoke in a strange bed, in an unfamiliar room, a month later, or perhaps a week, or perhaps only an hour. Her arm was pinned to her side with straps and every time she breathed a pain like none she'd ever felt went coursing up her side. Dimly, she became aware of a man, spooning something into her mouth.

Henry?

No, not him, some other—

Then sleep, heavy and intoxicating.

She dreamt of Henry, kneeling in a church. She dreamt of her mother, wiping her brow, whispering *my Ally girl*. She dreamt of a tart, the sweetest one she had ever tasted. She dreamt of her father, belting out a broadsheet ballad as he tinkered with an organ.

"Ally girl," her mother's voice kept interrupting the song, impatient.

"Ally girl, we must wash you up now," her mother insisted, and she was angry at her mother, and wished she'd hush, and then the pain came swift and bright and she opened her eyes and once again she was in the strange room but this time it was her mother who was standing over her.

She blinked, willing back the heavy, intoxicating sleep in which this awful pain could not reach her.

"No more laudanum for you, miss," her mother grumbled.

Real, unfortunately.

"Mama?"

Her mother folded her arms over her chest. "Well now who'd you expect, the Queen? Open your mouth and eat some broth."

Alice moaned as the pain came back to her, worse with the light.

"Where am I?"

"A nice farmer's house in Rye-on-Wilke. You were in a carriage accident. Nearly died, you did. Your arm is broken but the doctor says it will heal if you don't move it. Told him my girl needs use of it, for she's a right wonder on the organ and she can't much play one-handed."

Her mother spooned broth into her mouth. Alice tried to swallow it, but gagged. Her mother wiped her chin, like she was a child.

"How did you know I was here?" Alice asked, when she'd eaten enough to satisfy her mother.

"Your satchel was thrown from the carriage when you crashed, and they found Liza's letter in it. Figured you must have family in Fleetwend. William drove me here to tend to you as soon as we heard."

She felt a flood of terror, because she was trapped here in this bed where they could carry her away. "Mama, I'm not going back. I won't marry him. I won't."

"Oh, hush, Ally girl, you've made that clear enough. Besides, he's engaged to Liza."

"Liza! She's barely sixteen."

"Old enough to have the sense to know that a man offering security is not a great imposition she must endure. William wants to marry a girl who knows the business, and she's no light on the organ like yourself but she can keep figures and look after a workshop well enough. Besides, she likes him. We all do. Save for *you,* my changeling child, who prefers working in a brothel to using her God-given talent."

Her mother offered her another spoon of broth. Alice waved it away.

"Why did you come here if you're still angry with me?"

Her mother rolled her eyes. "If I had let you die every time you acted willful and perverse you'd not have lived past the age of two, Alice Hull. Always said you were a changeling, but you are mine, aren't you? Every bit as stubborn as your mama."

Alice was not sure whether to shout at her or laugh.

She decided to laugh.

She instantly regretted it. It was the devil on her arm. "Shit of dragons," she hissed.

Her mother shook her head. "I see even getting struck by lightning is not enough to cure your filthy mouth." But her mother was smiling.

And suddenly, Alice knew that everything would be all right.

Her family was not perfect, nor was she, but there was love here. She felt it. Hers for her mother, her mother's for her.

"Mama, I know it must seem odd, my life. But I promise, I'll be all right. I want to live in London. I have this wild notion that if I earn enough at Mistress Brearley's, I might compose music on my own."

Her mother shrugged. "Ally girl, I never thought you wouldn't be all right. Foolish maybe. But you'll land on your feet. Always do." Her mother paused. "William said you could still have the organ if you want it. Thought your pa would want you to have it, married to him or not."

Her mother reached down and straightened the harp pendant on her necklace, rubbing it for just a moment with her thumb. She'd known her mother long enough to know this was an apology of sorts.

"Mama, I'm sorry I lied to you about my work."

"Well, if you hadn't I'd have worried more. It's all worked out. Just want my girls to have at least as good a life as I did, mind. Didn't mean to have you running about the shire thinking I was dead."

Alice nodded. "That was unkind of you."

Her mother gave her a sly look. "If I hadn't, that handsome minister of yours may not have taken such a shine to you."

"Mr. Evesham? A shine? What makes you say that?" Her mother was a frustrating woman, but that did not mean she was not an observant one, especially when it came to eligible men taking shines to her unmarried daughters.

"He gave me a right scolding for my so-called abuse of you when you ran off. Seemed more upset than you were."

"He did?" It was sweet he had spoken out in her defense.

"Aye. And old Helmsley came and said he caught you with the minister in the church, sinning." Her mother paused dramatically. "I said, well that's my Ally. Never met a handsome boy she didn't want to sin with, in church or otherwise."

Her mother chortled merrily, and it was all so incredible that Alice laughed too, never mind the wrenching pain it produced in her arm.

Actually, she did mind. It hurt like her bones were being clamped in the teeth of a vicious dog.

"Oww!" she cried.

"That'll be the Lord punishing you, no doubt," her mother tutted, though there was affection in her eyes. "Corrupting a minister, agh. Were I not a godly woman I might be proud my daughter has such wiles, and her a wee thing with no bosom to speak of."

"You really thought he was fond of me?" Alice asked. She knew he'd felt something for her after they'd kissed in the church, and certainly by the time they coupled at the inn, but she'd wondered if he'd just been overcome by lust.

But her mother looked at her without a trace of doubt. "Gazed at you the way your pa used to. Like you was God's gift to us all."

Alice felt tears prickle in her eyes. "I miss him," she whispered.

Her mother rubbed the little harp again and sighed. "We all do, love."

Alice knew that her mother was speaking of her father. And Alice *did* miss Papa, every day.

But she had been speaking of Henry Evesham.

CHAPTER 33

LORD LIEUTENANT OUSTED ON VICE

Outrage erupted in the House of Lords yesterday following the testimony of Lord Lieutenant Henry Evesham, who concluded his investigation into the vice trade with shocking recommendations for reform. Evesham said strengthening regulation of the trade would be more effective than enforcing harsher penalties, and proposed a scheme to license prostitutes and brothel-keepers, suggesting a guild be formed to see to the health and interests of harlots and their customers. Evesham's testimony was interrupted by strong objections from members of the Committee on the Eradication of Vice, who rejected the findings of his report and dismissed him for gross failure of his responsibilities. Lord Spence, who convened the Committee, called the report "an affront to moral decency and an insult to the resources of the Crown."

—THE LONDON LEADER

As a man who'd spent his whole life dreading ambiguity, Henry found the swiftness and decisiveness of the judgment that fell upon him following his report a relief, if a painful one.

"Immoral dross," Lord Spence, the man who'd given him his title, had sneered at him while stripping him of it.

The papers set in on him by evening, crowing of his downfall. *Saints & Satyrs* took up the mantle of condemning him as merrily as he'd once condemned others from its pages.

Reverend Keeper arrived at the Meeting Rooms in a state of agitation, demanding to read the report for himself. His face tightened as he did so. When he finally finished, he looked at Henry like he might look upon a body at a funeral, and pronounced him thoroughly corrupted by his work.

"You are like a son to me, Henry," Reverend Keeper said. "I plead with you to renounce this and ask the Lord's forgiveness."

When he said that he could not, Reverend Keeper accepted his decision. Together, they said a prayer. And the reverend told him that forming a ministry circuit of his own within their connexion would no longer be possible.

Henry offered to clear out his rooms in the Meeting House. Reverend Keeper accepted.

Within days, most of his close friends had made clear that they must sever their connections to him. The loss of each relationship was like a wall falling down in a house he'd spent a decade building. He understood, of course, though it still hurt.

But the only response he truly couldn't bear was the one that never came at all. For there was really only one person whose opinion on the report he wanted: Alice Hull. And she had not replied to his letter.

He'd sent the report to her at the whipping house, with a note he'd spent so many hours writing he had it memorized:

Dear Alice,

When I found myself driving you to Fleetwend, I thought I had been put in your path because God was using me to lead you back to him. Now, I wonder if it was the opposite—that he put you in my path to show me a deficit in my own faith—to remind me that it is better to be humble than to be perfect, and to open one's heart in compassion than to close it off in judgment.

I have taken his lesson to heart, and I am grateful for it.

I see now it was wrong of me to ask you to repent, to hide yourself, to lie. For what is most Christian is to love, and serve our fellow men as best we can, and leave judgment to the Lord.

I send you this report as a request, one sinner to another: read it, and have faith in me.

If you cannot love a man like me, I will accept your choice and wish you happiness and grace in whatever path you take. But if you would have me, it would be the highest honor to make a life with you. Openly, without apology, acknowledging the full complexity of you, of me, and of us.

If you burn as I do, Alice, then please, my love:
Set me as a seal upon thine heart.

Yours in faith,
Henry Evesham

The final line was from the Song of Solomon, that biblical poem of longing between lovers that he'd always worried he was too fond of. Now, he wondered if he had not been fond enough—if he'd hidden from its expression of pure desire and soul-deep longing, out of fear.

He'd taken to reading it late at night, thinking of Alice.

Your lips are like a scarlet thread,
and your mouth is lovely.
Your cheeks are like halves of a pomegranate
behind your veil.

He liked to close his eyes and think of Alice as the woman in the scripture, wrapped in scarlet threads, blissfully eating pomegranate seeds, licking their juice from her lips in sensuous delight. He missed her appetite, the pleasure she took in everything from the taste of cake to the taste of rain to the taste of his own body.

He missed her touch. Her laughter. Her humming. Her lurid, awful cursing.

He was determined to give her time, not to rush to her and demand she reconsider her position on their future. But it had been a week of silence, and he was beginning to fear no response would come.

That the problem had not been his views, or hers.

That perhaps his love was simply unrequited.

And then, one morning, the errand boy from Charlotte Street came by his new lodgings with a parcel wrapped in paper just heavy enough that he knew it must contain a key.

It did. But it was not from Alice.

Henry,

I am writing to commend you on the bravery and compassion of your report. I am saddened that your findings were dismissed, for I know how much good they would have done. I have heard of the consequences you have faced, and wished to say you have a friend in me and my investors, some of whom might be able to be of use to you.

To that end, we'd like to host you for supper in my private dining room this Friday night at nine o'clock. Present this key to be admitted. I hope to see you there, and shake your hand.

With compliments,
Elena Brearley

There was no word of Alice. But nevertheless, he sent back an acceptance with shaking hands.

CHAPTER 34

"Child, we were worried you were dead," Stoker said, when he opened the door of the whipping house and found that it was Alice standing there.

He dropped his usual forbidding air and wrapped his arms around her, being careful to avoid the sling covering her arm.

"Mistress," he called over his shoulder. "Look who has returned."

The sound of Elena's measured footsteps coming down the stairs was one of loveliest bars of music Alice had heard in her entire life.

"Alice," Elena murmured, rushing close to inspect her injured arm. "I was worried for you. We all were. Your letter about the accident only arrived yesterday. We had begun to think you would not return to us."

"I nearly didn't, though not for lack of trying," Alice said. She'd been going mad, being treated as an invalid by her mother for a fortnight. She'd left as soon as the physician had given her his blessing to take a mail coach. "I've missed you all. I am itching to return to work."

Elena raised a brow at the sling over her arm. "We'll not be able to resume your training if you're missing your flogging hand, my dear. But I'm sure we can find a use for you. I'm glad to have you back. From your letter, it sounded like you had quite the journey."

"Well, I was trapped in the snow with Henry Evesham, my mother staged her own death to try to force me to marry, and I nearly died in a carriage accident. I don't think I shall be leaving London again any time soon. Perhaps not ever."

Stoker laughed. "It's good to have you back, Alice."

"Yes," Elena said. "And if it is any consolation for your troubles, you must have had an impact on our dear friend Henry."

"Oh?" She tried not to reveal by her expression that any mention of Henry's name was like a food that she had been craving for a fortnight.

Elena nodded. "Indeed." She stepped over to the small desk in the alcove where they kept the keys and post, and rifled through a pile of letters.

"Here. He sent this for you." She held out a thick envelope.

"Is that his report? Is it out?" Alice's stomach clenched. She wondered what Henry had decided to do.

"Oh, the first page should give you an idea," Elena said, with a smile that implied it was something unexpected.

Alice ripped open the document with her teeth.

A PROPOSAL FOR THE REFORM OF VICE

1—Preface to the Recommendations Herein

Though it is tempting to impose one's moral views upon society, at times the practical result would be counter to the higher duty of Government to support the health and safety of the citizens the Crown protects. Such is the case in considering the trade of pros-

titution. In the following pages I therefore propose, after careful study, the following enumerated acts to improve public health and safety; reduce costs incurred by disease and criminality; safeguard public decency; and establish a code of protections for prostitutes such as those upheld by guilds of other trades.

ALICE READ THESE WORDS THREE TIMES, SCARCELY BELIEVING HENRY could have written them. She could not have hoped for a more auspicious prelude if Elena Brearley had authored the report herself.

"Remarkable," Alice whispered, wondering how Henry had found it in himself to write such a thing.

Elena laughed softly. "Indeed. Whatever you said to the man, it must have worked. He's calling for nearly everything we suggested. Licenses, guilds, physicians."

Alice was stunned. "I hoped he might hear some of our arguments and soften his positions, but I never imagined he would propose something so radical. Won't he be pilloried for it?"

Elena sighed. "He was dismissed by Spence. The papers are making a mockery of him. The debate he's started may well lead to reform once the outrage dissipates, but I'd venture the reverend won't be asked to perform christenings any time soon. But then he, of anyone, would have known there'd be a price."

Yes. He'd known it, and he'd done it anyway.

"There was also this letter for you," Elena said, holding out another envelope.

Unlike the printed report, it was written in his hand. His writing, just the look of it, turned her chest into a muddle. She fumbled it open, and the words inside did nothing to ease her. She felt like she was back in the grips of laudanum.

She had to sit down on the stairs so she would not fall over.

"Oh dear, what does it say?" Elena asked, dropping to her knees in concern as though Alice might be injured.

Alice read it again. "It says," she whispered, "'If you burn as I do, Alice, then please, my love: set me as a seal upon thine heart.'"

Elena's eyes widened. "It must have been quite a carriage ride you had with him."

"I need to see him," Alice said.

Elena smiled oddly, looking stunned for the first time since Alice had known her. "Well, you're in luck. He's coming to supper this evening."

CHAPTER 35

As he had done a fortnight before on a dreary winter morning that changed his life irrevocably, Henry flicked his knuckle against a discreet door marked twenty-three, tense at who might open it. This time, when the footman answered instead of the dove-eyed woman, he felt the opposite of relief.

Where is she, he wanted to cry. *Please, just let me see her.*

"Your key?" Stoker drawled.

Henry handed over the new one he'd been sent. Instead of his previous sigil, with the cross, this one bore the emblem of the scales of justice.

A compliment, he imagined.

"Mistress Brearley awaits you in her dining room with her guests. I'll show you in," Stoker said.

He led Henry past the staircase and into a suite of rooms that had not been part of Alice's tour. They were less austere, more comfortably furnished, and slightly better lit, though they still had a rather dark and brooding quality. The walls were upholstered in black silk, and the tables were adorned with vases of dark tulips, as though the house lived in permanent mourning.

"Mistress Brearley's private apartment," Stoker murmured. "The dining room is just this way."

As they neared the door a tiny dog came bolting forward, chased by what at first appeared to be a cloud of pale pink ruffles. The dog landed at Henry's feet and began to bark at him ferociously, as though convinced Henry had come to steal the silver.

"Shrimpy!" the ruffles—or rather the woman who was bedecked in them—cried. "Oh, Shrimpy, it is just your old friend, Mr. Evesham! Do behave."

Lady Apthorp lifted the growling dog into her arms and, with a wink at Henry, showered his ears in kisses. "You remember Shrimpy, of course," she said.

"Little devil," Stoker muttered under his breath.

Henry did not disagree. The previous Christmas the benighted creature had become so thoroughly riled during an outdoor nativity pageant at the Apthorps' that he'd caused a small child to fall into a pond. A frozen pond. Which had required Henry, who had been officiating the festivities, to jump into the icy water and save the little boy.

The dog stuck out his tongue with a smile and barked cheerfully under his mother's affection, as though he had no recollection of attempting infanticide.

"Charmed to be reacquainted," Henry said.

"I'll take Mr. Evesham inside, Stoker," Lady Apthorp said. Stoker nodded and walked away, with a parting glare at the dog.

"Come, come," Lady Constance said, nodding at him to follow her. "Everyone is looking forward to seeing you. We've all read with great relish the delightfully *terrible* things they're saying about you in the papers." Her eyes twinkled.

She and her husband, Lord Apthorp, had been among the figures vilified in *Saints & Satyrs* during his tenure as its editor. Oddly enough, the experience had caused the Apthorps to fall in love, and they now counted Henry as a friend. It was Lord Apthorp, who had once been a master here, who'd introduced Henry to Mistress Brearley.

"I suppose I deserve a bit of reciprocity," Henry said, matching Lady Apthorp's dry tone.

Lady Apthorp laughed. "Oh, I'm only jesting. I humbly welcome you to the society of we who are ennobled by scurrilous gossip. You may find the first weeks trying but the notoriety becomes emboldening." She smiled at her dog. "One can do *anything* when one is already a villain, can't one, Shrimpy?"

"Not quite anything," Henry quipped, not entirely without self-pity.

"Ah, but that is why we wanted to celebrate you. I wrote to Elena and said we must see Evesham at once, for he'll need an entirely new life, and I'm just the person to arrange it for him. You *know* how I love to meddle."

"You are too kind," he said. And he meant it. He'd always liked Lady Apthorp.

"Our guest of honor has arrived," Lady Apthorp sang as she led him into the dining room.

"Ah, Henry," Elena said, rising from the head of her table. "Forgive us, we sat without you to escape the incessant barking of Constance's insufferable dog."

"Shrimpy is *not* insufferable," Lady Apthorp rejoined. "He is outspoken. Like our dear Mr. Evesham. Now then, who needs an introduction?"

The room held a small party of people who were all exquisitely dressed and intimidatingly attractive. None of them, to his profound disappointment, was Alice.

Mistress Brearley gestured at a tall, hawkish man dressed in black and a willowy woman with striking green eyes. "Henry, this is Archer and Poppy. As you know, I don't use titles here, but for the sake of clarity they are better known as the Duke and Duchess of Westmead. They are investors in the club."

Henry bowed. The duke, he knew, was Lady Apthorp's elder brother. Henry'd heard rumors of his affiliation with this place many years ago, but had never quite believed them. Both Westmeads smiled at him pleasantly, belying their public reputation for being terrifying.

"And you know Julian and Constance, of course," Elena continued, gesturing at the Apthorps.

"Of course, a pleasure."

"And I'm always the last to be introduced," an elaborately wigged man at the end of the table drawled, eyeing Elena with a petulant smile. Beneath his resplendent headpiece of black curls his face possessed the kind of devilish features—a split chin, slashing cheekbones, diabolical eyebrows—that would have made Henry figure him for a rogue even if he had not already recognized him as the notorious Marquess of Avondale.

"Oh, Henry knows who you are, Christian," Elena said in a tone of acute boredom. "He's familiar with all the worst men in town." She shifted her eyes to Henry. "It will surprise you not at all to learn Lord Avondale is the founding investor in my club."

"And a most *avid* member," Avondale supplied. "I'm a bit offended you never exposed me, Evesham. 'Twas certainly not owing to subtlety on my part."

Mistress Brearley shot him a withering look. "Behave."

"You're here, beside me," Elena said, pointing at an open place setting. Henry noticed there was a second open seat at the table, and tried not to lose his self-possession obsessing over whether it was for Alice. Surely not, for if she were attending this meal she would have already arrived, given she lived in the house.

He tried not to appear crushed as he sat down. "Thank you for the invitation."

Apthorp, looking so impossibly beautiful that, as ever, it almost hurt to look at him, shot Henry one of his beguiling smiles. "Getting by, Lord Lieutenant?" His eyes were bright with sympathy.

"No longer my title, I'm afraid. In the spirit of Mistress Brearley's etiquette, call me Henry."

"Well then, dear Henry, let me be the first to say I am utterly shocked at what you published."

Henry smiled. "You and the rest of London."

"It's brave, what you wrote," the duke chimed in. "Futile, I expect, but brave."

"Not futile," Apthorp replied. "The ideas are being discussed, and that's a start."

"I hope so," Henry sighed. "I plan to publish a longer work presenting more evidence, once the furor settles."

"It will settle," Apthorp assured him. "And while I'm sure life is not overly pleasant for you just at present, I have found that public acts of wanton foolishness have a way of working out." He smiled fondly at his wife.

Lady Apthorp, in turn, smiled at Henry. "I always thought you were gifted at prose, even if you are sometimes a terrible nuisance with a quill."

She paused to allow everyone to groan, for she herself was, infamously, a terrible nuisance with a quill.

"I make it my business to cultivate the most dissolute publishers as friends," she added. "I will introduce you around to all of them, so that they may fight for the honor of putting you in print."

"I'm sorry I'm late," a voice—*her* voice—said from behind Henry.

He whirled around.

Alice. His Alice.

Her dove's eyes were looking directly at him, shining.

"Oh, Alice, there you are," Elena said. "I thought you might have fallen asleep, and I didn't want to wake you after your ordeal."

Her ordeal?

"No, I was downstairs," she said, sliding into the seat beside him. "Helping cook with something in the kitchen. A recipe my mother taught me."

"One-armed?" Elena chuckled.

Henry belatedly noticed her right arm was tucked to her side with a discreet black sling.

"Alice what happened?" he cried, far too loudly. He felt all the eyes in the room lock on him at once with open interest, but he could not contain himself. "Are you all right?"

"Yes, yes," she reassured him. "I was in a carriage accident and broke my arm. But it's mending, and I'm fine."

She paused, and looked at him sideward. "I only returned to London this afternoon. It seems there is much I have missed." She smiled at him like there was no one else in the room.

She meant his letters. His report.

It was sinful to be glad she had endured a broken limb, but all he could think was *thank you, Lord.* For it meant, all this time, she had not been ignoring him.

"I'm so glad you are recovering."

What he meant was that he wanted to take her in his arms and carry her from this room and tell her all of the feelings rattling around his heart, but did not wish to make a scene.

He forced himself to keep his hands pressed on the tablecloth, so he would not do so anyway.

"I asked Alice to join us because I suspect she had a hand in shaping Henry's recommendations," Elena said to the other guests. “They recently took a rather ill-fated journey, and it would seem they had ample time to talk.”

Alice blushed and shook her head furiously. “Oh, no. Henry deserves all the credit for what he wrote. I merely railed at him a bit and horrified him with my cursing.”

“That’s not true,” he said, just to her. “I’d long been wrestling with contradictory ideas. You helped me see what was right. I’m very grateful.”

“You went much beyond what I had hoped for,” Alice said, looking pained. “I admire it, and I agree with you, but I can’t help but wonder why you did it.”

You know why.

“I simply found,” he said, looking into Alice’s eyes. “That I had to act in accordance with my heart. Whatever the consequences.”

CHAPTER 36

Given that everyone in the room was watching her and Henry in a state of abject fascination, Alice was grateful that Elena chose that moment to ring the bell summoning the food.

She was more grateful still when Henry, perhaps sensing that she was finding it difficult to maintain her composure, changed the subject.

"Lady Apthorp," he said, "I've been hearing such wonderful things about the latest production at your theater. Are you working on a new play for next season?"

"Do call me Constance," she said, "And as it happens, I am working on an opera. Or, at least, the libretto for one. An adaptation of *The Taming of the Shrew*. Except in my version, the one who will be tamed is the man."

Avondale arched a brow at Constance. "Kind of you to finally write my biography."

"You are far from tamed, judging by what *I've* been hearing," Constance rejoined.

He lodged a tragic look at Elena. "Perhaps. But she'll tame me one day."

He did not need to say who the "she" was. His obsession with Elena—who had for a decade been his whipping governess, and nothing else, despite his attempts at making her his mistress—was legend.

Elena took a sip of wine and pretended not to hear him, for leaving him unrequited was a torture for which he paid her handsomely. "When can we expect the opera to debut?" she asked Constance.

Constance wrinkled her nose. "Well, I'm still looking for a composer for the music. I'd like to find a woman, but it seems that the lady composers of note are quite trepidatious at the notion of associating with a scandalous person like myself. They must please their more sober-minded patrons."

"You should speak to Alice," Henry said. "She's a gifted musician."

"She *is?*" Elena asked.

Alice's eyes darted to her plate. It was kind of Henry to say this but she felt shy claiming her own talent.

"Yes," he said. "She plays beautifully, but her compositions are the real marvel. She'd not leave a dry eye in the theater."

Lady Apthorp looked delighted. "Oh good, I *live* to provoke tears! Would you be interested, Alice?"

Interested was not the word. It would be the opportunity of her life. But she did not want to promise more than she was certain she could deliver.

"I would love the chance, but I don't know many operas. I would need to study the music to be sure I could work with the form."

"Come visit me and have a look at my libretto," Constance

said. “If it seems we might complement one another, we can take in some operas together for inspiration.”

Alice glanced at Henry in disbelief. He gave her an encouraging smile.

“I would be honored. Thank you.”

Conversation turned to politics, and Alice scarcely listened. Normally a chance to dine with such interesting guests would have her hanging on every word, but with Henry beside her, she could barely remember her own name.

“Oh, what is that heavenly aroma?” Constance said, inhaling the air, which had begun to smell like cinnamon. A maid, Delilah, came in holding a tray of apple tarts.

“Oh, how beautiful,” Poppy said, admiring how they’d been shaped into flowers. “Give the cook our compliments.”

Delilah smiled at Alice. “Alice made these herself. Said she thought the guest of honor would enjoy them.”

Alice dared to steal a glance at Henry. He turned to her with raw emotion on his face.

Oh dear. She had meant for this to be a subtle gesture. She did not wish to embarrass him.

“My mother always made them with nuts and oats and butter in the crust—said it was healthier,” she explained, feeling hopelessly shy. “I thought you might find it a nice balance between sweet and savory.”

Henry took a bite and closed his eyes. He nodded like he was lost in silent prayer. When he swallowed, he turned to her, and said in a voice that was barely audible, “It’s the best thing I’ve ever tasted.”

The way he said it made her blush.

They were both, indeed, blushing and looking at their plates, neither able to stop smiling.

Archer cleared his throat. “I think,” he said kindly, “we should allow the guest of honor and Alice a moment alone." When Alice looked up, she saw that the fearsome duke was biting his lip and looking at Henry like he wanted to hug him.

Elena quickly stood, her dessert plate in hand. "Yes, let's… ," she gestured at the door, and everyone rose in a rush. Good-natured laughter followed them down the hall, and then she and Henry were alone.

They both looked at the middle of the room, stunned. Alice was not sure what to say.

"I had no idea you had been injured—" Henry began, at exactly the same time Alice blurted "I read your letter this afternoon—"

They both stopped, winced. Alice sank down in her seat and laughed, though not in mirth so much as in excruciation.

"You first," he said softly.

Well, she might as well not beat around the bush. It was clear that he was as disordered as she was, and if she did not come out and say what she was feeling one of them might have a conniption before she ever got the words out.

"Henry, when my carriage was struck—it was lightning, a sudden storm. Well, I don't actually remember much—not anything, really—except lying on the ground and praying for one thing. That I could have another chance with you."

He swallowed painfully, seeming unable to talk, so she continued. "And then I saw your letter, and your report … and it was like my prayer was answered."

She took a slip of paper from her pocket and slid it across the table to him.

"I wrote back to you. This is my answer."

His face crumpled as he read the lines she'd copied from the Song of Solomon.

By night on my bed I sought him whom my soul loveth: I sought him, but I found him not.

Henry—Set me as a seal upon thine heart.

He fell to his knees before her and took her hands.

"Alice. I love you. About everything else in my life, I am a mire of contradictions. But on this ... on this, Alice, I know it as I know my own breath."

She leaned forward and placed a kiss upon his lips.

"I have no other certainties either, Henry. But I love you, too. I do."

He squeezed her hand. "It was foolish of me to insist that we might have it easy. It won't be. I see that now, and I am so sorry I dismissed your concerns. And if, given all that has happened, you are not eager to take on— "

"I'm a working girl, Henry Evesham," she said, reaching up to brush his hair from his eyes. "I don't require ease."

"You're certain?" he whispered.

She paused, because she wasn't without worry. Far from it. "About how *I* feel. But I need to know you won't regret this. I would hate to let myself become attached to you, only for you to find you want a decent girl."

"You are the most decent girl I know."

He was sweet, but she was not going to let him ignore her point. "You know what I mean."

He nodded, and something crossed his face. "One moment. I want to give you something."

He rose and left the room, and she heard him conferring with Stoker. When he returned, he carried his satchel. He reached inside and removed his journal.

The one she'd taken.

"I've been searching my heart since we parted, Alice. All my thoughts are in this book. I want you to read it. The whole thing. And decide for yourself if you might trust me to be yours."

She took the book from him and ran her hand over its soft

cover. She loved this book. She'd missed her diarist. "I will read it right away. This very night."

"Once you do, write to me. And..." he smiled ruefully, "please know that I will be in agony awaiting your thoughts."

She hugged the journal to her chest. "I shall. I promise."

He smiled at her, and his eyes were filled with such yearning that she leaned in toward his lips. He put his hand behind her neck and murmured her name. Their lips met so softly that it was almost nothing at all.

But it was enough to leave her shaken. She knew she had to step away, or she would never let him leave here.

"Henry, I'm not going to join the others. I need... " She took the book and kissed it. "I need to read this right away."

She saw Henry to the drawing room, said her farewells to the guests, and walked in a blind daze up the stairs to her room. She climbed into bed and began to read. When she had finished, she turned back to the first page, and read it all over again.

He had copied passages from the Bible on female beauty. On men and women lying together. Verses exhorting love. And in the margins he had written his own thoughts, each framed as a confession. His notes were not formal, but personal and honest. Fears about what he might be capable of and what he might not be. Passages that aroused his body or moved his emotions. An account of the ecstasy he'd felt when coupling with her, and the tremendous fear that had gripped him afterwards.

It was a confession of a man who lived virtuously not because he was a saint but because he was a sinner.

But the passage she could not stop rereading was an account of the day she'd given him a tour of the whipping house.

All I could think, as Alice led me to that subterranean chapel, was of the story I've read in the gospels so many times. In Luke's account, "a woman who lived a sinful life learned that Jesus was eating at the Phar-

isee's house. So she came there with an alabaster jar of perfume. As she stood behind him at his feet weeping, she began to wet his feet with her tears. Then she wiped them with her hair, kissed them and poured perfume on them."

For years, I've pictured myself in the scene, and it stirred me shamefully. I was horrified at being capable of such blasphemy. And yet, I can't deny I still long for it. I can't stop imagining that if I were to tell Alice of this vision—or, dare I even write it ... ask her to indulge me in it—that I might reassure us both that we are suited. For if I could trust her with this part of me, and not revile myself nor her for it later, would she not know there is no part of herself she cannot trust me with?

In the morning, Alice sent the errand boy to Henry's rooms, instructing him to come see her right away. When he arrived, he looked so young and nervous that she wrapped her good arm around his neck without speaking.

"You read it?" he murmured.

"Twice. And it was beautiful. And I think you're exactly right."

He stepped back, searching her face. "Right about what?"

"About your vision," she said softly. "You want me to bathe and perfume your feet, like the woman in the gospel."

He flushed a bit, but he did not dodge her eye, nor deny that he wanted it. "You would do it?"

She smiled. "With pleasure, Henry. If you're certain."

"I'm not certain," he admitted. "It's very new, to even admit to myself … But I … I long for it. And if I can accept it, then perhaps, I hope …"

She took his hand and squeezed it, because his vulnerability so moved her that she could not look at him without also touching him.

"I have bad news," she whispered in his ear.

"What is it?"

"I'm afraid you will have to wait until I have use of my arm."

He stepped back, and smiled, looking more like himself. “Good. That will give me time.”

“Time for what?”

He straightened his back, and his confidence returned in full measure. “To court you properly, Miss Hull.”

CHAPTER 37

Broken arms healed slowly.

Sometimes maddeningly slowly, for it protracted the uncertainty, and the anticipation, between himself and Alice.

Sometimes deliciously slowly, for it left time for other things, simpler things that neither of them had ever done before, like visiting bakery shops to find the most perfect apple tart in London, or touring cathedrals to locate the most beautifully toned organ.

By day, Henry spent his hours turning his account of London's streets into a book. But in the evenings, he met Alice at Lady Apthorp's theatre. Some evenings, he went on to the opera with Alice and the Apthorps, and he delighted in watching Alice listen intently, jotting down ideas in her notebook, or whispering ideas to Constance about the work they were creating.

Some nights, they strolled about through London's pleasure gardens, singing broadsheet ballads to each other. On Sundays, he persuaded her to attend the new worship group he'd started, where she began arranging hymns.

And at night, he dreamed of her.

When his dreams were sweet, he woke up smiling. And when his dreams were wicked, he did not deny himself the pleasure of them. He wrote them down and sent them to Alice in letters addressed to Mistress Hull.

After one such morning, his note came back with a reply in her hand.

Mistress Hull has set your appointment for tomorrow at ten o'clock in the morning.

He knew exactly what this meant.

That night, he barely slept.

When he arrived on Charlotte Street the following day, Alice greeted him at the door. She was wearing her formal receiving dress and the sling was nowhere to be found.

"Mistress Hull," he said, bowing. She led him into a small room and made him sit, while she stood. Her face was stern. "Now then. You've come to me for a session. Tell me what it is you'd like."

He hesitated, unsure what to say, as he'd never bought the services of a whore. Her face softened, and she used her normal speaking voice. "Henry, are you sure you want to do this?"

(He was. He was.)

He nodded. "If I seem uncertain, it is because I have rarely allowed myself to do something I have wanted so dearly in my entire life."

Something changed in her eyes. Her expression was soft, calm, understanding. It was the face he once used when his congregants confessed their sins and worries.

She came and put two hands on his head. "You are safe with me, Henry. Safe."

Her gentle touch gave him a measure of comfort—enough to say exactly what he wanted.

She asked questions on several details he had not thought of—the temperature he preferred for the water, what she should wear, whether he wanted more touched than just his feet. It was strange to be asked such intimate questions in such a brisk, efficient way.

Alice finally nodded, satisfied she knew the full measure of his fantasy, and the limits of it.

"Stoker is waiting outside. He will take you downstairs," she said. "When I meet you there, I shall be the woman from your fantasy, and you shall be the weary traveler. If you find you want to stop, you need only address me as Alice, and that will be a signal to pause our session."

He followed Stoker through the quiet house to the room that had once haunted his dreams. It was exactly as he remembered it, except the scent of incense was stronger, and a chair had been placed at the center of the room in front of the altar, surrounded by candles.

A knock sounded at the door, and then Alice reappeared. (No, not Alice. Mistress Hull.)

She carried a wooden pail of water that gave off a fragrant steam and set it before the chair. Her hair was covered with a black veil, as he'd requested, and it made him instantly excited, despite his nerves.

She turned to him and bowed low, like a servant.

"You must be so tired from your travels," she said softly. "I want you to be comfortable. Can I help you with your coat?"

She moved behind him and pressed her fingers to his sleeve. Awareness rippled through him. It had been weeks since he had felt her touch, for he had asked her to honor his celibacy until he'd reassured them both that they could be together, without doubts or guilt darkening their intimacy.

But this did not mean he hadn't longed for her. Looking at her now, he felt he'd never burned so hot and bright.

"Sit down," she said, gesturing to the chair. "Let me ease your weariness."

She knelt at his feet and slowly, very slowly, untied the laces of his boots. He watched every movement of her fingers, felt each tiny change in the pressure of the leather around his shins and ankles. Sliding his feet out of those shoes was one of the most pleasant sensations of his life.

He closed his eyes as she rubbed her hand over the outline of his toes above his stockings.

"How your feet must ache," she said. "You've travelled so far." Her voice was sweet, feminine, a coo—nothing like the way that Alice talked, and even less like Mistress Hull. She was the maid, who only wished to serve him.

She was good at this. At reading beneath what he'd told her to the truth of the desire. For now he understood what had made him want this. He wanted to be loved and tended and nurtured for his goodness. It was his highest fantasy.

She moved her fingertips up to his calves and untied the stays beneath his breeches to release his stockings. He could scarcely breathe.

Her hands were bare, and he liked the feeling of them on his legs.

"Place your feet inside this tub, so I can wash away your troubles."

He did, and the water was so warm, and her hands on his toes and soles and ankles were so soft, so soft.

She smiled up at him from beneath her lashes. "Does that feel good?" she whispered.

He nodded.

It felt like mercy.

It felt like love.

She picked up a small gold cup filled with a liquid and poured it into the water. The faint fragrance he had smelled before grew stronger, filling the room with the scent of lavender and something spicier he couldn't place.

He squeezed the arm of the chair and closed his eyes. Between the warm water at his feet and the lovely smell and the pressure of Alice's fingers lightly kneading his ankles, he wanted to moan with appreciation.

She stopped, and he heard her hands come out of the water, and he opened his eyes. She was lifting the veil up over her head. She looked directly into his eyes and dropped it to the floor. And then she began to remove the pins that held her plaited hair in a knot at the back of her head.

A long, dark braid fell down over her breasts.

She unfurled the braid, letting strands of hair fall in waves around her.

He was transfixed by how she looked. *He wanted this. He wanted this so much.*

She took a phial from her pocket and removed the cork. She poured a scented oil into her hand, then massaged it into her tresses as he watched. He had to close his eyes again, because she looked so beautiful, so erotic, that if he watched her surrounded by all that loose, luxurious hair—he'd always loved long hair, dreamed of having a wife whose hair he could brush in the evenings—this would be over far too soon.

"Open your eyes," she whispered, pouring a generous portion of the oil from his calf, to his ankle, to his big toe. And then, using a fistful of her own hair, she began to massage it into his skin. The sight paralyzed him. That long, soft hair draped over him. The whisper of her breath on his skin as she lightly kissed the arches of his feet and caressed the space between his toes. He gasped in pleasure.

The stirrings became sharp and urgent as she murmured about his poor toes, his poor shins, his hard work, his many travels, and it felt so wonderful to be tended in this way that he wished she would touch more of him.

"Does it please you?"

Oh God, help me, but it does.

"Yes," he gasped out. He could feel his cock rising against the fabric of his shirt, dripping now at the sight of her and the tenderness and care she'd given him.

"Would you like me to bathe you?"

She was asking if he wanted more. And he did. He did.

"Please," he whispered.

She took his hand and led him from the room into another one he'd seen—the bathing room—dark, and hot, and filled with steam. The tub was full of scented water, and there were more phials and soft cloths piled all around it.

He was utterly still as she undressed him. Each whisper of her skin on his lit him like he was a lamp. With every garment that she dropped upon the floor he felt more nude, more open. Like he was being born anew, beneath her touch. Baptized into something he'd never known before, but craved.

Neither of them spoke as she led him to the tub. He sank down and watched her as she dipped her hair into the water and bathed his neck and shoulders, then his chest, his back. She moved to his feet and washed his legs and thighs. All that was left was his belly and his cock, which was so hard, so aching, it was nearly painful.

She teased his belly, moving slowly lower, so her hair brushed along his hipbones. His muscles rippled at the delicate sensation, and his cock jutted from the water.

She met his eye, a question in her expression. "How might I soothe you?" she whispered.

He knew she was offering to relieve his desire. But he wanted something different.

"Will you sing to me?"

Her eyes widened, and then she smiled, and the smile was his lover's smile, Alice's smile.

She took his hands in hers and began to croon a song he'd never heard.

Oft have I vow'd to love no one,
but when I think on thee,
I have no power for to give o're,
thy Captive I must be;
So many looks and graces dwells
between these Lips and Eyes,
That whosoever sees thy Face,
must once be made a prize.

As she sang, she began to run her hands lightly over his body, swirling the water around him.

Oft have I view'd thy comely parts
from head unto the toe,
Which makes me fry in Cupids flames,
the truth of all is so;
For when I lie upon my Bed,
in hopes to take my rest,
I cannot sleep to think on thee,
whom I in heart love best.

Her eyes were shining down at him as she sang those final lines. Dove's eyes. (Alice's eyes. His Alice's eyes.)

"Shall I wash more of you?" she asked, moving her hands toward his painfully swollen arousal.

(Yes. But not yet, my love.)

He took her hands in his and kissed them. "Alice, I don't want to make love again until you are my wife. It's a vow I made to God that is important to me."

She gave him a cockeyed smile that was thoroughly Alice's. "As you wish, Reverend. I can burn as long as you desire."

He stared at her. "Does that mean you will marry me?"

She laughed softly. "This was for you, Henry. For me, I would have married you a month ago."

He paused, an idea forming in his mind. "What about tonight?"

CHAPTER 38

Elena was in a session, so Alice simply wrote her a note. "Ran off to marry the minister."

She and Henry left the whipping house hand in hand, Alice carrying a single bag, and Henry nothing but the coat on his back. They hailed a hackney to a stable, where Henry rented a coach and team.

"Where are you taking me?" she asked, snuggling up beside him. "Gretna Green?"

"Somewhere better," Henry said enigmatically.

"I wonder how long it will take until an axle breaks, or we are stranded in a hail storm, or beset by highwaymen," Alice mused, as he took the road heading south, toward the coast.

"I'd like to see a highwayman try to get the better of you," he said, grinning. "Certainly you could out-curse him."

"Bloody befucked right I could."

Henry groaned, which pleased her very much.

Despite her prediction, the roads were good and mostly empty. The weather was mild. They did not encounter thieves, nor wolves, nor even a minor plague of locusts.

She was almost disappointed when Henry slowed the horses onto a wooded path leading up a hillside and said, "We're almost there."

At the top of the hill, the trees parted, and before them was a castle. An actual castle, pretty as something in a story book, complete with high turrets fit for a princess.

"What is this place?"

"Wait here," Henry said, grinning mysteriously. "I shouldn't be long, if things go to plan."

He strode up to a heavy wooden door and pounded on it. After a moment, a man about Henry's age opened it. He wore a dressing gown, like he had come from bed, and started in surprise. Henry pointed at the carriage. The man's face broke into a delighted grin, and threw his head back and laughed, slapping Henry on the back.

The two of them disappeared inside.

Alice waited, amusing herself by walking about the grounds, which included a pretty little chapel overlooking the ocean on the other side of the hill. The air smelled green and rich, like early spring, and the garden was noisy with birdsong. After a quarter hour Henry called her name, and she wandered back to the castle doors, where Henry was waiting with the man she'd seen before. This time he wore the robes and collar of a priest.

"Alice Hull," Henry said, "please meet Mr. Andrew Egerton, my dearest friend from university."

"A pleasure, Miss Hull," the man said, smiling at her like she was some kind of miracle.

"Mr. Egerton is an ordained minister, when he's not lazing about playing country squire."

"Mr. Evesham has persuaded me to issue a special license, in my capacity as a minister of the Bishop of Canterbury," Mr.

Egerton said. "I can marry you right now. If, indeed, you truly mean to marry Henry Evesham."

"I do," she averred cheerfully.

He grinned. "Then follow me."

And so she took Henry's hand and walked beside him to the pretty little chapel.

It had no organ, but that did not matter. For within ten minutes, they walked back out, still hand in hand.

Wed.

CHAPTER 39

Henry's heart was full to bursting.

God was good.

In their quick conferral Andrew had agreed to give him use of the dower suite of the castle, so that his bride might have a proper wedding night before they returned to London.

Andrew had had a word with his housekeeper to ready the rooms. When they walked in the door, Henry realized his friend's servants had done more than ready them.

The table was filled with roses and a bounty of fruit and cakes set out on crystal plates. The bed was tossed with rose petals.

"Oh Henry," Alice said, pausing at the entrance of the room. "This is too much."

He pressed her to his side. "It's our wedding day, Alice. Nothing is too much."

Oh, to have a bride to spoil. What fun.

"Are you hungry?" he asked her.

"No," she said. "I'm a bit tired from the journey."

"I have just the thing to revive you. Wait here."

Andrew's late mother had been prescribed bathing during a

long convalescence from a lung ailment, so her suite had a rather unusual luxury: a bathing room, with a deep soaking tub and steam troughs heated through a furnace beneath the floors. He had asked Andrew to have the bath prepared, so it would be hot for Alice.

The room was lined with pretty painted tiles and the floors were covered in soft carpets. The vents released warm steam fragrant with lemon peels and rosemary. He took some roses from a vase in the hallway and scattered the petals over the steaming tub. Feeling whimsical, he made a trail leading from the tub to the door.

He went back to fetch his wife. "Come. I have a surprise for you."

He led her through his romantic display, enjoying her delight in the rose petal trail and the scent in the air. When they reached the bath, he turned back to smile at her, but her face arrested him. She looked like she might weep.

"Oh, don't cry. I just wanted to bathe you, as you did for me. So you will feel as I felt. So cared for. So loved."

"That's how you felt?"

He nodded. And it struck him that all day, he'd not felt guilty, or sacrilegious, or perverse. He'd not lost himself in endless prayers, begging God's forgiveness.

He'd just felt loved.

"I'm so glad," she whispered.

"Then let me undress you."

He took his time with it. He removed her clothes slowly, caressing her skin, kissing her in secret places he'd never had time to fawn over, like the inside of her knee, and the ticklish bit beneath her armpit.

When she was nude, and he had taken down her hair and brushed it out, he lifted her and put her in the bath. He drew a sea sponge over her until she was rosy, and massaged scented oil into her flesh. She even let him wash her hair, and smiled as he played with it, marveling that this creature, this beauty, was his to love and care for.

"Paul the Apostle was right," Henry said. "It *is* better to marry than to burn."

"Henry," Alice said very seriously.

"Yes."

"Take me to bed."

CHAPTER 40

"Oh, Alice. Oh, sweet heaven," Henry said, as he entered her for the first time.

"Don't blaspheme in the marriage bed, Reverend," she chided, lifting her hips to allow her husband to more thoroughly consummate their union.

For an unschooled man he found a rhythm easily and filled her in such a way she did not have to seek her pleasure, it simply came in rolls.

The effortless intensity of it bathed her in a kind of inner light.

It was, indeed, like heaven—or as like it as a girl as wicked as herself was qualified to say.

Henry's eyes were full of something shining, and that certainty came over her again.

He loved her, she could see that. But he also loved *this.*

And castle or not, in this bed with him, she felt like a queen. For Henry's body was among the finest luxuries she'd ever had the pleasure of consuming.

When they'd exhausted each other, a lazy smile played about his lips. A rather proud one, if she was not mistaken.

"Why Henry Evesham," she laughed. "I believe I've made you into a satyr."

His mouth twitched up shyly. "I've always been a satyr. I tried to tell you."

She squeezed him. "And I thank the Lord for that."

Henry fell asleep in her arms. When he was softly snoring, she tiptoed out of the room and found a maid.

"I wonder if I could ask the housekeeper for a request upon breakfast?"

"Of course, Mrs. Evesham."

"An apple tart. With lots of cream and caramel. For my husband."

She went back into the bed and snuggled up beside Henry.

"Thank you," she whispered.

Perhaps she was thanking her husband. Perhaps she was thanking God.

The only certainty was that it was a kind of prayer.

THE END

HISTORICAL NOTES

Part of the pleasure of writing this book was investigating the absolute treasure trove of 18th-century broadsheet ballads and folk songs that survive in the historical record, many of which are filthy, or heartbreaking, or both. In most places I excerpted from these songs as they were written, strange-to-our-modern-eyes-punctuation and all, though I did take the liberty of changing a word or two here and there for the sake of clarity.

If you are curious about the songs that appear in these pages, you can find more about them here:

- The High-Priz'd Pin-Box (c. 1750): http://ebba.english.ucsb.edu/ballad/32500/citation

- Good Morning, Pretty Maid (c. 1750): http://www.contemplator.com/england/prettymaid.html

- The Flattering Young Man and the Modest Maid (c.

1700): https://ebba.english.ucsb.edu/ballad/34283/citation

And finally, a note on Methodism. Henry Evesham's faith is loosely inspired by the writings of John Wesley and other figures members of the 18th-century Evangelical movement in England. Please note that while I hope Henry's faith and concerns are in the spirit of the era, his version is entirely fictional. It is by no means intended as an authoritative portrait of the historical movement, nor a reflection of the Methodist Church as it now exists.

THANK YOU & WHERE TO FIND MORE

Dearest reader,

Thank you so very much for reading *The Lord I Left !* If you enjoyed Alice and Henry's story, **please consider leaving a review**. Your thoughts are a blessing to the community of readers looking for new books, and to authors like myself who very much want to match our work to people who will get a kick out of it.

If you would like to spend more time on Charlotte Street, make sure you have read the first two books in the series. There is *The Duke I Tempted (Book I)*—in which the secretly-submissive Duke of Westmead reluctantly marries his ferocious gardener (for convenience, of course), and then is forced to discover he still has a working human heart, very much against his will. And then there is *The Earl I Ruined (Book II)*—in which a singularly rebellious young lady accidentally ruins a supposedly boring man, conspires to save his reputation via a fake engagement, and discovers she is, in fact, the boring one, and also arguably in love. Whew!

The next book will star Mistress Brearley herself, and her nemesis cum patron cum paramour Lord Avondale, and will come out, let's say, who knows … because I have not yet written it! If you would like to stay in touch regarding (wait for it….) *The Rogue I Ravished,* you may subscribe to my newsletter. It purports to be about book news, but I must be honest: it is often just pictures of my cat wearing a bow tie.

If "who knows" is too long to wait for your next Scarlett Peckham joint, than allow me to suggest my upcoming book, *The Rakess* (out April 27, 2020.) It is the first in my new *Society of Sirens* series from Avon, about a group of radical, libertine ladies who weaponize their scandalous reputations to fight for justice and the love they deserve. *The Rakess* is inspired by Mary Wollstonecraft, acute feminist rage, and every swashbuckling rake book you ever read in the mid-to-late 20th-century. I've included a little taste for you on the following pages.

Love,
Scarlett

AND NOW FOR A WHOLE NEW ROMANCE SERIES!

Sneak Preview of THE RAKESS, Coming April 2020

She's a Rakess on a quest for women's rights...

Seraphina Arden's passions include equality, amorous affairs, and wild, wine-soaked nights. To raise funds for her cause, she's set to publish explosive memoirs exposing the powerful man who ruined her. Her ideals are her purpose, her friends are her family, and her paramours are forbidden to linger in the morning.

He's not looking for a summer lover...

Adam Anderson is a wholesome, handsome, widowed Scottish architect, with two young children, a business to protect, and an aversion to scandal. He could never, *ever* afford to fall for Seraphina. But her indecent proposal—one month, no strings, no future—proves too tempting for a man who strains to keep his passions buried with the losses of his past.

But one night changes everything...

What began as a fling soon forces them to confront painful secrets—and yearnings they thought they'd never have again. But when Seraphina discovers Adam's future depends on the man she's about to destroy, she must decide what to protect... her desire for justice, or her heart.

SNEAK PEEK AT THE RAKESS

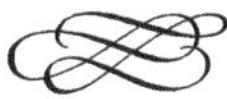

Kestrel Bay, Cornwall
June 1797

At the ungodly hour of half past two on a sun-braced afternoon, Seraphina Arden stood before her looking glass in her flimsiest chemise, squinting against the glare coming off the ocean as she removed pins, one by one, from her coiffure.

She unspooled a long curl from above her temple and arranged it to trail over her left breast, drawing the eye to the hint of pink one could just barely make out through her thin lawn shift. She untucked another tendril from her nape, letting it unfurl down the middle of her back. The effect was louche, as though she had been grabbed in a passionate embrace.

Perfect.

She was the very image of an utterly ruined woman.

Henri enjoyed that kind of thing, if she recalled.

It had been years since their last encounter, but the memory of those nights in Paris still made her breath catch. Even mediocre painters had a facility with their hands that elevated the purely carnal to an art form—and Henri's work was celebrated on three continents.

She draped a cloak around her shift and set off down the coastal path toward the abandoned belvedere at the border of her property and Jory Tregereth's. As weather-wizened as a ruin, perched precariously among the cliffs, the old folly afforded a magnificent view of Kestrel Bay, if one didn't mind steps overgrown with tufts of purple fumitory weeds and winds that nearly knocked you over as you climbed.

The air smelled like her childhood—like brine and sand and pollen. A heady, salty scent that made her ill at ease. She had come here to remember how that era of her life had ended, but now that she was here, each reminder of it smarted.

Henri would be good for her. He would remind her who she had become, and distract from the unpleasant reminders of what she'd lost.

She ascended the steps carefully, wincing against the bright, flat glare off the Kestrel. At this time of day, the light hit the cliffs in such a blinding arc it was difficult to parse the sky from the sea.

But she only had eyes for Henri.

He'd come early. He was leaning against the balustrade with his back to her, absorbed in sketching cliffs. Oh, but he was picturesque. Like a chiaroscuro, with his dark clothes and hair cutting against the misty vista of the ocean. She'd forgotten precisely how well formed he was: long and lean with those broad shoulders and strong arms and clever artist's hands. She couldn't make out his face, but in silhouette his jaw was better made than she remembered. The two years since their last assignation had agreed with him.

Something inside her lit, in a way it hadn't since that night six weeks ago, when Elinor had disappeared and all the pleasant parts of life had faded into numbness.

"Henri," she said.

He didn't turn, unable to hear her over the roar of the violent, salty air whipping off the ocean. Which gave her a delicious idea.

She draped her cloak over the rail of the belvedere, toed off her shoes, and crept forward, silent, silent, across the floor until she was just behind him. She placed a single finger at the bottom of his neck, below the knot of satin ribbon holding his raffish hair into a queue. That spot that lit up all the other spots that wanted touching.

No man could resist it.

She would know.

"Henri," she whispered in his ear.

He leapt, arching his back toward a marble column behind him as though she was a cutpurse who'd assailed him rather than the woman whose bed he'd traveled hours to make use of. His sketchpad clattered to the floor. His face was obscured by the shadow of the column, but his hand caught her wrist and dragged her forward, toward the light.

She bit her lip at the pang of anticipation. He remembered how she liked it: rough.

"What in Christ's name?" he growled in the low, clipped vowels of a Scot.

A Scot?

He stepped forward into the light, and his face was as harshly handsome as it was completely unfamiliar.

Who was he?

She wrenched her arm out of his grip and stepped back, clutching herself to block his view of her . . . her *everything* . . . through the filmy fabric of her shift.

She glanced up into his face, trying to place him, hating herself for worrying that he was someone from her past, someone who might say something cruel or reach out and—

Her bare foot landed on the page of his discarded sketchpad. She glanced down. It was not the cliffs he'd been drawing.

It was the jointed beams beneath the belvedere.

She glanced back up and caught him staring at her.

And there was such a terrible hunger in his eyes that they could have been her own.

ADAM ANDERSON TORE HIS GAZE AWAY FROM THE WOMAN WHO HAD nearly sent him toppling over the low stone balustrade and shrugged his coat from his shoulders, holding it out to her so that she might use it to cover herself.

"I beg your pardon, madam. Here, take this."

She had been clutching her barely shrouded body protectively, as though he—not she—had been the one to pounce.

It was not an effective means of restoring her modesty. Standing as she was in that fierce shaft of light, her thin gown was transparent, swirling luminous around long, finely made legs that rose into lavishly flared hips and a dark thatch of—*Christ*.

She held his glance for a long moment. And then she dropped her self-protective posture, something like amusement blooming in her eyes, and padded calmly back across the stone floor in her bare feet, ignoring his attempt at chivalry.

"Who are you?" she asked idly.

Her gait was defiant, the shadow of her buttocks swishing from side to side beneath her gown in bored, unhurried time.

He felt a flash of irritation at himself for continuing to ogle her.

But that gown. The way it swirled around those legs beneath it.

Stop.

"I'm Adam Anderson," he said to her back. "Mr. Tregereth's architect. Forgive me if I've disturbed you. He did not mention this building was in use."

The woman reached for a cloak she'd left tossed against the railing. She arranged it around her shoulders and glanced back at him, her expression wry. "And I imagine he would not approve of it had he known."

Her face was arresting. Slanted black brows, an elegant slash of a nose, green eyes smudged with heavy lashes. It was a face he could have made a feast of drawing, in the days when he still drew women and not window fixtures.

"Tregereth is not demolishing the belvedere?" she asked. "That would be a shame. It makes a pleasant little ruin and I enjoy looking at it from my window." She pointed up to the weathered but grand house that stood a half mile up the coastal path, at the promontory of the cliffs.

He'd been told the place was abandoned.

He gestured at a cracked piece of the stone floor that had begun to list, sloping down toward the cliff's edge. "This foundation needs rebuilding. It's not steady. You should be careful, coming here alone."

"Did you think, Mr. Anderson," she asked, widening her eyes, "that I intended to be alone?"

His sketchpad caught the wind and threatened to sail over the ledge. She stopped it with the toe of her bare foot, then bent down and handed it back to him.

For a brief moment, their fingers touched. The hairs on his forearms stood, as though she'd sent a current through him.

He wrenched his hand away, and she watched him do it, abrupt, a touch delayed. Something knowing rippled through her eyes and the corners of her mouth turned up.

She met his eye. "If a gentleman should appear here in search of me, send him up to my house. And if you would be so kind, don't mention this to Tregereth. He has never approved of my visits."

She winked, turned around, and strode up the steps in her bare feet, holding her slippers in her hand.

"Forgive me, madam, I didn't catch your name," he called after her.

She turned back. "Seraphina Arden," she said with a low, theatrical bow and laughter in her eyes. Laughter that implied, *Of course that's who I am, you dullard.*

Belatedly, he recognized her angular silhouette from the woodcuts sold in stalls along the Strand etched with the words *The Rakess.*

The woman climbing back up the cliff in a state of scandalous undress laughed at him because she should need no introduction; she was one of the most infamous women in all of England.

ACKNOWLEDGMENTS

Thank you as always to Sarah, Natanya, and the team at NYLA for helping me make this book the best it can be, even if, say, it happens to be Christmas and you have the flu and the entire romance industry is burning down around you. Thank you to Kerry Jesberger who continues to perform magic tricks with the ethereal covers she makes for this series. Thank you to Peter Sentfleben for editing the manuscript and being excited about this book even when I wasn't. Thank you to my family for enthusiastically reading my books even though they contain extremely elaborate sex scenes and general wickedness—I love you, even when you are not being Best of the Bunch, and certainly when I'm not. Thank you to Emily for being my boss. Thank you to Lauren for being my fitness instructor. Thank you to Nonie for being my bow tie model. And thank you to Chris for being my husband.

ALSO BY SCARLETT PECKHAM

The Secrets of Charlotte Street

The Duke I Tempted

The Earl I Ruined

The Lord I Left

The Society of Sirens

The Rakess

ABOUT THE AUTHOR

About Scarlett

Scarlett Peckham is a *USA Today* bestselling author who writes steamy historical romances about alpha heroines. She lives in Los Angeles.

She loves chatting about books on **Twitter**, turning them into pretty pictures on **Instagram**, and doddering around haphazardly on **Facebook**.

You can find her here:

Website: https://www.scarlettpeckham.com/

Newsletter Signup: http://geni.us/TheScarlettLetter

facebook.com/ScarlettPeckham
twitter.com/scarlettpeckham
instagram.com/scarlettpeckham
bookbub.com/authors/scarlett-peckham

CPSIA information can be obtained
at www.ICGtesting.com
Printed in the USA
LVHW010014200620
658570LV00010B/938

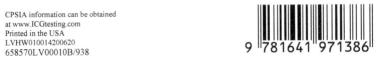

9 781641 971386